# FALLING FROM GRACE

# FALLING FROM GRACE

*a novel*

## MEL FOSTER

*Falling From Grace*

© 2024 by Mel Foster

Editors: Jade Heiss, Dianna Graveman
Cover and Interior Design: Emma Elzinga

Indigo River Publishing
3 West Garden Street, Ste. 718
Pensacola, FL 32502
www.indigoriverpublishing.com

Ordering Information:
Quantity Sales: Special discounts are available on quantity purchases by corporations, associations, and others. For details, contact the publisher at the address above.

Orders by US trade bookstores and wholesalers: Please contact the publisher at the address above.

Printed in the United States of America

Library of Congress Control Number: 2024911098
ISBN: 978-1-954676-96-1 (paperback)     978-1-954676-97-8 (ebook)

First Edition

With Indigo River Publishing, you can always expect great books, strong voices, and meaningful messages. Most importantly, you'll always find . . . *words worth reading.*

They say it takes a village to raise a child.
Well, the same can be said for birthing a book.
There are so many people who played a part in this journey.
Some small parts. Some larger.
But combined, every piece of advice, every bit of feedback,
every encouraging word contributed to this moment.
Thank you to all of you. You know who you are.
I am eternally grateful.

– Mel

Cast all your anxiety on him because he cares for you.
1 Peter 5:7 (NIV)

**1**

*Catalina, Arizona, 1995*

Mama said a lot of things can kill you in the desert. That She's been the death of many long before me and will continue to be so after I'm gone. It takes a certain kind of person to see past Her grittiness and find the beauty in Her violence. From a young age, even my mama knew that I was one of those people. That Her simplicity spoke to something in me. Something I couldn't ever see. Only feel. And though my love ran deep, it didn't make Her any less relentless.

The morning sun blasted through the passenger side window, searing my right arm and bare legs. And though it burned, it didn't stop me from resting my cheek on the sill to watch the small dust devils swirling across the dirt like rattlesnakes on the hunt. They never lasted long but kept me from staring at the brown-eyed stranger with pasty skin and eyes ringed with dark circles in the side-view mirror. Kept me from remembering how Mama took any opportunity she had to express disappointment that I wasn't blessed with her sun-kissed hair or pretty blue eyes. But no matter the miles of white lines and the never-ending stretch of desert, nothing was truly enough to forget the bad. Everything had an end.

In the time it took for me to sit upright and look away from my reflection, the dust devil had died. Stretching my long legs, I shifted and twisted, trying to adjust the weight pressing against my pelvis. My lips sputtered in defeat. I tried to get my mind off my bladder. First by counting the cars on the road and then by humming to the song on the radio, but neither worked. I looked over at Pa.

The bags under his eyes were big and dark enough for a prairie dog to hide under. A kind of tiredness that only a cigarette and a drink could cure. And my nose still crinkled each time Pa lit up. No matter how old I got, it was just as bad as the first time. It was one of those things that never got better. With the cigarette hanging out the corner of Pa's mouth, he reached over and fiddled with the radio stations, stopping at the sound of Brooks & Dunn singing "Boot Scootin' Boogie." Pa's beat up '69 Ford 100 bumped and clanged along the road, keeping time with the music. After he took a second drag, he flipped his Wildcats baseball cap backwards. Why he turned it on the second drag and not the first or third, I still didn't know. There were always reasons for why Pa did the things that he did.

"Thanks again for drivin' me. You didn't need to. It's only a mile and a half to the gas station."

"Hey now, what kind of dad would I be, huh?" Pa said. "To let his little girl do such a thing?" He patted my shoulder twice before focusing on the road, taking another drag of his cigarette.

Whenever Pa would call me his little girl, there were two things I wanted to do. One, I wanted to hug him. Two, I wanted to scream at him. But all I wished for were the words that I hoped would come after: *You're the greatest thing I ever did in this life. I'll even stop drinking for you.* Just once, how I would've loved to hear that. At the end of the day, though, it was wishful thinking, nothing more than the wisp of a willow tree. My eyes glanced between his face and hand, gathering enough courage to say what I really wanted. I was always afraid of hurting someone as it wasn't their fault they had bad habits.

Especially Pa.

When he took that fourth drag, I bit my bottom lip and said, "You know . . ." and caught Pa's glance. "I read in *American Baby* that cigarette smoke increases the risk of asthma."

He snorted, propped his tanned arm on the windowsill, and carelessly flicked the burnt ash outside. "But ain't, uh . . ." He hesitated and let out a chuckle, long enough to make up some new excuse. "Ain't asthma hereditary?"

Before I could correct him, he said, "Your ma smoked when you were still in her belly, and you grew out of it. Either way, it'll be wheezin'."

"It's not an it. It's a baby, Pa. So will you put it out?"

Pa looked at me and back at the road, taking another drag as if he hadn't heard me. There was a time when I loved how the corner of his mouth twitched, not knowing then what it really meant. Now I knew better. The day I told him I was pregnant, the corner of his mouth twitched. I knew at that moment he would never like the baby. He would never like me again. From that day on, he saw me like Mama and his hatred grew even more.

He wasn't always like this. Pa used to buy me Jose's Pollo Tacos and a root beer float every Friday after school. Now, everything about him that I used to love was the thing I hated most. And I wondered if this was what my mama felt like when she was pregnant with me. My attention turned to admire how the sunflowers on my dress stretched across the curve of my belly. I hadn't believed I'd ever be capable of feeling or giving this baby the unconditional love she needed, a love that ceased to exist between my own mama and me. But the moment I heard her tiny heartbeat, a bond formed so quick and so strong it still made tears well in my eyes. It was the most beautiful sound I had ever heard. My life had found meaning, and it wasn't just my own freedom I thought of anymore.

It was ours.

A heavy weight settled in my chest. Still, my baby and I had a roof overhead and food in the fridge. That overshadowed all thoughts of escape. I stared at the blurring landscape of desert in the side-view mirror. Vultures circled overhead waiting for their next meal. Playing with the strand of hair that slipped from my scrunchie, I looked at Pa again. His gaze stayed fixed on the windshield.

"Did I tell you that Arlene gave me a scrapbook yesterday for when the baby's born? You know, to put pictures in it." Reaching down beside my feet, I grabbed my bag, pulling out the July edition of *American Baby*. "And I was thinkin' of some names for the baby. You wanna hear 'em?" I asked, searching to find the right dog-eared page among the other dozen like it.

I resisted the impulse to stick out my tongue like a six-year-old trying to figure out how to unscrew the cap on a Coca-Cola bottle. My fingers hastily flipped the pages, and I beamed as I landed on the right page, pointing to the list. "See, Pa, I circled the top two in red marker. Look."

"Why don't you have a top three like a normal person, Grace?"

"I like even numbers, and they sound better, that's why," I answered. Reading down the list of names, I asked, "Whaddya think of Daisy?"

"Eh."

"Faye?"

He looked straight ahead and exhaled sharply, the irritation building in his eyes like water simmering in a pot. Unsure of what to say or do, I bit my bottom lip. Pa scrubbed a hand over his face like he was exhausted.

"Pa—"

"Grace, I just got off my night shift. I've had only four hours of sleep, and after I drop you off, I have to haul ass back to Uncle Wayne's and lug five thousand pounds of limestone to Scottsdale."

"I thought Dave was—"

"Dave's gone missin' again, so I'm covering a few of his shifts. So gimme a break, okay?"

"Pa, I really didn't mean . . ." I said, hoping the softer approach would twist his wing, but paused as his eyes peered at me, warning me that his patience was unraveling. "Sorry, Pa." I turned away and rolled the window down all the way to allow the hot air to blast my warm and sticky face.

The sound of him releasing a breath caused my eyes to drift over at him again, catching the inevitable twitch to the corner of his mouth. All he had to do was look at me with those unpredictable eyes, and doubt and fear settled into my head as I readied myself for the worst. Would he finally do it? Do what he did to my mama and leave me a scar of my own? But no matter the times I believed he'd finally do it, he never acted on it. Something in him seemed to always stop him. Something that cared.

"Hey, have you heard back from your ma at all?" Pa asked. When I didn't answer, he exhaled and said, "Alrighty then, I take that as a *no*," and two streams of smoke expelled through his nostrils.

After we drove five more minutes in thick silence down the dirt road, there they were: a dozen trailers sitting in the middle of nowhere. During the day, it was quiet. There was this feeling that nothing was alive. Mama always said every morning, "The early bird catches the worm," and her words still held true. Nothing made a sound. Nothing moved except the ripples of heat vibrating. The heat was always up and ready to devour anyone by nine a.m. But by night, our trailer park became like the desert.

Unpredictable and lawless.

Pa turned down the middle row of single-wide trailers. A smattering of mesquite trees surrounded them, offering much needed shade and relief with their unpretentious beauty.

Time, and the strong winds of the Arizona desert, hadn't been kind to some of the homes. Others looked as though their owners took great effort and pride to continue cleaning windows and maintaining the little patch of land. Where one trailer would be lined with potted petunias and white lawn furniture, the next would be in shambles, waiting to collapse on its concrete footings.

Ours was the fourth one down. Our home. Yet every so often, I allowed myself to wonder what my life could be with a real lawn and a white porch with a yellow umbrella. Even if I were lucky for such a future, Mama says I'd still be the same; once trailer park trash, always trailer park trash. What made up for it all was the one thing that this place had that no other did: the sweeping panoramic view of the Santa Catalina Mountains in the distance. It was the one thing about this place that made living here tolerable.

"Looks like someone moved into old Mr. Lawson's place," Pa said as he pulled up in front of the trailer. I leaned forward as far as I could for a better view and spotted a black pickup truck parked in the driveway beside us. "Let's just hope they don't play that damn jazz music all night."

"It wasn't so bad," I said as I slipped on my sandals. Pa rolled his eyes. "It wasn't."

He shut off the truck, saying, "Uh-huh. Hey, don't forget your bag of snacks. You're eatin' for two now."

"You know that's a myth, right?" I opened the door. "I ate like I always did in the beginning but by the second trimester they tell you to up your calories by three hundred fifty and on the third—"

"Jesus Christ, Grace, I don't care." Pa climbed out of the truck. "It really is one thing after the other with you. I need to take a piss, so just wait a dang second." He rushed into the trailer.

I pushed myself up from the seat, using the door for leverage. The hot metal frame stung my fingertips, and I yanked my hand away just as the magazine slipped out of my bag and tumbled onto the dirt. "Dang it," I said, shutting my eyes and wiping the sweat from my forehead, trying to ignore my throbbing feet.

At an unflattering angle, I bent over and reached as far as I could with my fingers to pick up the magazine. Catching the corner, I slowly stood upright and groaned, placing the magazine on the hood of the truck. Just as I gathered enough energy to move, Ray stormed out of his trailer. He slammed the door, muttering the usual gibberish that would make most people gape in horror. Ray took the saying *The quickest way to a man's heart is through his stomach* by living it proudly with his big belly and plump cheeks. He tripped over the step stool and chucked it at Arlene's lawn chair. Placing his hands on his sides, he looked over, finally noticing me. I waved and kept my other hand firmly planted on the magazine to avoid losing it. By now, the June edition was surely buried underneath a foot of sand and dirt.

"Mornin', Ray."

He wiped sweat from the tip of his red bulbous nose. "How long you been standin' there?"

"Not long."

"You going or not?" Arlene yelled from the inside the trailer. "I don't hear you leavin'!"

"I'm goin'! Stop gittin' your knickers in a twist! I'm talkin' to Grace!" Ray shook his head, regarding me. "I tell ya, that woman's gonna gimme another gray hair. You want me to pick up anything for you? I'm goin' into town."

"No, I'm fine, Ray."

"You sure?" he asked, glancing toward Mr. Lawson's trailer. "Hey, you know who just moved in?"

"No. Do you?"

He took another glimpse across the road and shrugged. "Your guess is as good—"

The door creaked open, and Arlene stepped outside onto the makeshift patio, carefully holding a red plastic cup with her freshly done nails. She leaned against the door frame and stared down at Ray, who stood there not moving.

"What, woman? I'm on my way. Grace and I were just talkin'."

"Did you ask Grace if she needed scrapbook supplies? They're havin' a sale," Arlene said.

Ray wiped the sweat from his forehead and placed his hands on his sides. "No, I didn't, and you didn't tell me nothin' about no sale."

"Yes, I did."

"No, you didn't."

I watched the volley of bickering words fly back and forth like a ball in a tennis match. After eighteen years of living across from each other, not much had changed. Still, I reckoned, if it weren't for them, I wouldn't have come to know a little about the one thing in this world that was *Love*. A good kind of Love. They may not have much, but that Love carried them through thick and thin. That's what everybody wants in this world. A person who loves them and all their imperfections.

Arlene reached into the back pocket of her white capris and took out several coupons cut to perfection. "Cut them just last night, so don't go twisting my words now," she declared as Ray took them from her hand. "And did you fix your hearing aids like I told you to do a week ago? You're basically deaf without 'em."

"No, honey, I just turn them down when I'm around ya," Ray muttered. He leaned toward me, saying in a hushed tone, "You'd think she would've figured that out by now. Only been doin' it for the past three years." He flashed me a grin, but it quickly disappeared as he looked back at Arlene. And like each time Arlene saw or heard Ray do something she didn't like, her lips thinned into a tight line.

"You know, it wouldn't hurt to hear *thank you* or *please* once in a while," Ray said. "Just sayin'."

"What did you say?" Arlene asked. Ray looked at his feet and cleared his throat. She folded her arms as her eyes drifted toward me and softened, a smile spreading across her face. "And how are you and that baby doin', sweetie?"

"We're doin' okay," I said.

"You drinkin' enough water? I don't want you faintin'."

"Yeah, I am. And how are you doin'?"

Arlene looked at Ray, who wore a clumsy smile. "Oh, you know. Another day in paradise. And Ray, don't forget to get some supplies for Grace, okay? They'll be in the craft section. Got it?"

"I still have some, Arlene," I reassured her.

"See? Told ya," Ray said.

Arlene unfolded her arms, saying, "Well, just hurry back, will ya, before you drop dead of heat exhaustion. Don't go over the speed limit, and for God's sake, Ray, don't light up when you drive. You remember what happened last—"

"Honey, I think after over thirty years of driving, I'm gonna know a thing or two," Ray declared.

"Uh-huh. And Grace, you gotta tell me when you finally pick a name for that baby."

"I will, Arlene, don't worry," I said.

Arlene turned back inside, but not without giving Ray one last dirty look. "Fat dumbass," she muttered and shut the screen door behind her.

I glanced over, expecting Ray to roll his eyes and mutter gibberish again. Instead, his cheeks were red, and a big toothy grin had spread across his face. My nose and brows scrunched in confusion. It was as if her hateful words had given him a spark of energy, and he was now anxiously excited, like a kid who was promised ice cream after dinner. He looked at me and jerked his thumb at the trailer, saying, "That means this boy is gittin' lucky tonight. She can't resist this tub of jelly." He patted his gut, and I held back a smile.

Ray reached into the front pocket of his Hawaiian shirt and took out a lighter and a pack of Camels. He gave one last look at the new neighbor and retrieved a cigarette, placing it between his chapped lips. He jerked his head and said, "Well, whoever they are, I like their taste. That truck there is a Toyota. Reliable as they come." He opened the car door and climbed in with a grunt. Something cranked and sputtered as the gears shifted, but before driving off, he asked again, "You sure you don't need anythin' at all, Grace? Can't live off Slim Jims forever, you know."

"I'm fine, Ray. Bye now."

He rolled his eyes and smiled before speeding down the dirt road. I fanned the cloud of dirt from my face just as a small gust of wind blew the magazine off the hood of the truck. "Gosh dang it!" I jogged around the truck and bent down as far as I could, giving no second thought to my lower back. As my fingertips snatched the corner of the magazine, a deep ache shot through my hips and feet.

Holding my back, I slowly stood upright. As I shook the dirt off the cover, I caught a glimpse of someone in the new neighbor's driveway. A man passed by the driver's side window, walking to the tailgate with a small limp to his right knee. By the looks of him, I bet he could reach that shelf where Pa always kept the Oreos. He was slightly stocky but muscular enough for people to do a double take. If I had to guess how old he was, I'd say late twenties, but from the few strands of gray framing his face and the faint lines at the corner of his eyes, I wondered whether it was the sun or the hardships of life that seemed to have aged him too soon. His eyes flickered over, and he halted in his tracks.

I awkwardly smiled, waving. Instead of waving back, he just stared at me quietly. Was he pissed off, or was this just his usual face? His eyes lowered to my stomach and back to my face again. And I knew I couldn't hide the red on my cheeks. I had gotten used to people staring at me but never in this way. I expected a scowl or a look of disgust, but the man simply looked away as if it didn't matter, removing a box cutter from the pocket of his worn denim jeans. He pushed the long, dark brown layers from his face, sweat dripping down the side of his cheek. Little bits of sunlight glared off a pair of dog tags resting against his broad chest, causing my eyes to lower as he lifted a box into his arms. I looked up again. He turned away to leave.

"If you need help with anythin', you can ask the Johnson's."

He stopped and looked over.

"T-they're right over there." I pointed at Arlene and Ray's trailer. The new neighbor glanced across the street and then back at me.

"Grace!" Pa yelled and I turned, expecting him to come outside. I looked back to see the new neighbor duck his head under the door frame, letting the screen door shut behind him. Pa hopped outside, tugging on his left boot. "What are you still doing out here? Get inside before you drop dead in this heat, will ya?" Pa snapped.

"Wait, Pa—"

He pushed past me and headed to the truck. "What is it now? Uncle Wayne's gonna beat my ass again if I don't get there in time. You know him."

"Pa, just wait," I called out and struggled to keep up with his long strides. "I need to give you something. Please."

He stopped in his tracks.

I dug into my bag, hastily searching through the mess of crumpled articles from baby magazines and the July *Reader's Digest*. "Just gimme a sec, I know it's in here."

Pa tilted his head to the sky, looking for patience. He didn't seem to find any, so he proceeded to walk away and climb into the driver's seat. After finding a small list and a few dollar bills in my wallet, I jogged over and knocked on the window. "Pa. Pa, come on, please. Please. It's not much, but I need 'em."

Pa stared straight ahead. His dull eyes seemed to study each speck of dirt on the windshield as if each one represented a mistake in his life.

"Pa, please."

He opened the door, and I stepped back, my eyes moving higher as he stood. Though he was just a couple inches shorter than Uncle Wayne, Pa could still knock someone into next week. He looked at me like a helpless dog who kept interfering in every aspect of his life. It was that look that always made me want to cry. Pa stepped forward and snatched the list from my hand. Taking one glance, he let out an exhausted sigh and threw down his baseball cap, scrubbing a hand over his face.

A twinge of guilt sat on my chest as he pinched the bridge of his nose. It used to be Mama's kryptonite. Now, it was mine. Moments like this instinctively caused the little girl in me to feel sorry for him. And this time I knew what I did wrong. "I forgot I had it when we went to the gas station. I'm really sorry, Pa," I said sincerely, hoping for him to look at me the way he used to. Now he looked at me the way he looked at Mama. As a blurry shape with no features. "Please, Pa. I really am sorry. I—"

"Why do you gotta do this to me, Grace?" Pa asked, taking me aback from his sudden soft tone. I opened my mouth to speak further, but it was as if the wind itself had whisked away the last thread of patience in him. "I'm really tryin' to do everything I can for us. Don't you get that? Without Uncle Wayne, I'd be on the freeway begging for scraps. And you'd be right there with me while your ma is off doing God knows what. Christ, the apple really doesn't fall far from the tree, huh?" He pushed himself off the truck, pacing back and forth. "I'm tryin', Grace. Every day."

"I know, Pa."

He turned on the heel of his boot so fast it gave me whiplash to suddenly find his wide furious eyes glued to my face. "You say you know, but you don't do nothin'! You're just as stupid as your mother!" he yelled, his face flushed red, throwing the crumpled list on the ground.

I wanted to convince myself it was the sun that made his face so red, but deep down I knew it wasn't. It was the burning anger, directed at me for making him put his life on hold. In some ways I did understand that anger, and in some ways, I didn't. There were moments, though few and far between, when courage stirred in my throat to say what I've been aching to say since I was a little girl. But then Pa would spew those words—words I had no reason or right to object to: *You'd have no one. Where are you gonna go?* and *I'm the only person who still loves you.* Words that left me feeling guilty for ever having the idea to leave. I swallowed, unable to move.

Arlene stepped out from the trailer. "For the Love of Christ, Bill! Stop your yakkin' and do what your daughter says!"

Pa looked at Arlene. "Woman, I'm gittin' sick and tired of you thinkin' you got a say here!" he yelled. "So why don't you go back inside and leave us the hell alone. You got that?"

Arlene lifted her manicured nail and pointed straight at him. "One day, Bill. One day, you're gonna git what's comin' to ya and it ain't gonna be pretty, but I hope to the Almighty, I'll still be alive to see it," she said and turned to go back inside but not before giving Pa one last look.

"That bitch is always sticking her nose in places where it don't belong, and that's on you, Grace." Pa wiped his nose and picked up his baseball cap, placing his hands on his sides. "That's on you," he stated in a hushed tone, shoving the tip of his pointer finger in my face. A screen door creaked open, causing Pa to turn and lower his hand. "Oh, mornin', neighbor. Didn't see you there."

I looked over and saw the new neighbor standing there at the end of his porch, his eyes focused on Pa. Pa cleared his throat, offering a reassuring smile that most might believe enough to help them carry on with their day. But as the man took the last step down from his porch, letting the door shut behind him, his eyes flickered to me. Flustered by his attention, I looked away, expecting the pitiful look that always came my way. As if they knew my life and my secrets. But what I never would've guessed was for a man as intimidating as he was, providing little to no reaction—apathetic even. As if this was another day for him, just as it was for me. I glanced over to see him now observing my pa.

"Those, uh, dog tags?" Pa asked. "My buddy's brother is in the Army."

"Pa, leave the man—"

"You ever killed anyone?"

"Pa!" I exclaimed and gently hit his arm. "What is wrong with you?

What makes you think you can ask such a thing?"

"Stop your bitchin' and whinin' and just get in the dang trailer, will ya? So I can get to work." Pa snatched the money from my fingers and gestured to the door. "Go on now. Go." He shoved me back.

The man moved forward but halted mid step.

"Come on. Go. Move your fat ass. Move it before you really drop dead." Pa gave the new neighbor one last look. "What? You got somethin' to say? Or are you gonna just keep starin'?"

The neighbor's face was stolid and focused as he turned away, just slowly enough for me to make out the slight bump in his nose and the strong angle of his jaw. He picked up a box from the porch and went back inside.

"You see that?" Pa jerked his thumb and climbed into the truck, saying, "Ya think someone would've told him by now that starin' is rude. Keep away from him, got it? Men like that are a hit and miss. They're dangerous."

"Got it, Pa," I promised reluctantly, picking up the crumpled list from the ground. "And if you can, please, stop there after work. I'd really appreciate it," I said, sticking my head through the window, holding out the list. Pa rolled his eyes and grabbed it from my hand, waving it in front of me before throwing it on the passenger seat.

"And, Pa, don't forget—"

"Can you get outta the way so I don't run you over? And fix the awnin', will ya?"

I stepped back as the tires skidded out on the dirt.

It was moments like this when I wished I had smelled Mama's chocolate chip pancakes that one morning instead of the exhaust of her car leaving. Before I allowed the memory to dwell too long, I made my way into the trailer. The cooler air hit my face, relieving my burnt skin. It was then I found myself standing in the middle of the room. Trapped. Every time I stepped in here, time ticked slower. Everything was in slow motion, and I was stuck just like my mama. She was there, but not really. From a young age, I promised myself that I would never be like her. Yet, here I was.

Just as tired and broken.

After grabbing a Slim Jim, I took the step stool from underneath the kitchen sink. I headed outside and set it down, carefully centering my feet on top to reach for the awning rod. Standing on my toes, my fingers still strained to reach the lever.

"How many times do I have to tell you that it's not safe for you to be doin' that?" Arlene exclaimed, and I looked over to see her walking up to my side with arms folded in disapproval. My mouth tugged into a smile with the Slim Jim still between my teeth. "Git down from there. It ain't safe."

"I got it, Arlene. Don't worry," I said and unsecured the lock to extend the awning. "See?" I stepped down and hooked the awning rod into the strap loop. "There isn't nothin' for you to worry about."

"There isn't nothin' until there's somethin'. Why can't your dad do it? He can't keep makin' you do these things. One wrong move, and you'll break your neck, Grace. Heck, if you keep it up, you're gonna end up with a little story of your own in Reader's Digest. Now why you smilin'? It ain't funny."

"Nothing bad's gonna happen. You gotta stop worrying. He's just too tired to do it when he comes home, Arlene. He had to put it up last week because of that bad storm. It's hard for him, ya know? I can't do much anymore. I'm gittin' fatter by the week. So, if I can help him out, I wanna."

"Grace, you know I love ya, but you'd think by now, he'd be a bit smarter. And the same goes for you, too. You can't be doin' these things. You got a baby now. And just 'cause you can do it, doesn't mean you should. Now move over. I'll take this side. You get that one. Alright?"

"Arlene."

"Don't Arlene me."

After we pulled the fabric taut from both sides, we tightened the rafter knobs and adjusted the awning's height. I tied the strap into place. Arlene wiped the dirt off her hands and assured the arms were stable. "And you'd think your dad would also learn where and when not to open that big mouth of his."

"It's just who he is."

"Sweetie, no one is just like that without a good reason. I'd bet my money it was your mama who done him that way. Now, I better not see you out here again. And if I hear ya call yourself fat again, I'm gonna throw a fit. Got it?"

"Got it."

Arlene nodded, saying, "Good, that's good. Now I'll be down a few rows at Miss Taylor's. Gonna watch some Days of Our Lives. So if you need me, holler. And drink some water. It's hotter than hell out here."

"I know, Arlene."

"I know you know."

She smiled and turned away, heading down the street, her hips swaying to and fro. Over the past eighteen years, Arlene and Ray were the one constant and stable thing in my life. They had become my family—and God forgive me for saying this—but Arlene had become more of a mama to me than my own. I sat on the step underneath the awning with my legs in a wide stance to compensate for my belly. Relieved to be in the shade, my eyes closed. But even with an eight to ten-degree drop in temperature, it still didn't stop the sweat from sliding down my cheek. Yet, at that moment, I didn't really mind it. For once, it was silent. And all I could hear was the soft rustle of the mesquite trees and the song of the cactus wren.

That sound, unlike the many others that existed here, had become one of my favorites. Without it, there was no desert. I opened my eyes and stared at the empty road ahead, taking my first easy breath. Looking over, I saw that a sixty-pound black-tipped German shepherd had taken refuge underneath the new neighbor's truck, protecting himself from the summer heat. His large tongue reminded me of a strawberry popsicle melting in the sun. I took a bite of the Slim Jim, searching for any sign of its owner. When my eyes fell upon the animal again, he was standing at attention, his big ears directed straight at me. He didn't move, but the wag of his tail dismissed any worries I had.

"You want a bite?"

Ripping off a piece, I held out my right hand and patiently waited for him to approach on his own terms. He hesitated but walked over until his wet snout hit my palm to gobble up the treat.

"Well, aren't you sweet? Tico would have bitten off my finger. He's the chihuahua who lives three trailers up the street. He's cute, but between you and me, I already like you better," I said. "You got an owner? I don't see a collar on ya. I'd take you, but my pa doesn't like dogs. He thinks they're dirty. Don't go off now, alright? I'll be right back." As fast as my sore feet could muster, I rushed into the trailer and returned with a bowl of water. "There you go, buddy. The best filtered water in all of Arizona." I sat down, watching his tongue eagerly lap at the water.

Shuffling footsteps made me lift my head. Walking up to his trailer was Mr. Emerson in a sweaty white tank top and boxers. Even from several feet away, I could smell the sour odor seeping from his skin. He did a double take and halted.

"Mornin', Mr. Emerson."

"That a dog, Callaway? If you think about letting that mutt anywhere near my property, I'm gonna—"

"You're gonna what?"

"He's a fleabag."

"He's not hurtin' anyone."

"He's gonna shit on my property."

"You shit on your property," I muttered beneath my breath and rested my chin in my hands.

"You hear me, Grace?"

"I hear ya!" I shouted.

He grumbled and stormed inside his trailer, slamming the door. I took another forceful bite of the Slim Jim. The animal yowled in protest. "Hey, don't worry, I'm not gonna forget about you," I reassured him and handed him a second piece. After he finished chewing, he circled around two times before collapsing underneath the shade by my foot. "I know how you feel, buddy." I reached over, gently scratching the side of his stomach. His left back leg started to shake. "Oh yes, that's the spot. That's the—" I stopped as he abruptly sat upright. "What is it, boy? You hear somethin'?"

He turned his head to the direction of a sound.

I leaned forward as much as I could, spotting the new neighbor stepping off his porch. He set down an empty box and tried to flatten it out with his boot. Unsuccessful, the man threw his head back and sighed in exhaustion, placing his hands on his sides. I hadn't noticed it before, but now that I did, I smiled at the sight of his hairy arms. They weren't gnarly, but there was enough to make me silently laugh. Must be miserable in this heat. He glanced right and left before blowing a high-pitched whistle into the air with his index finger and thumb. The dog barked, causing him to look over. I waved.

In the ten seconds it took for the animal to return to his side, he had not spared a wave in return nor acknowledged the booming music coming up from the road. Sir Mix-a-Lot's deep voice loudly sang Baby Got Back with a rattling engine as its chorus. I looked over, expecting either Mr. Emerson's or Arlene's son. A beat-up red VW Jetta sped up the dirt road.

"Mama?" I said in disbelief and stood upright but not without glancing over once again to the neighbor's trailer.

He was already gone.

# 2

Tires came to a harsh stop, spewing dirt and dust as something in the underbelly of the car clunked. No matter the times Mama had visited, it was nevertheless heartbreaking for me when she left again. Every time was like the first time all over again. And the child in me still clung to the hope that one day she'd walk up to me, open her arms, and say, "I came back for you, baby girl." But from the overdone makeup and her rum-soaked eyes, I learned to never hold my breath on such a hope. As Mama used to say, "When you start to expect, that's when the disappointment starts."

At least she still had her curly blonde hair going for her.

Mama stuck her face out the driver's side window, smiling as if she had just left for a quick run to the market and returned with a six pack of Pepsi. "Well, look who it is! Is that really you, Grace?" she asked, seemingly surprised. She shut off the radio, stumbling out of the car in a pair of shorty shorts, a low-cut Wildcat T-shirt, and pink sandals that were just as bright as her eyeshadow.

"Hi, Mama."

It was hard to miss that Mama's two greatest assets were supported by not one but two bras. It was those two reasons that had done in my pa. At least that's what Pa said. She lowered her sunglasses to the tip of her nose, letting her eyes wander to my belly. "You're bigger than the last time I saw ya. Wasn't I just gone for a week?"

Whenever I believed I was used to it, someone said or did something that brought me right back to those first months when the baby bump started to show. While the other girls stood at their lockers, applying layers of lip gloss and fluffing up their hair, I was stretching my shirt over my growing belly just a little bit more than the week before.

"Now why you lookin' at me like I ate the last french fry off your plate? I thought I'd at least git a smile outta ya or a hug. I did come all the way down here, sweet pea. I must've been in that dang car for five hours, I'm tellin' ya."

"I'm not your sweet pea anymore, Mama."

"Hey now, you're always gonna be my little girl. I may not be around a lot, but I'm still your mama, and the Lord is watchin'. And what are you doin' out in this heat? You got a baby now. You shouldn't be out here."

"I was out fixing the awning. Arlene helped me."

"She still around?"

"Yeah, she's sweet."

"You know that's what I said about your daddy and then you popped out." Mama glanced around. "And where is your daddy? I don't see his truck. I've got another bone to pick with him."

"At work."

"He got a job now?"

"Mama, why you here?" I asked. "If you're here for money, then you can go back to wherever you came from and try beggin' there," I replied curtly and turned away.

"Well, Lord Almighty! I swear, you're becoming more and more like your daddy every day. You even got that look he gets in his eye when he says it. Like daddy, like daughter, you know what I mean?"

I stopped and looked back. "I'm serious, Mama. We don't have anything we can give you. So you can go on home."

"Hey now—"

"Goodbye, Mama."

"Hey, I did come all the way down here. You really ain't gonna invite your mama in? I gotta pee. All that drivin'. We can even catch up on our girl talk. You still make that sweet iced tea of yours with those orange slices? I'd love a glass. Now move, I'm burstin' here." She slid past me into the cramped trailer and threw down her bag. She ran down the hall, disappearing into the bathroom just like the times she'd work a night shift.

I looked back one last time but saw no sign of the neighbor or his dog and stepped inside. Mama's loud groan of relief traveled from the hall to the kitchen. I set out the pitcher of sweet iced tea and took out two glasses from the cupboard. After I searched for any dust particles in either glass, I filled each one to the top. I carefully positioned a yellow umbrella and straw in mine and brought it to the table. Sitting down, I propped my feet on the chair across from me with a sigh. I stared at the umbrella and pushed it around the glass.

Sinking into the chair, my lips sputtered, and I asked my stomach, "This is as fancy as it's gonna get, isn't it, baby?"

I looked down the hall at the sound of the toilet flushing and the sink gurgling. There were many things I wanted to ask my mama. Things I couldn't ask. Where had she gone this time? How long was she gonna stay? But there was that one question that outweighed all combined, left unanswered for the past nine years: Why didn't she take me with her? Every part of me wanted to scream and cry, but I knew if I threw a fit, she would hop right back into that car. I set the glass on my belly and took a much-needed sip. The crisp but sweet orangey taste cooled my body, and my shoulders dropped, gently hitting the back of the chair.

"Good Golly, I'm sweatin' like a sinner in church." Mama came out wiping the smudged mascara underneath her eyes with a wet washcloth and said, "Your Uncle Wayne still datin' that girl Kathy, or did she finally have enough?"

"You could say that. He's with Tina again."

"So he knocked her up." Mama snorted and opened her bag on the counter, fishing out a cigarette and her lighter. "I gotta tell ya, you'd think with how that man drinks, his swimmers would be slowin' down by now."

"Well, I don't know what to tell ya, Mama," I said, resting my chin in my hand. "He's your brother."

After the fourth flick of her thumb, Mama lit the cigarette and took her first long drag. And like each time, she leaned back against the counter and crossed one leg over the other, folding her arms. Just like Pa, Mama wasn't always like this. There was a time Mama and I would dance together in the kitchen to songs on the radio. Life didn't seem so bad then. Especially when she made her chocolate chip cookies. Whenever I fell down or scraped a knee, I would sit anxiously at the kitchen table, and Mama would begin tenderly mixing the cookie dough, as if that dough contained a special magic to make me forget about the pain. And each time I bit into that gooey, chocolatey goodness, the pain wasn't bad anymore. Yet, as good as those times were, they were few and far between.

"So, who was that tall drink of water who moved into old man Lawson's place? He looked mighty fine, even from behind, and I know he ain't related to him. You can't get that from Mr. Lawson."

"I don't know. I get the feelin' he doesn't talk much."

"Well, let's just hope he doesn't play that jazz music. Your daddy hated that," Mama said and took another drag. She opened the fridge and stuck her head inside, resting her hand on the frame, holding the cigarette between her fingers. "You got anythin' worth drinkin' here that's not apple juice or sweet tea? I know your daddy's got to have something." She grabbed a carton of milk and twisted off the cap, taking a whiff. "How are Gramps and Gammie doin'?" she asked, rummaging through the fridge. "They come by at all?"

"I haven't talked to Gammie since she said she wouldn't have a whore in her family, Mama."

"Well, I guess it's safe to say Gammie hasn't changed much then."

Other than the annual Christmas card my mama used to send in hopes of receiving a few dollars in return, I never did know one thing about them. And I know I never will. Gramps and Gammie didn't like helping lost causes. Too much work, they said. Even when it came to family.

"I just thought you woulda been halfway across the country by now, sweet pea, instead of stayin' here living with your daddy."

"You didn't give me much of a choice, Mama," I stated without thinking, catching her head turning just a fraction.

For a moment there was a flicker in her eyes that reminded me of that morning after Pa had first hit her, when we were on Highway 77, just ten minutes from home. My five-year-old self watched in terror as Mama swerved into oncoming traffic. But just as quick as it would take for my pa to finish a beer, the thought didn't last long, and she quickly swung the wheel back. I still find myself wondering what made her change her mind at the last second and if she truly felt that was the only way out. I never held it against her.

In fact, I understood even more now.

Mama looked back at the fridge.

"You know, you lived with him."

"Now that was different. A shoulder to cry on is a dick to ride on, sweet pea. I gotta say, though, I'm glad your daddy stepped up. Took him long enough. He's always been a lazy you-know-what. Have you eaten anythin' yet? Cause from the looks of this fridge, I'm guessin' you haven't. There isn't enough in here to feed a baby. You want a sandwich? I think there's—oh here it is! That little bugger was hidin' behind the potato salad." Mama threw down the tub of food on the counter and stood upright with a can of beer, shutting the fridge with her hip. "Your daddy know your birthday's comin' up? I didn't see a cake in there."

She snapped the tab off the can and poured it into her iced tea.

"My birthday ain't for another two weeks, Mama. And I don't wanna have a cake. I don't like cake, remember?"

"He could git you somethin' at least," she said. "You really still don't like birthday cake?"

"No."

With my chin resting in the palm of my hand, I looked over at our neighbor's kitchen window that lined up perfectly across from ours. Even though our screen wasn't the cleanest, I was able to still make out his broad-shouldered shadow passing by. Not even a day here, and he already reminded me of Mr. Lawson. Unfriendly. Unsociable. Someone who preferred spending more of his time outside with nature rather than with people. I imagined that years in the desert had caused him to forget common courtesy and manners. But if he was just an unpleasant man, I could deal with it. I watched as he propped his leg on a chair, holding a bag of something against his knee. It wasn't his silence that made me curious. It was the wanting to know why. Was he silent because he's given up on people? I wasn't sure if I cared either way. But what if he's just like me?

Lonely.

"Aw, geez, I thought you woulda outgrown that by now, Grace," Mama exclaimed.

"What? I stare at things that are interesting."

"Yeah, and curiosity killed the cat. So stop bitin' that thumb of yours. And sit up straight."

It was then I realized I had been biting my thumb all along. I quickly lowered my hand and sat upright.

"You remember what I told you, Grace? Stranger danger. I don't want you spying on the new neighbor, you hear me? You did it with the Parrishes. And yes, I did know about you spying on him and his wife. You even did it with the Johnsons. You were a weird child. Always lookin' at everybody. So stop it."

"I think you and Pa have more in common than you think, Mama."

"You're not funny, Grace."

"I thought that was pretty funny."

"You don't know the man."

"He has a dog, so how bad could he be?" I claimed, realizing how ignorant I sounded.

"Grace, don't be stupid," Mama declared as she placed the leftover turkey sandwich in front of me as if she were giving a dog its bowl. "Here, you need to eat. Gotta keep you healthy to keep that baby healthy, ya hear?"

"Thanks, Mama."

"You're welcome, sweet pea." Mama awkwardly patted the back of my shoulder. "I gotta get goin', though. Gotta hit the road. It was fun catching up on our girl talk. We should do it again." She flicked the cigarette into the sink and turned on the faucet, fanning the smoke out the window.

Picking at the piece of soggy lettuce, I said, "And where you goin' this time, Mama? Louisiana? California?"

"Who knows? But that's the excitin' thing about life. You never know where you're gonna end up," Mama replied with a bright smile and bent down to stick her head back in the fridge, conducting one final sweep to see if she missed a can of beer. "Ah, ha! Jackpot! I knew you were holding out on me, Grace." She held up Pa's six-pack that he had bought the night before and shut the door.

Something sickly stirred in my belly, and it wasn't morning sickness. There was one thing that kept Pa happy, and it was a six-pack waiting for him at home. Mama was no longer around to take the brunt of his anger. Yet, that didn't stop her from randomly showing up for brief visits over these past nine years. I'd like to think I've learned how to handle that side of him. Mama never figured it out. I don't think she wanted to. Mama always seemed to bring out the worst in him, and all she had to do now was take his favorite thing in the world. And when that happened, I found myself wondering how long Pa could continue to hold back. Would he enjoy seeing me vulnerable, like a raw open wound that was picked at with a jagged fingernail? If he did, I knew it wouldn't make a difference to lock the bedroom door before he returned home. I slowly pushed myself from the table and supported my lower back with my hand, letting out an exhausted sigh.

"Ooh, goodie. And it's my favorite, too. Maybe your daddy had a sixth sense I was comin'."

"I doubt it," I said as politely as I could muster. "Please put the beer back, will you, Mama?"

"Grace, calm down. It's just beer. It's not like you'll be drinkin' it. Now you gonna walk me out or not?"

I followed Mama to the car and watched the pack of beer swing back and forth around her hooked fingers. At that moment all I wanted to do was scream and beg her to take me instead. How can something so simple as a six-pack of beer make a person spiral? Even if I did tell her everything, I had nothing on my body to prove it. Any proof I had was intangible. She suddenly halted in her tracks and pulled back her shoulders, preening like a prairie dog. I looked and saw the new neighbor walking to his truck. Mama began her predictable head to toe sweep, assessing his impressively tall and muscular figure.

"My, my, it seems like things are really gittin' interesting around here, huh?" she said not so discreetly, nudging my shoulder as she allowed her eyes to wander up his strong, sweaty arms.

"Mama—"

"Hey, you!" Mama called out, and the neighbor halted. "Yeah, you, I'm talking to you."

"Mama," I pleaded.

She smacked the side of my arm. "Oh, hush, Grace. It's called being neighborly."

He shut the tailgate and picked up the last box, stopping in his tracks once again at her next words.

"Ain't never seen you around here before. You local? I'm Miss Callaway, but you can call me Leanne." Mama smiled, twirling her finger around one of her tight blonde curls. I glanced between them, unsure of what to say. He was as quiet and dull as Ray was the day he watched old Mr. Taylor put up that BUSH sign in his front yard. And from the looks of it, I knew he'd never like my mama just as I knew Ray would never like Mr. Taylor after that.

"Hey, you deaf?"

"Mama."

She folded her arms, dropping one hip. "I asked you a question. It's called common courtesy. Ever heard of it, gimp?"

"Mama!" I exclaimed.

Without a word, he walked away, and Mama threw her arms out in disbelief as the screen door shut behind him.

"What a prick. Doesn't know a good thing when he sees it," she scoffed and climbed into the car. "Your daddy didn't know it, either. No man does." She turned her head just at the right angle for the sun to catch the scar at the tail end of her brow, a constant reminder of her own past with Pa.

If I stayed much longer, I was sure I'd become a canvas of bruises just like Mama had been.

The ignition sputtered.

"Well, say hi to your daddy for me, sweet pea. You should feel lucky he's helping you out."

There were many things I wanted to say at that moment, but I knew how it would make her feel. Like the searing heat of summer, no matter how well I thought I knew my mama, her words never ceased to burn me. I often asked myself which one was worse, but I knew I'd rather take the burn of the sun than have the little girl in me break a bit more. Like with my pa, I had to stop making wishes that weren't ever gonna come true. My mama had done the best she could with what little she knew. But there were some days I wished we didn't share the same blood. And I questioned that bond. A bond that should never be questioned between a mama and her child. Mama knew it too, and sometimes I believed she felt the same way about me. The day I was born with brown hair and big brown eyes, just like my pa's, I had become a daily reminder of her biggest regret from her junior year of high school.

"Okay, Mama. Drive safe."

"And you remember what I told you? They're all just leeches sucking us dry, and when they're done, they just move onto the next pretty thing. All just waitin—"

"Mama."

"I'm serious, Grace. It's hard to say no when God makes 'em like that. And remember. No spying."

"I know, Mama."

"Yeah, you say that. But you still go ahead and do it. And when I come back here, you best have a name picked out for that baby. Alright, sweet pea?"

Mama waved and sped up the dirt road, blasting the radio at full volume. Every part of my body wanted to run after her, crying out for her to stop. But I knew she wouldn't hear me, not just because of the radio, but because she would choose not to. The day she left, the love for me went with her, too. Turning away, I stepped back into the trailer and shut the door. After closing the blinds and grabbing my iced tea, I lowered myself onto the rocking chair that Uncle Wayne had unexpectedly given me. I propped my feet on the ottoman and tilted my head back, allowing my eyes to fall over to the fridge.

It wasn't the worst thing that could happen. The worst was when he's good to me, when he occasionally brought me a hamburger or simply smiled at me in the morning. Those good days almost made up for the bad ones. On good days, I didn't hear that little voice in my head, screaming at me to get out. Maybe I didn't want to. But on the bad days, I wondered what was wrong with me.

The whir of the swamp cooler and the waning light of day sliding down the wall had lulled me into a deep sleep until a fleeting bright flash hit my face, and I opened my eyes, rubbing the crusts from them. A truck's engine settled, and I slowly sat upright, stretching out my achy legs. It wasn't until I heard the familiar muffled voice of Jorge Hernandez singing *"La Puerta Negra"* that I knew who it was. And in the time it took for me to stand, Pa stepped inside and yelled a slurred goodbye to Uncle Wayne. I searched for any sign of a Minit Mart bag in either of Pa's hands but found none. Strands of his shaggy brown hair stuck to his forehead and specks of dirt sat across his cheeks. My nose scrunched from the foul smell of burnt popcorn and the reek of alcohol and sweat. Pa kicked the door shut with the sole of his boot and took a swig of beer, still shuffling his feet side to side.

"Hey Pa—"

He continued to sing loudly, and spread his arms wide. Unlike my mama and me, Pa had to sing and dance at the same time. He could never just pick one. *"Baila conmigo!"* he called to me, setting his beer on the counter.

"Pa—"

He grabbed my hand, swung me in a circle, and shimmied his way to the kitchen, still singing. Other than a six pack of beer, it seemed like dancing and singing were the two things in this world that he still loved doing.

"We got anythin' to eat? I'm starvin'."

"I made some sandwiches and some tomato soup. It should be warm still. I left the lid on."

"That's it, huh?"

"It was all we had left, Pa. The potato salad wasn't any good."

He nodded and ripped off a piece of paper towel.

"How was your day?" I asked, carefully choosing my words to not disrupt his good mood.

He replied with a shrug and patted the now wet towel on the back of his red and sweaty neck. "Oh, you know. Just one place to the next. Uncle Wayne says hi by the way. He's happy you're likin' that chair he gave you. It helped out with the last one when she got pregnant." Pa balled up the towel and waved it around before chucking it at the trashcan only to watch it bounce off the rim. "Dagnabbit," he said as he let out an exhausted groan and flung his head back. "I can never throw with my right. I swear."

I hesitated, fighting off the urge to ask if he had had the chance to stop and buy what I needed. "And how is Uncle Wayne?" I asked, hoping to appear sincere, but because of the expression on Pa's face, I didn't hold my breath.

"He's fine, fine as any man could be with all the problems he has."

"And Tina?"

He lifted a brow and looked over at me with a suspicious glint in his eyes. "Why you askin' so many questions about them?"

"I don't know." I cleared my throat. "I'm guessin' Uncle Wayne is picking you up today?"

"You mean tomorrow."

"Pa, it's after midnight."

He looked up at the green flickering numbers on the microwave and clicked his tongue. "Well, look at that."

"You could've just stayed at Uncle Wayne's," I reminded him as calmly as I could, carefully bending down to pick up the wet piece of towel and throwing it in the trash. "I bet he would've let you sleep on the couch again."

Pa snorted, saying, "While he fucks Tina in the other room? Yeah, no thanks. Once was enough for me."

"Don't you know how dangerous it is to drink and drive? You know on average one person is injured every six minutes in a—"

Pa threw his head back in a fit of uncontrollable laughter, followed by a spasm of wheezing. He gasped for breath, clutching his chest as he tried to recenter. After spitting into the sink and wiping his mouth, he spoke with a strained voice. "Y-you're funny, sweetie. Not even a year ago, you were out there in the desert drinkin' with that boy of yours. And look what that got ya," he said, gesturing to my belly.

I bit the tip of my tongue, knowing there wasn't anything I could say to change the truth in his words.

"You're a hoot, you know that? Just like your ma. Oh, God. My sides hurt. Whoo!"

"Pa, I'm serious."

"Uh-huh." He lifted the lid off the pot of soup and stuck his pointer finger inside, swirling it around. Pa sucked off the layer of soup and popped out his finger, saying, "You want a bowl?"

"Pa—"

"Oh stop your worryin'. Nothin' bad's gonna happen to me. Cause if it did, you'd be alone. And you don't like to be alone. You wouldn't even know what to do if I left. You don't even know how to change a tire or how to take care of yourself, Grace. Let alone a baby." Pa bent down, sticking his head inside the fridge. "Hey, you sure you don't want a bowl? It's good."

He was right.

Yet there was something about the way he always said it that crawled under my skin. As if I'd never be capable of surviving without him. I pulled my shoulders back and stood straighter, like I had something to prove. His head tilted, like a dog trying to make sense of something. It was then I knew he had seen the empty space in the back of the fridge. He sucked the excess tomato soup off his finger. An audible "pop" sound pricked my ears. Every following second passed in silence, suffocating me with the uncertainty of what he would do next. I waited for the shivers up my spine, but they never came.

"So, your ma was here. How'd she look?"

"She's still blonde."

"I thought that bitch would be dead by now, but I guess she's not." Pa snorted and shook his head, violently swinging the door shut, placing both hands on his sides. He looked around for something to smash, seizing the half bottle of beer from the counter, launching it at the wall. "She's like a fucking cockroach! Mooches off me! Just like you! All you fucking women are the same!"

"I'm sorry, Pa."

"You bet your sweet ass you're sorry."

"I am," I replied, immediately regretting my tone with his sudden silence.

"You think I believe you? You let her come in here and let her do what she wants. You don't do nothin'. You never do. You just let it happen." He sneered, and his glazed but furious eyes pierced into mine. When did it happen—when did I become his dog? Just how much did I have to endure just for the promise of food and shelter? If it was just my stomach to feed, I'd already have left.

"I'm sorry, Pa."

He shook his head, about to turn away, leaving me to hope that he would just drop it. "Pa—"

"You're a dirty liar just like your fucking mother!" he shouted, fury contorting his face until he was almost unrecognizable. "You're lucky I haven't thrown your sorry ass out! I stepped up with your mama, and now you, because that's what my father taught me. I'm the problem solver, you got that? Without Uncle Wayne, we'd be on the side of the road. You got it? And you know what, you should be grateful. You should be down on your fucking knees thanking me when I walk in that fucking goddamn door everyday!"

As his booming voice ripped through my ears, a shot of spit landed on my cheek, and I wondered if my face looked anything like Mama's when she stood here facing him in these moments. All I saw was a man angry at the world who couldn't ever be the pa I remembered when I was a child. It broke something in me that I never knew existed. Tears welled. His harsh words burned any good memory I had of him into ash, never to be mended or taped together for the millionth time. The Johnsons' porch light flipped on, causing Pa to go quiet. And for a split second, half of me expected he would just hit me right here and now. He twisted his body over the counter and looked out the window, shutting the curtain closed with a forceful swing of his arm.

"Guess who's on her way? Damn that bitch and her hearin'." Pa stormed down the hall towards his room, muttering, "Can't ever mind her own damn business. Always gotta stick her nose in places where it don't belong." The sound of a dog urgently barking only added further to his frustration. "Just perfect! I bet it's that new neighbor's!"

Before I could speak, there was a knock.

"Get rid of her, will ya? And tell that dog to shut up! Some people got work in the mornin'!"

Patting my cheeks, I wiped any tears that had escaped. Something I had seen my mama do countless times before. And just like it was for her, it was harder for me each time. When I opened the door, Arlene stopped pacing back and forth and regarded me with *that look*. A look she once showed my mama. Even down to her very hand clutching the collar of her pink robe. And the mix of hairspray and night cream wafting up my nose. Everything was the same. But now I wasn't hiding behind my mama's leg. I was my mama now. Arlene exhaled and lowered her hand from her chest.

"Sorry if we woke you up again, Arlene."

"Never mind that. You okay, sweetie? If you wanna, I could make up the couch for you."

"No, I'm okay, Arlene."

"You tellin' me the truth now, Grace?"

I nodded.

She peeked past my shoulder, scouring the inside for anything out of the ordinary or out of place. Her eyes then fell upon the shattered bottle behind me on the kitchen floor and regarded me knowingly. I glanced at the smashed bottle near the kitchen table. Neither of us spoke for a long drawn-out minute.

"Alright, well, if you need anythin,' just holler." Arlene took one last look before leaving.

"Night, Arlene."

"Night, sweetie."

I shut the door, standing in the middle of the kitchen. The thought of scrubbing the sticky layer of cheap beer off the linoleum floor made my knees ache. Quietly, I made my way to the bedroom and peeked in through the door. My eyes followed the sole of pa's boot hanging off the bed with his upper body splayed on the duvet. I cautiously sat beside him on the edge of the bed. A suffocating stillness hung in the air as I searched for the right words that would keep me and my baby safe just a little bit longer. I watched the back of his head until I had enough courage to speak. That head I used to hold onto when I would be on his shoulders and point at the blanket of stars. Now it's just something I wanted to shoot open to find the answers as to why he does the things he does. But the child in me wanted to beg him to love me like he used to. To hold me and tell me he cared and that everything would be okay.

That I was worth it.

"I'm sorry," I said sincerely, remembering Mama's words.

His head turned just a fraction, but the rest of him stayed still. I looked at him and found his dark, lifeless eyes staring back at me. Tendrils of panic curled in my stomach, wondering if this would be the moment.

Would he finally hit me?

"I didn't ask you to do all this for me ... maybe I do sometimes take you for granted. I'm sorry."

Being pricked with those shards of glass in the kitchen would be a far better punishment than saying these words to please him. I never knew saying a word could feel so disgusting. Like taking a drink of sour milk. It's what Mama had to do to see with both eyes the next day and not wear a sweater in ninety-degree weather. A man like Pa always needed to have the last word.

He slowly sat up and swung his legs off the bed, running a hand through his messy hair. His chest raised high and deflated as he exhaled deeply, pinching the bridge of his nose and squeezing his eyes shut.

"I'm sorry, too. I've just had a long day, Grace. I'm tired all the time. I can't remember the last time I had nine hours of sleep." The vulnerability in his voice struck a chord in my heart.

"I'm sorry," I said softly. "I'm sorry."

I didn't know what made me do it, but I placed my hand on his cheek and wiped the one tear that had fallen. Perhaps it's because whenever he's regretful, he reminds me of the pa I used to love. Whenever he frowned, I wanted nothing more than to hug him until he smiled. Yet the absolute worst part wasn't the helplessness or the despair that would set in when he threatened to leave. It wasn't questioning my sanity every day when he would look at me a certain way or smile at me like he used to. It wasn't the exhaustion I saw in my young eyes when I caught my reflection in the mirror. It was his ignorance. His refusal to acknowledge what he'd done to my mama. Even though I lay here beside him, it wasn't the pa I knew when I was a child. Now he's just a man who holds my fate and freedom in his hands and could decide at any moment to squeeze me a bit tighter. It would be easy. Boom and lights out. And he knows it.

He's always known it.

# 3

Every morning, like clockwork, I sat in my yellow lawn chair by the porch to watch and admire the rising sun. To remind me that there was something greater to look forward to every day. As the small ball of fire in the eastern sky increased in size and shine, a smile spread across my face. Nothing was more pleasant to the senses than the sunrise. It took all the bad thoughts away. It was just me, the desert, and my baby.

That's all that existed and mattered.

The gentle progression of the first light broke against the horizon and saturated the hills. Puffy, colorful streams of orange and dark purple cast their brilliance against Her mountains. While it was easy for me to find the beauty in Her every day, there was nothing more beautiful than the sound of that soulful cry. A cry that resonated deep in my soul. I sat up higher hoping for a glimpse. Mama used to say hearing a coyote's howl meant good things were on their way. I'm still waiting for that day, but at this moment, its long drawn-out howl made me yearn for freedom, adventure, and the complete trust in the pack. In the wild, everything was simpler. One knew where they stood in the world. Even if they had fallen.

After savoring the moment a bit longer, I stood from the porch and returned to the trailer. Peeking down the hall, I watched Pa shift in the sheets as the sound of the door closed behind me. Relieved to see him still in a deep sleep, I slowly removed a five-dollar bill from his wallet on the kitchen counter. I lifted the banquette cushion and took out the box of Pampers Arlene had given me. I carefully pulled back the tape from one end of the box and shoved the money inside. Glancing down the hall one more time, I returned the box to its proper place, quietly closed the seat, and adjusted the cushion. With a skip to my step, I began the mile and a half walk to the gas station.

Not even five minutes in, every nook and cranny of my body began to sweat. My feet throbbed and pain shot through my calves, but the promise of a stocked fridge and a box of apple juice kept me going. It was the closest store with food and water, nestled right on the corner of Highway 77 and Golder Ranch Road. I pulled two large strands of hair to the back and secured them with a scrunchie. In twenty minutes, I saw the small station and its big red and blue letters spelling out Minit Mart. Even from afar, anyone could tell the roof was on its last legs, struggling to fight off the strong elements that Arizona storms bring. Dried grass sprouted from the cracks in the cement. I picked up my pace, heading down the small decline and wiping the sweat from my forehead. Motor oil and processed food permeated the air as I pushed against one of the heavy glass doors and stepped inside. Tim Rushlow and the Little Texas gang softly sang "Kick a Little" through the static of the radio.

I turned and saw Sam behind the counter, focused on a July edition of *Rolling Stone*. His round black cheeks were plump and full of life. Sam was one of the three people in this world who never once looked at me with any hate or judgment. And sometimes, between him and Ray, they restored a little hope in me that not all men were bad. Sam lifted off his reading glasses and reached into the pocket of his shirt, taking out a small cloth to clean the lenses, careful not to tug the cord leading to his thrifted treasure, a Sony Walkman. I walked over to the counter and leaned forward, pulling the right earmuff off. He bolted in surprise and scrambled to catch his headphones, placing a hand over his chest.

"Mornin', Sam."

"How many times are you gonna do that to me?"

"Till you stop wearin' those things."

"I take medicine for heart palpitations, you know. One good scare, and I could drop dead. Then you'd feel really bad."

"I told you it's not safe, Sam. What if someone robbed the place? You're gonna get shot. Didn't you read that story in *Reader's Digest* last month? Some guy walked in and shot up—"

"I'm not gonna get shot, you worry wart. You gotta stop readin' those things. They're gonna make you paranoid, if they haven't already," Sam muttered as he finally caught his breath and glanced over to the door, wiping the bottom of his nose. "And where's your daddy? I don't see that truck of his out there. I swear, Grace, if you keep doin' this, one of these days you're gonna end up with a *Reader's Digest* story of your own." He continued when I opened my mouth to reassure his worry with a little white lie. "And don't give me that hooey of keeping in shape and exercising. Cause guess what, you can get nine hours of sleep every day, exercise till your bones ache, and eat tofu, but you're still gonna die. And never lose those extra twenty pounds." He patted his belly.

I stifled a laugh, and like what I always had to do on any day I came in here, I looked at the dozen keychains on the counter. Something that always fascinated me. Such a simple, crafted piece of metal holding all the important keys to a person's life in one place, all carried on this thingamajig, and God forbid if one loses it. Since I was a child, I wanted one of my own. Even though it was small, it represented something greater than itself. And my favorite was the one with the Saguaro charm, Arizona's state flower. But I still never had the courage to take it. Fiddling with the keychain, I smiled. My eyes then fell toward Sam who gawked at me, and I pulled myself away.

"When are you gonna buy that thing? I swear, just let me give it to you already. It's been months. How much thinkin' do you have to do for a keychain?" Sam placed his hands on his sides.

"When I get outta this town, I'll get it."

"Grace, the only people that leave this town die. Ya hear about that poor sucker just yesterday who died from heat stroke? Obviously underestimated how much water he needed for the climb up Camelback. That's the second one since last week. It's August, for heaven sakes. People are nuts. But . . ." he began with an exhale, putting on his reading glasses, leaving me waiting for his next inevitable words. ". . . as my pop would say, Grace. Natural selection at its finest."

"That ain't nice, Sam."

"You know I'm right."

"Okay, Sam, whatever you say. Now I gotta pee. I didn't go before I left." I speed-walked to the bathroom.

"And when are you gonna name that dang baby, Grace?" Sam called out. "It's not gonna stay in there forever."

"I don't know!" I hollered.

After wiping every bare part of my body with a wet paper towel, I left the bathroom revived with my skin now freshly cooled and ready for whatever the day might bring me. I shared a smile with Sam before he returned to a customer, and I made a straight beeline towards the boxes of apple juice. As I wandered through the aisles, my mind was peacefully empty, sipping on the juice box. I lifted my gaze from the shelf and spotted a familiar black truck pull up alongside a gas pump.

The man climbed out and made his way over. He had a slight limp to his gait but that didn't detract from his imposing physicality. There was something daunting about his movements, as subtle as they were. He was even taller than he appeared from across the driveway. It was like witnessing a lone coyote that had strayed far from its habitat stepping foot into civilization. He walked confidently but was also wary, evaluating each person and car that arrived. My pa once said that if I ever crossed paths with a coyote to remember that I could not outrun him. Stand your ground, look him in the eye, and let him know you're not taking your eyes off him.

To anyone else, he was just a man at a gas station. But if they looked closely enough, he was on guard, patrolling and taking in his surroundings. If one thing were to be out of place, he would be the first to know.

And though my mama and pa had always told me not to look at people, it was their certainty of someone that made me all the more curious about them. And for some inexplicable reason, the sound of the bell caused my heart to quicken as I watched him step inside, still unable to look away. He seemed to have already completed a day's work from the bits of white paint on his boots and arms and the few strands of sweaty hair stuck to his forehead. His eyes flicked toward me, and my neck whipped away so fast I thought I had injured myself. I nibbled the top of my straw and once again slowly allowed myself to take a gander as he walked up to the counter, reaching into his back pocket for his wallet.

"Can you put fifteen on pump four?" he asked in a slow but deep drawl. "And also, do you got any corn nuts?" He turned his head just a fraction over his shoulder, noticing me. But this time I didn't look away.

I stared at him longer than it took for the sun to rise. At least it seemed that way to me. But during what had only been three seconds for my mind to come to a standstill, a smile had crept onto my face that stretched from one side to the other, showing every single tooth. He looked away but not without sharing another glance and rubbing behind his left ear. As tempted as I was to keep watching him, I knew, just like in the desert, there were always limits. I ambled over to the refrigerated section, slipping a carton of eggs and a carton of milk into the basket. Finding the last two packets of Applegate turkey slices, I moved on to the next aisle where all the sweet and savory favorites awaited anyone with a sweet tooth. Snickers or Razzles? So difficult to choose. After grabbing two bags of potato chips instead, I made my way up to the counter, expecting to see him.

Even by the time Sam had rung up my last few items and started to bag them, there was no sign of him. Then, unexpectedly, the scent of turpentine, wood, and sweat assaulted my senses. My nose scrunched. Looking over my shoulder, I saw him behind me, holding a bag of corn nuts and a bottle of water. My head turned back to center.

Sam glimpsed between us as he bagged the last item. "Thirteen fifty-five," he said.

Reaching into my small purse, I counted out the dollar bills and change. My fingers paused, struggling to remember how much I had already laid on the counter. Biting my bottom lip, I went to retrieve two more dimes but stopped to look at Sam for guidance. He nodded and said, "You got it. Two more dimes and a nickel."

I nodded, saying, "Right," and reached back into my coin purse. "And another penny—"

The man brushed past me and stepped forward, saying, "Look, I'll just pay for whatever she has. I need to get goin'." He laid down two crumpled twenties on the counter. "Just keep the change."

"Hey, there's no need for that. I have my own money," I said as he turned away without so much as another look. "Hey, I'm talkin' to you," I called out just as the door snapped shut behind him.

Unsure of what else to say or do, I stood there, taken aback. Any time I received an act of random kindness now, every bit of me hated it. Pity had disguised itself as kindness as far as I was concerned. What had the man gained by doing that? As sad as it was, people didn't do things without hoping for something in return. People were never as selfless as they claimed to be. At the end of the day, those little acts of kindness only existed for them to say that they did it. That way, they could sleep a bit better at night.

"Looked like he was in a hurry. He moved faster than the drop of a hat." Sam said, adjusting his glasses on the bridge of his nose. "That fella new around here? Ain't never seen him before."

"He's my new neighbor."

"Too bad you can't choose your neighbors."

By the time I grabbed my bags and gave Sam a small smile, the black truck was nowhere to be seen.

"Thanks, Sam."

"Have a good day, Grace. Stay cool, ya hear me?"

"I hear ya." I walked out of the station but not before giving him a quick wave goodbye.

The moment I stepped outside, a strong gust of dry wind hit my face, and my legs sizzled like eggs on a skillet. Arizona was just a vault of hot air. I stepped onto the asphalt to begin the mile-and-a-half walk back home. To please my curiosity one last time, I stopped and glanced around, unexpectedly finding the truck sitting at the corner of Golder Ranch Road. Even if he was a good man, my stomach twisted just like the times I would walk home from school and watch every car passing by, frightened that one of them would stop. And despite the words Mama had repeatedly ingrained into me from a young age—*Don't talk to strangers*—my feet kept walking towards him. His dog spotted me, and his ears perked.

Even then he hadn't seemed to notice me yet. He just sat there, letting the engine idle, scratching behind his left ear, looking elsewhere. The glare of the sun hit the windshield in just the right spot, making it difficult to discern any of his features. But I could see the tips of his fingers tapping the wheel.

"What are you doin'?" I asked.

He flinched and looked over, seeming hesitant to say something as if he was truly surprised that I had approached him.

"Uh, I—"

"You what?"

He opened his mouth to speak, but I didn't give him a chance.

"You're not *that* guy, are you? The one that the cops are lookin' for? Last month in *Reader's Digest*, some girl hitchhikin' had to survive in the desert after some guy clubbed her over the head and left her for dead. They still haven't found him. So you better say somethin', or else I'm gonna start screamin'. Cause I know you ain't lost."

"I . . ." he began, struggling to find the right words. I stood there, suspicious, waiting to hear what he had to say next. "I was just wonderin' if you, uh, needed a ride?" His voice was gentle but guarded.

"I don't take rides from strangers," I said and walked away before he could respond. "Bye, now."

"Look, I didn't mean . . ."

I stopped and turned around to look at him. His truck door had opened. And my eyes slowly moved higher as he climbed out and straightened his spine to its full extent. I was right. He could really reach the top shelf where Pa kept the Oreos. "If I scared ya, I'm sorry. I didn't mean to. Really. I just . . ." he stammered and cleared his throat, shifting his stance, rubbing the back of his neck.

If I didn't know any better, I'd reckon he was the one who was more at unease. And why he seemed reluctant to look at me for anything longer than several seconds, I didn't know. Not only that, but he really wasn't a man of many words. The silence could've stretched home and back by now. I could see him growing impatient, frustrated by his own inaction. It was as if I was the first person he was attempting to communicate with after breaking a long vow of silence. Like I had done after the first year Mama had left. All I had wanted, deep down, was someone to talk to. Desperate for a friend, a companion, even just a person to smile with. I was lucky I had Arlene, Ray, and Sam.

Though he didn't say much, he still had all my attention. His stance shifted again before he muttered, "Okay, forget it, just, uh, forget I said

44

anything," and turned away. His dog stuck his head out the back window and whined, wagging his tail. As naive as it was, I couldn't help but think: *How bad can he be if he has a dog like that?* My mama always said you learn the most about a person by reading in between the lines.

But what if I can't find the lines?

He then abruptly turned around and faced me, saying, "Look, I just can't in good conscience leave you here or not ask ya again. It's . . . it's hot out here. And I don't want somethin' bad to happen to you. Especially with you bein' that way."

From the look in his tentative brown eyes, I knew he expected me to turn him down again, but I wondered if a part of him still hoped for the possibility of me saying yes. And though he was a stranger, I found myself considering his offer. But just as my pa said, men like him are a hit and miss. Any man is. However, I truly believed if he really had wanted to hurt me, he would've already done so. And this was another opportunity I had to not listen to Pa. I was free to say and do whatever I wanted. And the thought of the long stretch of road ahead and walking any further made my muscles ache. "Okay," I said. "But if you try to do somethin', I'll scream. You got that?"

"Okay."

"Okay."

We lingered there for just a moment longer before he made the first move and turned away. I hesitated at first but followed, struggling to keep up with his long strides as he made his way around the truck. As he opened the passenger door, I immediately stepped back without thinking. The dog's whine settled any remaining doubts just long enough for me to lift myself onto the seat. The man watched me struggle to move into what I'm sure was a very unattractive position. My foot slipped on the sidebar, and he quickly stepped forward just as I caught myself on the handle.

"I'm fine. I've done this before. I don't need a man's help," I said, trying to convince myself more than him.

I slowly but surely pushed myself onto the seat. A mix of beer and dog hung in the air, oddly soothing my nerves. He shut the door and circled around the truck, eyes scanning the perimeter, without so much as even moving his head. I fought the temptation to sneak a good look at him and smoothed my bunched-up dress just as he climbed inside. He checked the side mirror before accelerating, and I sat back in the seat hoping to appear relaxed. His dog stuck its head out the window, enjoying the last minutes of tolerable heat. I was completely alone with him. In his truck. Maybe later I'd tell myself I should have thought longer before agreeing to this. I should have counted to ten and waited until I regained my sanity and evaluated the pros and cons like a thoughtful, rational adult.

Though the sound of the radio played in the background, a thick silence descended over us. We shared a glance, and he shifted in his seat, stiff, before sticking his hand into the bag of corn nuts. Like a fly buzzing around my ear, the loud crunch and static of the radio began to irk me. He propped his arm on the windowsill and exhaled a deep breath through his nose. Even though he appeared calm, there still lay an unmistakable tension in his hands and face. Was he always this way, or was it just me that made him this way? He rubbed the back of his ear, and my eyes lowered to the sunlight reflecting off his dog tags and then to his arms. Anyone would pray to not be held in a chokehold in those. Half of me felt uncomfortable to be alone with him. He was, after all, a man. Yet, the other half was undeniably and shamefully curious about him, and I hated that I was. The last time I felt this intense curiosity I ended up looking at two pink lines on a stick two weeks later. I looked out the window and at my lap, then at him again, unsure of what to say or do.

"You know, my friend Stacy Maguire got in her neighbor's truck when she was thirteen and didn't come back until she was eighteen," I said. He stopped chewing and slowly looked over at me, astonishment twisting his face. "I-I mean, she was fine. She just ran off with a boy she liked. Even asked me to come with her. I said no. Obviously," I stammered.

He nodded and turned away, tapping the wheel.

The apple of his cheek and his lips twitched as if he was holding back a smile, which I didn't have time to fully witness since he had returned his attention to the road. But what he didn't know was that I caught a small glimpse of that smile from the reflection in the side-view mirror. It was awkward. It didn't fit him, as if the muscle hadn't been used in a long time. But most of all, the light of day reflected the humor residing in his eyes. The sight of it all made me relieved to know there was a human inside.

Every year at Christmas, Mama would take out her watercolors and paint a prickly pear cactus on a card for my grandparents. It was one of her favorite plants because it was spiny on the outside but sweet on the inside. This man somehow reminded me of that cactus. Would there be something lurking deeper beneath that stoic and quiet exterior? Something sweeter? He faced the road, popping in another handful of corn nuts. With each crunch, the harder it was to resist biting my bottom lip.

"He's a handsome dog, by the way," I said. "What's his name?"

"Harley."

"I always wanted a German shepherd growing up, but my pa always said no."

"He's a Belgian Malinois."

"Oh."

"Look, kid, I don't wanna—"

"I'm not a kid," I said. He stared ahead, unresponsive, as his brows slowly pinched together.

"I'm not. You got that?" I repeated in a firmer tone, causing him to glimpse at me peculiarly.

Other than the sound of his finger tapping the wheel, the crunch of the corn nuts, and the radio, there were no other words or looks exchanged. I kept my mind occupied with the clear view of the Catalina Mountains ahead of us. As we passed the dirt road and turned right, I spotted my trailer in the distance, expecting Pa to stumble out in his dirty white tank top and boxers, inhaling the fresh air with a cigarette between his lips. An unsettling feeling churned in my stomach, and I asked, "Can you stop here?"

We caught each other's glances. And just as I expected him to ask why, he pulled off to the side of the road just three trailers down from the Johnsons'. He lowered his hands from the wheel, sitting back against the seat.

*Say something, Grace*, I thought. "Anyway, um, thanks for givin' me a ride."

He cleared his throat. "No problem," he said, rubbing behind his left earlobe again, giving me an awkward but faint smile.

I opened the door, carefully climbing out with a grunt of effort. Harley whined and sat up from the backseat. "Bye, Harley."

He barked.

I shut the door and took only a few steps forward before I paused to watch him as he turned into his driveway. He killed the engine and climbed out of the truck with Harley, not once turning to look back. My eyes followed his quick movements, and I blinked as he shut the screen door with more force than normal. If a sweetness did lurk inside him, it was rooted deep, as Mama would say.

As I passed by the Johnsons' trailer, I stopped at the sudden sound of Ray saying, "Mornin' Grace." There he was sitting in Arlene's pink fold-out chair with his bunions on full display and a cigarette hanging out the corner of his mouth.

"Mornin', Ray."

"How's you and the baby doin?" he asked.

"We're fine."

"Good. Good." Ray nodded as his knowing eyes drifted to the new neighbor's trailer and then to my face. "So, I see you met the new neighbor." He jerked his head toward the truck.

"Uh-huh."

The thought of my pa waking up at any minute now began eating away at my nerves.

"What's he like?"

"Um . . ." I paused, trying to come up with a simple answer. "H-he didn't really talk much."

"Huh." He nodded and scratched his chin before tapping the excess ash of the cigarette into a tray, putting it out. "Well, hey, you wanna take a load off with old Ray?" He slid over his fold-out chair, eagerly patting the seat. "Come on. Sit. Before Arlene wakes up and gives me the stink eye. I don't think your dad will be up and 'round for another good half hour. He's not gonna know."

"I'd really like to, Ray, but I need to get these things in the fridge." I gestured to the bags in my hand.

He slumped back into the chair with a scowl, muttering and shaking his head. "I swear, no matter how old I get, women still be breaking my heart. I'll be dead, and it'll still be breakin'."

"You'll live, Ray," I reassured him. "And Arlene told you no smokin' in the morning, remember?"

"Been smokin' this brand since I was thirteen. You don't see me coughing up a lung," he said defensively.

"Not yet."

He rolled his eyes and sputtered. "Not yet, she says. Not yet. All you women think you know what I need but you really don't." He mumbled the last line, but I heard it loud and clear.

I smiled. "Bye, Ray."

I headed into the trailer, shutting the door behind me. The smell of aftershave and soap filled the small space, confirming the very worry I had outside. I let out a breath and allowed my body to relax as I set the bags on the counter. My pinched feet slid out of the sandals and my toes wiggled in relief. I bent over, placing the carton of milk and eggs in the fridge. *Thump. Thump.* I looked up and saw Pa sticking a foot through one of the pant legs of his jeans.

"Mornin', Pa."

"Where did ya go? You weren't on the couch."

"The gas station." I stood upright, shutting the fridge. "And when are you gonna get some new jeans? Those don't fit you."

"When I win the lottery," he answered, struggling to fasten the button, muttering an array of expletives. He inhaled deeply, sucking in the bubble of belly fat, and secured the button. He let out the breath, staring down at the protruding fat spilling over his waistline, and patted the jiggly flesh. Pa hadn't taken Mama's leaving very well. We both hadn't. Pa snagged a black T-shirt off the chair, sniffing underneath each arm. "Besides, it's not like your dresses are gittin' any looser either, girlie." He pulled the shirt over his head. "So what were you doin' at the gas station?"

"Just picking up what we needed. Sam says hi."

"Uh-huh. I saw that new neighbor and his mutt just now. Like we need another dang dog here. Just more shit to step in."

Ever so slightly, I turned my head, watching Pa sit down. As his strong fingers looped and tightened the strings of his boots, I knew I'd give myself away if I found the courage to speak. One crack of my voice, and he'd know I'd done something wrong. Something he didn't like. Just like with Mama. There was a time when being his little girl was easier. But now there wasn't much I could do. Even in these moments. All I could do was just try to breathe and pray nothing would give me away.

"Tico's one thing. But I swear, Grace, I don't like the look of that dog. It's why I don't want you doin' what I know you're thinkin' of doin'. You're too old for that. So stop it already." Pa gave one final tug to secure the laces of his boot and stood from the table. The sound of a car's horn caused him to lean over the counter and peek out the window. "Right, well, there's Uncle Wayne. Don't wait up, okay? I have a double shift again, and I might not be back till tomorrow."

"Alright."

"Hey, you okay?" His voice was unexpectedly soft. And instinctively that scared little girl inside me surfaced. I shook my head, unable to form a sentence in my head, let alone find my voice.

"I think it's just morning sickness," I replied, trying to convince myself rather than him. "I still get it sometimes."

"Well, throw up, will ya? You'll feel better, and you'll look better." Pa fetched his baseball cap off his chair and stopped at the door, giving me one of his rare smiles. Even on the days Pa acted chipper, there was still a sadness lurking in his eyes. The same kind Mama always had. All their smiles were little white lies showing me how easy it was to hide the pain of an unfulfilled life. And I'd bet all the money stashed in the Pampers box that Pa wouldn't return home sober. His demons were always waiting at the bottom of every can of beer. "Hey, you know I love you, Grace."

"Love ya, too, Pa."

I leaned toward the window and listened to him whistle as he climbed into Uncle Wayne's truck. The moment the front tires churned the dirt and sped down the street, my knees began to wobble, and I slowly sank into the corner between a cabinet and the fridge. I exhaled loudly and deeply, unaware I had been holding my breath. My chest began to rise and fall at an uneven pace. Tears clouded my vision as I cried, wanting to run and pack up everything I had. But what was worse was knowing I never would. I'd stay on the floor just like Mama did. Allowing the slowness of time and self-torture to paralyze me. And then, sooner or later, I'd exhale in resignation once again, brush myself off, pull back the tears, and clean up the shattered beer bottle from last night.

# 4

The mornings Pa would stay at Uncle Wayne's had become precious. It was a luxury to be able to sleep in the one bed with my arms and legs splayed wide across the sheets. But even though Pa hadn't been here the night before, he still left a suffocating stench, reminding me that this was his territory the moment I opened my eyes. Maybe if I shut them again and whispered a prayer, I'd wake up in the middle of springtime sitting on a porch of my own, underneath my umbrella, holding my baby girl and drinking my sweet iced tea. A morning like that didn't sound so bad. No morning ever sounded bad with her in my arms. As much as I yearned to continue pampering my aching muscles some more and daydreaming of the what-ifs, the growing light outside willed me to leave the confining walls of the trailer.

With the first glimmers of light catching the edges of the mountains, my problems didn't seem so big, and no matter what life threw at me I could still stand tall and strong, just as those mountains had for millions of years. Shutting my eyes, I emptied my mind to fully bask in the soul-catching howl of a coyote in the distance. When the light of day had touched across all the land, a sudden movement in my belly caused me to look down. And like the first time I felt her tiny hand or foot kick, I smiled just as big. It was a feeling I could never grow tired of. "What?

You hungry, baby? You know, I reckon Sam's wonderin' where we are. So let's go and get some food and keep him company." I pushed myself off the step and slowly stood, supporting my back with my left hand, feeling another sudden movement.

"Well, aren't you just a ball of energy this mornin'."

After a much-needed trip to the bathroom, I walked out of the trailer and slipped on my sandals one at a time. I stepped off the makeshift patio and took not even one step before I had to stop. Using the post for stability, I lifted my right foot and my fingers reached down as far as they could, untwisting the plastic strap of my sandal. I sighed in relief as my nose caught a whiff of black coffee and a hint of motor oil. At first I looked at Arlene and Ray's trailer for the source of the smell. The kitchen curtain was still shut. Even the porch light was on. Lowering my foot, I walked forward and saw a cup of coffee and a paper plate with a slice of toast sitting on top of an old milk crate across the way.

I halted.

Next to it was a pair of Timberlands underneath the neighbor's truck, once tan but now covered in layers of motor oil and dirt. Harley sat by the right tire, standing guard and watching his owner, ears raised to the highest point I'd seen. My neighbor then pushed himself out from underneath the truck and dusted off his hands, standing upright. After wiping the sweat from his forehead, he cleaned the grime off his hands with a dirty cloth before reaching for the toast. Only then did he turn around and lean his side against the truck, ripping off a piece. Harley stared up at him, all the more hopeful. The man's mouth moved, but I couldn't hear the words. It was obvious he was talking to Harley. That said, it was the first time I'd ever seen him so relaxed. And much to my surprise, he even smiled. As silly as it was, a part of me hoped that maybe one day someone would smile that way at me, a smile that spoke of a bond that only two like-minded souls shared.

He tossed the bread and watched Harley catch it with ease. He did a double take my way, and suddenly his countenance changed. He shifted his stance as he stood straighter. It was then I realized I had intruded.

"Mornin'."

He rubbed the back of his left ear. "Mornin'."

The sound of his voice was low and soft, and I almost mistook it for the wind. He then looked to the ground, sticking one hand in the pocket of his jeans. Even from afar he seemed hesitant to acknowledge me, possibly more so than he had been just yesterday in his truck. And that's all it took for the stillness to stretch further and further between us.

"Well, bye now."

"Hey, um, do you . . ." he began as he stepped closer to speak, but instead he cleared his throat as if another part kept him from doing so. I stared at him, wondering what he possibly had to say to me. But whatever it was that brought him to a complete standstill, it quickly passed as he said, "Right. So, well, just—just be careful, will ya?" He remained still for another moment before turning on the heel of his boot and striding back toward the trailer, head down, rubbing the back of his sweaty neck. Harley looked at him and then at me before quickly following him to the door.

I didn't know how long I stood there, confused as to whether I had said something to offend him. Was it because I had intruded? But when I heard the sound of his door slamming, a sound I was becoming all too familiar with, my feet moved. And I wholeheartedly believed right then and there that any future interaction would be fleeting and never more than just a hello. Just when I thought I had seen a sliver of the sweetness that lurked under his sour outer core. I wasn't sure if I cared, but nonetheless, a part of me couldn't help but question it. It wasn't until I was further down the road that keeping my curiosity and uncertainties at bay didn't seem so much of a struggle anymore as his truck had now become small enough to fit in my pocket.

By the time the morning rush shoppers had bought their quick fix of coffee and talked with Sam, I still hadn't shaken my neighbor from my thoughts. Even the sound of Tracy Lawrence singing *"Alibis"* on the radio wasn't enough to lure me into a sing-along. And every so often, I'd raise my head, a small part of me expecting to see the neighbor's black truck pull up in the gas station lot.

Looking away from the window, I saw that Sam had just passed Mrs. Anderson her bag of toiletries and tobacco products. Her frail and wizened gray hair was pulled into a tight bun, stretching the crow's feet further back from her eyes. Though they held a certain brightness, there was still a lack of spirit in them. And for a brief moment, I wondered if that's what people saw in mine. Sinking into the fold-out chair and propping my swollen feet on the counter, I returned my attention to the August edition of *Reader's Digest*.

"You two have a nice day now. Nice seein' you again, Grace. Tell your daddy I said hi," Mrs. Anderson said, giving Sam and my feet another quick once over as she left. I lifted my chin, watching her.

"Well, isn't she just a peach."

"Not her fault she was raised that way, Sam. You know that," I said and sat upright with a sigh. "You could say, though, it's her fault for not breakin' that nasty pattern."

"Not everyone can change, Grace. Takes a certain kind of person. And there's not a lotta people like that out in the world." Sam sat on the stool, opening up his magazine again.

Dark shadows circled his eyes and gathered at the creases of his downturned mouth. I recognized the exhaustion his body exuded. No matter how many times he denied it, even after living here all his life, I knew he played with the idea of packing up his family and leaving. I wanted to pry, but I knew he would just say what Mama used to say: "I'm fine, Grace." Turning away, I stared at my feet, wiggling my toes in my sandals.

"Hey, you sure your daddy isn't gonna come in here lookin' for ya?

By now you're usually headed back home."

"For the second time, Sam, I'm sure. He stayed at my Uncle Wayne's again last night, or at least I hope so. You know how they are. Those two together are bad news."

"Alright, well." Sam exhaled and shut his magazine, providing me his full attention as he said, "Wanna share another story from that 'bible' of yours?" He gestured toward my *Reader's Digest*, seemingly interested.

I sat upright with a burst of energy and lowered my feet from the counter, anxiously finding the page I had left off on.

"I know I say this all the time, but that stuff is gonna get to you sooner or later."

"Oh, hush, you love it, too," I replied and found the page, sitting on the edge of my seat. "Here's a good one. This one was a speedboat in Florida that nearly severed a diver's arm. He was in the water for almost a half hour until someone found him. Can you believe that? The driver of the boat visited him in the hospital, and they fell in love. Six months later, he divorced his wife and a year later married the driver. Now they're expecting their first child. Well, ain't that sweet."

"You really can't make this stuff up, I guess," Sam said, nestling the earmuff of his Sony Walkman against his ear.

I placed the magazine down on the seat and slowly pushed myself up with a grunt. "I need to pee. That last juice box set me over. I gotta say, though, I do feel bad for the wife. Does marriage mean nothin' anymore? I swear, Sam, this is why I don't wanna marry. Nothin' good comes from it."

Sam snorted and shook his head.

"What's so funny?"

"As I've said before and will say again, Grace, it takes two people who are in love for a marriage to work," he stated for a matter of fact. "And you ain't even nineteen yet, by the way. You got your whole life ahead of ya. I said the exact thing when I was your age, and ten years later, I married my wife. Are there days when she pisses me off? Good golly, yes. But I know I piss her off, too."

"Well, my mama always said it takes a certain kind of man to handle a Callaway woman."

"Yeah, well, parents don't know everything."

"If my mama was right about one thing, Sam, I think she'd be right about . . . uh-oh." I halted at the sudden urge to hurl. I tried to hold it back, but it fought back harder, and I raced to the bathroom, pushing past Sam.

"Grace?" he asked, worried.

After patting my heated face with a cool paper towel, I returned to the counter with an exhausted sigh, tightening the string of my dress around my waist. Sam looked up from the magazine, concerned. I placed my hand on the counter for extra stability, fighting against the wobble and ache of my body and knees. Taking one last breath, I shut my eyes to recenter myself.

"You okay?"

I did a thumbs up.

"You need some water?"

I nodded, holding my back. "I don't think the baby liked the fourth Slim Jim," I said with a soft laugh.

*Ring.*

I looked toward the entrance. A group of teenage boys walked in with Wildcats jerseys and baseball caps, filling the air with their boisterous laughter. One of the lankier boys had hoisted himself on the back of another, piggyback style, and they charged down the aisle. It's funny how seven months could seem like a different lifetime. And seven months was all it took for me to forget about them, like they had seemed to forget about me. I turned to go sit with Sam when the bell rang again. It was Mason. He was here. And taller than the last time I saw him. His white T-shirt was tighter across his chest and arms now.

Mason looked over, and his face dropped. Every nerve of my body kicked into high gear, and I made a sharp turn down the candy aisle, hoping he hadn't seen me.

"Hey!" he called out. "I saw ya, Grace!"

Just as I made my way to the end of the aisle and peeked around the endcap, Mason slid in front of me. He caught his breath, propped his arm on top of the shelf, and smiled at me with his perfectly straight, white teeth.

"I gotta say, Grace, you still move just as fast as you used to." He pushed back the fallen strands of his brown hair and then gestured to my white dress. "Oh, hey, I like the little flowers you have there. It's pretty. I thought you didn't like—"

"It's the only thing that fits me."

"Oh, well, you look good," he said and cleared his throat.

"And you're taller."

"Well, I hope I am. It has been a while." He grinned big, showing off his left dimple. That smile made all his boyish features shine even more. His eyes were the same clear green that I've always loved since I met him. Those two things, mixed with the sweet talk he learned from his father, made me ultimately and shamefully putty in his hands. All he had to do was flash a toothy grin and wink that right eye, and it made any girl catch her breath. His smile disappeared once he knew he hadn't pulled the reaction he had wanted out of me. "Can we go talk outside, Grace?"

Be it from his friends' loud laughter or the desperate gleam in Mason's eyes that had already bent my better judgment, I said, "Alright."

I followed behind him to the door and glanced over at his group of friends who were at the slushy machine debating over the cherry or blueberry. Mason held the door open, and I stepped outside into the hot air, keeping myself underneath the awning. My eyes slowly adjusted to the brightness of the sun. Mason cleared his throat, scratching the middle of his chin. Though he had changed physically, his little quirks hadn't. And it still took all I had to not slap him across the face.

"So you're, uh, five months preg—"

"Seven."

"Seven, right. You got any names yet?"

"What are you doin' here, Mason?" I asked, trying to hide the irritation in my voice.

"I came to get—"

"No, I mean right here. Right now. What do you wanna talk to me outside for? I got nothin' to say to you."

"I wanted to talk to you."

"And it took you seven months to wanna talk to me?"

"I was busy."

"*You* were busy?"

"Hey, you're the one who stopped coming over, Grace," Mason stated in a low hushed tone. "I did try and talk to you. You'd always run the other way. Like you did just now. You've never made it easy for me to get through that wall of yours. Ever. You even stopped coming to school. So don't try to blame it all on me."

"Were you bullied every day?"

"No, I—"

"Were you stared at every day?"

"Grace—"

"And anytime I saw you in the hall, you just looked at me like I was some embarrassment. You don't know nothin' about what I've been goin' through. Were you laughed at? Were you called a whore? Did you get called fat? No. You didn't. I can't even go into a store now without someone looking at me like my baby's an abomination. Your mom and dad were the ones who told me to stop hanging out with you," I said, noticing Sam watching us from the counter. "They said I was a bad influence," I continued, facing Mason. "And what did you do? You did nothin'."

"Hey, I'm not having an easy time either with you being knocked up and all. You know why I couldn't tell them about it. My dad would beat my ass and knock me into next Sunday, Grace. You know it."

"It's called a baby. Not an 'it'. A baby." I turned away, making a straight beeline to the door. He caught up with me with little to no effort and grabbed my arm. I yanked it back. "Don't you dare touch me, Mason."

"Okay, okay. I'm sorry. I shouldn't have said that. That was wrong of me," he admitted. "It's just . . . I've been wanting to talk to you for a while now, Grace. I've been messed up about it. And I get why you don't want anythin' to do with me. I get it, alright? Really. I do. I wasn't the best boyfriend there. But I wanna try again. Like old times. Can we, please? And I swear, if I do something that pisses you off, we can cut it off and I won't bother you ever again. I promise."

A twinge of guilt weighed on my chest from the anxious gleam in Mason's eyes. "Well, alright, I guess."

In spite of everything, a part of me still held onto that hope that every person had in this world. For a brief moment, Mason had almost made me forget the crater that had dug itself in my chest. That I had spent my childhood building a series of walls around. That moment was all I needed to think that maybe it was okay now. Maybe it was okay to knock down the wall just a bit for him. I could rebuild. I've done it before. A smile spread across his face, and just as he was about to speak, his group of friends piled out of the station with large slushies in hand. Their laughter went quiet as they looked toward us. Two boys gawked at me as the other two directed their attention to Mason, bewildered.

"What? You got somethin' to say, Grady?" Mason asked.

"No." Grady cleared his throat. "How you doin', Grace? It's been a while since we last saw ya."

"Fine, and you?" I asked.

"Asked Mary to the Pima County Fair this week," Grady said proudly with a grin. "She finally said yes."

"That's this week?" I asked.

Mason smiled toward me and said, "Yep, this Friday."

I nodded, catching one of the boys giving me a prolonged once-over. His eyes set on my belly.

"Anyway, uh, we're gonna go wait in the car, Mason." Grady flashed me a forced smile before leading the group away. "Nick, come on. Nick. Stop starin'!" He snapped his fingers. Nick quickly turned and caught up to the three boys, head down. Mason and I watched them huddle into the Jeep.

Mason exhaled. "I guess I should get goin' before they die of heat stroke, huh?" He retrieved his keys from his pocket and said, "You know, those big pretzels that you like will be there at the fair. Or can you not have that?"

"I can have it."

"Good, 'cause I was thinkin' we could go with them. In separate cars of course. Cause I-I know you don't really care for Grady's driving. Especially when he's had a few too many . . ." He flinched when one of the boys honked the horn. "I'm comin'!" he yelled. "For fuck sake. I'll pick you up at nine. Alright? This Friday." He stepped off the sidewalk. "You still live with your dad, yeah?"

"Yeah."

"This Friday. At nine o'clock. Don't forget." Mason smiled, jogging across the lot over to the Jeep.

From a young age, words had lost their meaning to me. Someone could say they'd do something, but it doesn't mean they'd do it. As much as I wanted to feel a bit of passion, hope, and maybe, even, love, I knew at the end of the day, Mason would never love the baby as much as I would. If by some miracle we did work out, I'd only be giving my baby girl the same father as I have now. And no matter how badly I wanted to experience the one thing that comes close to magic in this world, there was nothing more important to me than keeping her from having the same kind of father. Either way, I'd never find something as good as this baby. I headed inside, relieved to feel the cool air. Sam looked up from his magazine.

"I take it that was the baby daddy you don't like talkin' about?"

"What does your gut tell you?"

"Funny. Very funny. But whatever you two were talkin' about out there, he better have told ya that he's gonna help you and that baby, Grace. Boy needs to step up."

"Sam, my mama told my pa the same thing, and look at how he turned out. I don't wanna give that to my baby. And as much as I don't like the boy, he don't deserve that either. Nobody does."

"Grace, I'm not tellin' ya that you need him. I know you don't. I'm sayin' no matter how many books or magazines you'll read, it's not gonna tell you everything. Take it from me. I have three kids, and I still don't know what to do with the third one. Now sit your butt down and rest those feet. Just lookin' at you is making me tired."

I smiled and walked over to the counter.

"Anyone ever told you that you're sweet, Sam?"

"Only you, and my wife when I take out the trash. Now come on, how about you read me another story from that magazine of yours? I know you got another one in there. Let's hear it."

As the sky dimmed, Mason now occupied my thoughts instead of that new neighbor. Though I had played that scene so many times in my head till I lost count, it was as if I had seen a ghost that had come back to remind me of what I did. It was like looking into a past reflection of myself. And I wondered if this was what Mama felt like whenever she saw Pa. There was a sense of relief, then a little terror because I hadn't the slightest clue what to say or do next. I thought the burning anger had been swept away since the moment I heard my baby's tiny heartbeat. At least that's what I thought until today.

"Alrighty, Sam. See you tomorrow."

"You sure you don't want me to drive you home? I could close up shop for ten minutes. I don't mind."

"I'll be okay. And I have water." I reassured him one last time and waved goodbye before stepping outside.

Despite the throbbing pain shooting from my feet to my calves, my mind was captivated by the palette of colors accumulating in the sky. Rivers of pastel pinks and blues stretched across the horizon. No matter if it was dawn or dusk, my mind always found a sense of peace. It was one of the few times I truly enjoyed living in a place like this. I didn't even hear the rebellious teenagers and the bass of their low riding cars. For once, it was almost quiet. Then a delightful smell of burning charcoal and sizzling meat wafted up my nose, becoming more potent with each step I took. A puffy stream of smoke came from outside Arlene and Ray's trailer, dissipating into the sky the higher it traveled. Even as a little girl, I swore that I always tasted Ray's secret barbecue sauce hanging in the air. I picked up my pace as Ray stepped out from the trailer with a platter of hot links ready to be grilled, humming to himself.

"Evenin', Ray."

He turned, and his face lit up. "Well, howdy, Grace. Haven't seen you all day. Hung out with Sam?"

"He does have the strongest A/C around."

"He does, for sure. Here. Come sit. Keep me some company while I fire these babies up."

"You havin' a party or somethin'?" I asked as he placed half a dozen hot links on the grill.

"Nah, Arlene wanted me to get started on these before we head on over to Paul's and have dinner with his family. You want me to make a plate for you and your dad? I got a couple extra."

"We could always go for one of your patties, Ray. You know that.

63

Especially my pa." I sat down at the picnic table with a relieved sigh and set my legs on either side of the seat to compensate for my belly.

"Speakin' of your dad, I haven't seen him since yesterday. You know where he ran off to?"

"I think he stayed at my Uncle Wayne's," I answered, resting my elbow on the table.

"Again?" he asked, shaking his head. "What do your dad and Uncle Wayne even do over there?"

"I don't know. And I don't wanna know," I said and sat upright in anticipation as he flipped over a patty and coated it with his secret special sauce. Arlene and I reckoned, even on Ray's deathbed, the recipe would die with him. "Can I have that one?" I pointed. "That one looks good."

"I know you want this one."

"And—"

"Well done with two slices of cheese. I know what you like." Ray grinned and tapped his noggin with the prongs. "I still remember. Haven't lost my memory yet," he proclaimed proudly and did a double take across the way and waved. "Oh, howdy there, neighbor. Good evenin'."

I looked over, spotting the new neighbor walking to his truck. He halted and regarded us, standing like a deer in headlights. It reminded me of the first time Ray had come face to face with a javelina. Till this day, Arlene and I are still convinced he did in fact stop breathing.

The man gave us a quick, bland smile and glanced between us one last time before hastily turning away, fiddling with his left ear. Ray and I shared a quick look as he climbed into his truck and fled down the dirt road.

Ray clicked his tongue and returned his attention to the grill, nodding. "Well, alright, then. Guess you weren't kiddin' when you said he didn't talk much."

"He's odd."

"Everyone's odd in some way, Grace. That's what makes the world so interesting. Doesn't mean he's a bad guy."

"I wasn't saying that," I said truthfully.

"You thought I was the boogie man."

"Ray, I was five."

"Still, it took ya a long time to say hi to me. Didn't stop you from watchin' me and Arlene, though. I'd always see you sittin' on your porch or in that chair of yours. But now you love me," Ray said with a toothy grin. "And love my food. Can't ever get enough of it. Funny how that works out, don't it?"

Rolling my eyes, I smiled and pushed myself up to stand beside him to watch the most important process of crafting the perfect hamburger. The condiments. After he carefully laid across two crisp pieces of lettuce, two slices of tomato and onion, he smeared on a layer of mayonnaise before setting the bun right on top. Everything had its place and was done with intention. Ray stepped back to admire his work and threw the towel over his shoulder, placing his hands on his sides.

He nudged my shoulder. "I gotta say, those are some good-lookin' burgers if I do say so myself."

"Thanks, Ray."

"You want some fries?"

"I can heat up some at home. Thanks, though." I gave him a quick side hug and carried the paper plates in my hand, walking away. "Have fun at Paul's. Say hi to Arlene for me, okay?"

"Will do, Grace!"

After making a trip to the bathroom and baking half a bag of fries in the toaster oven, I sat on the porch with my full plate of food. And though Arlene and Ray had taken off down the road ten minutes ago, the smell of burning charcoal still hung in the air. I stretched my achy legs down the steps and took my first bite, savoring the spicy but sweet sauce that coated just enough of the meat. Ray's burgers had become the equivalent to my mama's chocolate chip cookies. I took another bite and sucked the excess sauce clean off my thumb, then looked up to see Harley sitting at the bottom of the porch. Leaning forward, I searched for any sign of the neighbor's truck.

It was nowhere in sight.

"Does he know you're out, or is this your little secret you keep from him?" I asked Harley.

His large ear twitched.

"You know, not everyone here likes big dogs like you. You gotta be careful," I said. Harley tilted his head one way and the other, whining. "I know. It's a problem." I tore off a piece of the greasy meat and held it out for him. He approached and retrieved it from my fingers. "You want another?"

Harley sat down, determined and hopeful. In seconds my hand was covered in slobber when I offered him the second piece, his tongue made of sandpaper. Little lines of drool fell from his prickly chin as he chewed the thick meat. "Pretty good, ain't it? I would eat them every day if I could."

Two loud engines in the distance caused me to raise my head. I then spotted Pa's truck and Uncle Wayne's flashy red pickup behind him. Harley turned his head, curious as to what grabbed my attention. I pushed myself to stand just as they pulled up. Both their trucks backfired, and I waved the smell of exhaust from my face. Harley's ears raised. From the tinted windshield I was unable to make out Uncle Wayne's face. He killed the engine just as Pa stumbled out of his truck with a case of beer.

"Grace, what's that dog doin'? I told you, I don't want that mutt shittin' on my property."

Uncle Wayne jumped out of the truck.

Even without his boots on, Uncle Wayne was just as tall as the new neighbor but didn't pack as much muscle in his blue T-shirt and denim jeans. His hair was slicked back, giving any woman the assumption he loved things in place and to be in control. And he did. The days Uncle

Wayne started paying more attention to me were the years my chest started filling out and the childhood plumpness had left my cheeks. After I turned twelve, his hugs grew longer, and his hands wandered in places that I was still learning about. It was then I knew a man like my Uncle Wayne couldn't ever be a saint no matter how much preaching he did in church. And though Pa and Uncle Wayne weren't blood-related, one could say their inner demons had a lot in common. I still wondered what would've happened to me if Pa hadn't opened the door when he did two summers ago.

"That the dog you told me about?" Uncle Wayne asked.

Pa jerked his head to Harley. "That's the one."

Uncle Wayne lowered his aviators and spat out a piece of chewing tobacco onto the ground. "You weren't kiddin'. That is one funny-lookin' German shepherd." He stepped back to fully regard Harley, who stayed still, staring at him. "Never seen one like it. Not even my buddy's dog looks like that."

"He's a Malinois," I corrected him.

His eyes fell toward me, and his tongue slicked across his teeth, letting out a small chuckle. "Those are the dogs that, uh, sniff out shit in the Army, right? Like landmines?" Uncle Wayne drifted his attention back to Harley. "Hey, buddy." He stepped closer and went to stretch his arm forward but immediately paused at the sound of low growling. "Whoa. Alrighty, then." Harley's ears had fallen back. The little hairs on his back stood at attention, and his upper lip was now lifted into a snarl, baring his teeth.

Pa chuckled, saying, "Guess it doesn't like you."

"Shut up, Bill."

"Grace, get the mutt off my property already, will ya?" Pa threatened, leaving no room to negotiate as he walked past me, smelling as if he had already started on that case of beer. "I don't want him takin' a shit."

"Harley, go." I snapped my fingers. Harley whined. "Go." Harley

FALLING FROM GRACE

gave me one last look before bolting off to his porch.

"Seems it listens to ya," Uncle Wayne said, his eyes wandering across the way to the trailer next to ours. "Hey, Bill, you said it was that new neighbor's dog, right? The one that don't talk much."

"That's what I told ya, ain't it?" Pa shook his head. "Oh, hey, is that Ray's food? Got any left?"

"Yeah, yours is in the fridge," I answered.

"Good, I'm starvin'. And thanks again, Wayne. Have a good night." Pa tipped his hat before taking it off to fan himself.

"No problem, Bill."

Uncle Wayne and I watched Pa head into the trailer, and the moment the door shut behind him, we looked at each other. Any time I was left alone with him, something always shifted in the air. And even now it still left me sick to my stomach. Like the day Mama was sweeping the porch, and a little voice inside her told her to scoop me up and run. If she hadn't, I don't know what would have come from that big, nasty scorpion standing behind me. Uncle Wayne reminded me of that scorpion. Sometimes it wasn't the rattle of a snake that made people scared. It was the things that never made a sound and that sneaked up on them.

"It was nice seein' you, Gracie. Keep an eye on your dad for me, alright?" He gestured toward the front door. I don't know why I hated it so much when he called me that. It was just a nickname. A nickname that he loved saying. "And tell him he needs to wake up bright and early tomorrow. I don't wanna be late again."

"I'll tell him."

"Hey, you still likin' that chair I gave you? Your dad told me you are. Three things I learned with my last wife was to always have a chair on hand, food in the fridge, and to never leave a pregnant woman unattended. Never doin' that again, I tell ya. That woman never let me live it down."

"I am. Drive safe, okay?" I turned away and muttered, "Like any woman would ever wanna be alone with you hangin' around."

"What was that?"

"Nothin'. Tell Tina I said hi, Wayne."

"Will do." Uncle Wayne nodded and let his eyes do a quick sweep of my body, allowing a suggestive smile to touch the corners of his mouth before he turned to leave. "You look good, Gracie, even with a bun in the oven." He climbed into the truck and shut the door, but not before saying, "You have a good night now."

# 5

This morning's sunrise hadn't eased or cleared my mind. Not even the coyote's howl was enough. There were some days when my mind was just bad enough that nothing could help it. Nothing could keep me from remembering that each time I now looked in the mirror, I didn't recognize myself. When did it happen? When did I start looking like Mama? My lips weren't as pink as they used to be. Even my eyes weren't as bright. But most of all, I was tired and broken in ways that no one knew about. Parts I thought weren't capable of ever being broken. What I hoped for was that maybe someday someone would ask me how I really was doing and hold me as I cried on their shoulder. Not wanting anything in return. No expectations. Just a simple expression of love.

And that's all I wanted from my pa when he grabbed the bag of food from my hand as I stood there on the porch in my bare feet. "Christ, you couldn't have moved any faster? Didn't you hear me? I called you three times."

"I was in the bathroom. Sorry, Pa. Morning sickness. I told ya I still get it sometimes."

Pa rolled his eyes. "Yeah, and I'm gonna be late again." He walked back to the truck where the driver side door was still open.

As Mama once said, Pa never trusted anything that bled for five days and lived to tell about it. He put the truck in reverse and drove off. I waved the dust from my face and sat down on the step, wiping the bottoms of my feet. From all the mornings I'd sat on this porch over the past eighteen years, nothing much had seemed to change since Mama left. The dirt still burned on the hottest of days, and the warm breeze swayed the mesquite trees in the same direction. Yet what was different was that I couldn't see the happy faces in the clouds anymore, and after the sun rose, all the colors of the day seemed dull till the sun set. But what I could always count on was the smell of Arlene's biscuits and blackberry jam wafting through the air, knowing the smile it would bring to my face. Today though, it was my second smile. The first was when I watched the cloud of dust settle on the road as Pa left.

What would it be like?

To see this trailer fixed in the rearview mirror. To see this place fade until it melted into the horizon. Able to go anywhere. To be free, like I always wanted. I'd always wondered if I did leave, would I ever have the opportunity to see the ocean? To escape from the heat? Something that Mama and I used to daydream about. That even beyond wide stretches of desert, water did really exist. Would it be like seeing one big sky?

Yet, as much as I wanted to escape, it wasn't my own life anymore. Nothing was as simple as getting in the car and driving off to Lord knows where when I was two months shy of pushing out a baby. Exhaling, I made that promise again. A promise I had made to myself, but now I knew I had to see it through. Not just for me, but for her. "One day, baby girl . . . one day, I'll get us outta here."

The neighbor's truck came up the road and turned into his driveway. I sat upright. As he climbed out and walked around to the back of the truck, my eyes couldn't help but follow. Like each time I'd seen him, my heart quickened. He had all the things no girl my age should want or like in a boy. He didn't have bare arms. His shoulders were broader. And he couldn't hide the troubles of life as easily as one could when blessed with youth. He made his way to the porch with a heavy box and set it by his door. Even the way his back muscles flexed underneath his white T-shirt was different. He stood and headed to the truck to shut the tailgate, running a hand through his disheveled hair. And just as I thought I had gotten away with staring at him, he stopped in his tracks and his eyes landed on me.

I pulled my shoulders back, gave him a small smile, and waved as I said, "Mornin'."

"Mornin'."

And just as I expected, no other words were exchanged. It was becoming the longest staring contest of my life. But it wasn't just him, now, that was unsure of what to say. He stood there for another moment, and just as I gathered enough courage to say something else, he quickly walked away with his head down. He scratched the back of his left ear. I watched him, my curiosity only growing.

"Mornin', Grace."

I turned so fast that I felt a brief moment of whiplash.

Arlene had stepped out from her trailer with pink rollers still in her hair and a spatula in her right hand. "Have you and that baby eaten anything yet? I made those scrambled eggs you love. And those biscuits."

"Really?" I grabbed my sandals and pushed myself up. "I thought you only made 'em on Sundays."

"Well, let's just say it's Sunday then. How about that? Now come on. I don't want 'em gittin' cold."

She waited by the door and helped me up into the trailer.

No matter the years, nothing could ever mask Arlene's hairspray and perfume from seeping out of the wood panels. Not even her cooking. Ray and I reckoned if it weren't for the two built-in bookshelves that proudly showcased Arlene's antiques, the smells wouldn't be as tolerable. The table was already set with plates of perfectly toasted bread, sausage links, and biscuits. And last but not least, Arlene's famous homemade blackberry jam. "It smells really good, Arlene." I sat down in the kitchen booth.

"Well, I hope it tastes just as good." She smiled and returned her attention to the sizzling pan on the stove.

Whenever Arlene had her back turned, she strangely resembled my mama. Down to the lopsided roller in the back of her hair and to the way she'd place one hand on her hip. And for a moment, I had my mama again. A moment where I could imagine she hadn't left me. That she loved me. That this food lying before me was hers. Like the basket of biscuits that I never had the heart to tell Arlene I didn't like. But the day after my mama left, I was sitting in the same place I was now when they suddenly tasted better. That's when I learned that on the bad days, the little things become the big things. Like Arlene's smile that was just as warm and filling. She set a plate of steaming scrambled eggs in front of me and sat across the table with her glass of iced tea. Eager, I sat upright and reached for the saltshaker. But before I could give it a shake, Arlene eyed me with a look of disapproval.

"What are you doin'?"

"I'm using the salt."

"No, you're not. What makes you think I didn't put salt in them? So give it."

"But—"

"No buts. Give it." Arlene grabbed the shaker from my hand, placing it far from my reach." I swear, you think you'd know by now that too much salt is bad for you." She shook her head, stirring the two packets of sugar into her iced tea and tapping the spoon once on the rim.

"I do know."

"You say that, yet you still keep eatin' it with everything, Grace. Like those Slim Jims."

I rolled my eyes.

"I saw that."

Smiling, I spread a layer of blackberry jam across the fluffy dough of the biscuit. Only after adding two forkfuls of egg onto the perfectly layered biscuit did I take a bite. The delightful mix of sweet jam, cheesy eggs, and a pinch of salt was now a taste I could never grow tired of.

"Good?"

"Best scrambled eggs ever."

"Good. That means I haven't lost my touch," she proclaimed with a nod, setting the spoon on her napkin. Her fingers smoothed the crinkled corners, seeming to dwell on something important. "So I saw your mama's VW driving away that day when I was on my way back from Mrs. Taylor's." Arlene treaded carefully as I stopped chewing. "Did everything go okay? I haven't had a chance to ask you."

"Yeah, I guess so," I answered, tucking a strand of hair behind my ear before taking a bite of eggs.

She looked at me just as she did whenever Ray denied double-dipping into her jam. Her lips puckered and she nodded, still smoothing the crinkled corners of the napkin. "Well, whenever you wanna talk about it, I'm always here to lend an ear. You know that, Grace. Okay?"

"Thanks, Arlene."

She smiled.

Ray emerged from the hall with the blue buttoned-down shirt and khaki shorts Arlene had given him a year ago for his birthday. And with her hand underneath her chin, she admired him. He halted and flashed a toothy grin.

"What? You see somethin' you like?" Ray spread his arms wide and slowly spun for her to take him all in. "Didn't know your man could still clean up good, huh? And can you believe that these fit? I give it a week." He patted his gut. "Mornin', Grace."

"Mornin', Ray."

"How are you and that baby doin'?" he asked.

"We're good."

"Good. That's what I like to hear." Ray made his way to the kitchen and lifted the pot of coffee, taking his sweet time emptying every last drop into his travel mug. "That bread for me?"

"Just how you like 'em. Some butter and some sugar. You gonna join us? You look like you're on your way out. Where you goin'?" Arlene asked, watching him secure the lid back onto the mug.

"Well, I was thinkin' of popping over to the hardware store. We need a few things. The leg's busted on my chair. And there's nothin' much else to do right now that doesn't involve dying from heat stroke," Ray said, leaning against the counter. "I swear, if someone tells me to stay cool one more time, I'm gonna throw a fit. Dry heat, my ass," he muttered as he took a sip of coffee.

I held back a laugh, but my belly shook anyway as I took another large bite from the biscuit.

"Why don't you ask Mr. Taylor if he needs anything? I'm sure he'd love to go for a ride," Arlene said. "You haven't gone over there with me in a while. They're always askin' me where you are."

"Honey, I love you, but I don't think Mr. Taylor and I are meant to get along in this life. And that's fine by me. I just should've known sooner." Ray shrugged, lowering the cup from his mouth. "Like the day he put up the BUSH sign in front of his trailer. Three years later, it's still up. Guess what, the election's over, buddy. And there's no way I'm sharing space with that man after what he said to me. I still have half a mind to go over there and smack some sense into him."

"What'd he say, now?" I asked.

"He keeps goin' on about that new neighbor. Just because he doesn't drive an American-made truck doesn't mean he doesn't love America, Larry. And those engines run just fine if not better—"

"Ray."

"I know. Let it go. Okay, I'm gonna git goin'." Ray kissed the top of Arlene's head. "I'll also take a couple of these for the road." He reached over and grabbed two slices of bread. "Have fun, girls."

"Bye, sweetie."

"Bye, Ray," I said with a mouthful as he left. "You'd think people like Larry would find better things to do than talk bad about people. It ain't nice, Arlene. He don't even know him."

"So I take it you and him did talk when you were in his truck the other day?" she said.

I stopped chewing and looked up at her, knowing there was nothing I could say to convince her otherwise. Like the time I was seven years old and stuck my finger into an outlet, a small shock of electricity stunned me into a mental blank for five seconds. Was this her intention? Lure me in with her cheesy scrambled eggs and then the second after Ray left, cleverly find a way to begin the interrogation? Arlene's gaze stayed fixed on me as her pinky tapped the side of the glass.

"How'd you—"

"Ray told me."

"Gosh dang it."

"Grace—"

"You gotta know I was just fine walkin' back home, Arlene. But there he was, sittin' in his truck. And I didn't really wanna walk. The more fat I get, the more my feet hurt. It's a real pain."

She set down her glass of iced tea, exasperated. "What did I tell ya about callin' yourself fat?"

"Sorry." I rested my chin in my hand, picking at the scrambled eggs with my fork. Looking back at Arlene, I waited. Would she say I was two fries short of a Happy Meal like my mama would? But instead she just shook her head and reached across the table for another packet of sugar. "Shouldn't you be tellin' me not to do it again? That I was stupid? He could've been a bad guy, Arlene. You never know. I really could've winded up with my own *Reader's Digest* story."

"Well, was he?" she asked, emptying the sugar into her glass of iced tea. "A bad guy?"

"No . . . no, he wasn't," I muttered and dropped the fork. "But that doesn't mean I wasn't stupid, Arlene. You know what my mama would've done if she found out I did such a thing?"

"Quit sayin' you're stupid, Grace. You weren't stupid. You wouldn't have gotten into that man's truck if you weren't trusting that gut God gave you. It's there for a reason. You know that. We don't know nothin' about him to say he's a bad man. Now don't you dare give me that sour look." Arlene pointed at me. "You know very well what I'm talking about. You were the same way with Ray when you were little. Remember? It took you a while to warm up to him. I think you were six when you actually smiled at him."

"Yeah, yeah, I know."

"That might've been the greatest day of Ray's life. When you finally smiled at him."

"Really?"

"Sweetie, Ray loves you like his own. And I do, too. It's why I know even if I did tell you to stay away from that neighbor, I don't think you'd even listen to me. You're still young in that respect. I say to do one thing, and y'all do the opposite. It's a vicious cycle. My three boys were like that. Told my second youngest to not knock up his girlfriend. And what'd he do? He's now married to her and on their third kid. All I'm gonna say, Grace, is that I think he's more scared of you than you are of him."

"I guess. He don't really look at me," I said, picking at my scrambled eggs. "I don't blame him though. Not a lotta people like lookin' at me. Even when they do, there's always a look in their eye."

"But I saw him talk to ya just now."

"I wouldn't really count it as talkin', Arlene."

"Well, either way, you gotta admit . . ." She stirred her iced tea before continuing. ". . . he looks mighty fine in those Levi's. And don't think I didn't see you starin' at him earlier out there. So don't try lyin' to me."

"I—"

"Hush."

I sat back in the seat, defiant, and looked out the window. "Believe it or not," Arlene began as she slowly slathered a layer of butter on her biscuit, "there was a time when Ray looked pretty good in those. I think he knew it, too. Always had that big grin on his face, bless his heart."

"He did?"

Arlene laughed heartily. "Oh, he did."

※

Two days passed. While I had found solace in the mundane routines of watching the sun rise, eating breakfast, and walking the mile and a half to the gas station, there was still enough time in the day for me to think about him. And when I did, the rational part of my mind often wrangled the other to keep quiet. Mama told me nothing good came from being curious. It was one of the few things she was right about. Cause here I was. Pregnant and stuck with my pa just like she had been with me. Sitting on the step, I watched Pa's truck drive away. After giving myself ten seconds, I pushed myself up.

"Alright, baby girl, you ready to head over to Sam's?" I caught my breath. "I swear, you're gittin' bigger every day." I dusted off my tank dress and slid my feet into the pair of sandals.

By the time I was at the end of the road, I was grateful for the white T-shirt underneath to protect the tops of my shoulders from being burned. The sun seemed to burn brighter than ever. And no matter the hand on my back for support, with every step I took, a throbbing ache shot up from my feet to my spine. Taking a much-needed break, I stopped to catch my breath. A strand of hair fell in front of my sweaty face, and I blew it away. My throat was already parched. I wiped the sweat from my forehead.

Exhaling, I went to take a step forward. It was then my insides twisted like licorice, and a broken cry escaped me. Thirty long seconds of pressure passed, and the muscles finally relaxed. Breathing out, I slowly stood upright and took a few more steps. The hum of an engine caused me to lift my head, but before I had a real chance to look, that same pain returned across my lower back. I bent over again, holding my thighs. The ground spun, and I began to quake with fear that something was wrong. My eyes opened at the sound of tires skidding to a stop and a pair of hurried footsteps.

"Grace!" a familiar voice called out, full of worry and panic. A whine quickly followed.

"Harley?" I croaked just before heaving onto the ground. The hurried footsteps came to a stop. A hand then gently pulled the hair back from my face, and the other kept itself on my arm to keep me steady. "Oh, God, that didn't taste so good. I think it was those chicken—" My eyes squeezed tighter, persevering through the pain as it spread across my lower back again. I stifled a cry, holding my head down. "Sweet baby Jesus, it's never hurt this bad," I groaned, struggling to breathe through the pressure.

His breath seemed close to my ear, but his concerned voice sounded far away. I put my hand on his arm, afraid I would fall if I didn't, and to reassure myself he was still nearby. "Seven months . . . she shouldn't be coming," I stammered over my frantic breathing. "I-It's too—"

"Grace, look at me." His voice was calm and gentle. Bit by bit, my vision began to clear as I focused on him. And for some inexplicable reason, the look in his brown eyes resonated with me. "I need you to pull yourself together. Can you do that for me? The stress isn't good for the baby. Okay?"

I nodded, still unable to take a steady breath.

"Now I want you to inhale for four. Hold it for four, and let it out for four. Okay?" His tone was soft. I nodded again. "You gotta breathe. Just like this." He inhaled, and I followed with a shaky breath, then held it and released it as he did. "Now do that a few more times. I'm sure the baby's fine. I think you're just dealin' with some Braxton Hicks right now. Nothin' you gotta—"

"No, no." I shook my head, my breaths coming and leaving in short and fast intervals. "They never hurt this bad before. Really—"

"Hey," he said calmly. "Grace, you gotta breathe. In for four and out for four. Remember?"

I inhaled and held my breath for four counts and then released it. And bit by bit, the tightness in my chest loosened.

"There's nothin' for you to worry about. I know it feels real bad, but Braxton Hicks can get worse for some, uh, women, when they're closer to their due date, and sometimes it's just the baby shiftin' around. That's all," he reassured me with not even a slight tremor or hesitation in his voice.

The look in his eyes was so certain, and once again I believed everything would be okay without so much as a second thought.

"I wanna get you some food and water. If you don't feel better, I'll take you to the doctor. You okay with that?"

"Uh-huh."

"Can you stand?"

I nodded, but as I stood the ground began to spin again. "I think I'm . . ." I began to fall back.

"Grace!" He grabbed me swiftly and pulled my arm over his shoulder, starting to walk us to the truck as fast as he could.

"Baby, my baby," I mumbled, my legs becoming weaker.

"Don't worry about the baby. I just need to get you some water and something to eat."

He opened the passenger door, helping me onto the seat with little effort. I watched him hastily grab a bottle of water from a cooler in the backseat. The urge to heave returned again. He shook the water droplets off his hand and was about to twist the cap off when I slumped forward, letting my head fall on his shoulder. My muscles relaxed like syrup being poured on a stack of pancakes. Soap, the tang of sweat, and even the faint note of Harley tickled my nose. His scent made my whole body relax, all the way to my tippy toes. Even the beat of his heart and the rise of his chest. And for some reason, I fought the impulse to cry. He reached up, pressing his cool palm against the side of my forehead.

"Am I . . . am I a bad mother?" I asked unexpectedly, my lips trembling at the thought.

His chest deflated, and he lowered his hand. "No. No, you're not a bad mother. Stuff happens. Now, you really need to drink some water. And not all at once. Okay?" He twisted the cap off. "Just a little bit at a time."

I nodded, taking the bottle from him. Only when I took that first small sip did he say, "Alright just keep doin' that." He shut the door and jogged around the truck. Leaning back, I was all the more grateful for the cool A/C to help fight off the nausea. Harley whined and licked my face, and I patted his side.

"I'm okay, buddy. Don't worry." I took another sip of water and exhaled in relief, not realizing just how badly I had needed it. Placing my hand over my belly, I closed my eyes and tilted my head back.

While the hum of the truck kept me from dozing off, I couldn't bring myself to look away from my belly. I was relieved to feel her little legs still moving inside me. Was this what my mama felt like? Sad? Scared to take care of another life when she didn't even know how to take care of herself? Angry for ever allowing such a thing to happen to her? But no matter how afraid I was of becoming like my mama, I didn't want to be alone. I'd been alone all my life, and this was my chance at happiness. All I knew was that for my own selfish reasons, I could never hand my baby over to another family. I wanted to be the one to see the first smile on my baby girl's face and to feel those little fingers wrap around mine. Looking away from the window, I quietly reached into my purse and took out the small folded piece of paper that had my top two names written on it. Slowly, I unfolded it. I glanced over, catching his gaze, and I turned over my palm to hide the note.

Unable to help myself, my eyes focused his way again, and I watched him shift in the seat, keeping his elbow propped on the windowsill. Every several seconds he'd let his thumb rub to and fro across the heavy stubble on his chin like he was thinking real hard about something, and based on the subtle crease in his brows, I believed it. Just as I believed that unfamiliar feeling that came from just the look in his eyes and everything he had said to me. The feeling of being okay but not knowing why. Since I was a child, nothing had ever been okay. Any time anyone told me everything would be okay, they ended up being wrong. It was just something to say to make me feel safe, even though I was far from it. Like with men. Men had always scared me. I never knew what it meant to feel safe with a man until Ray. But the more I looked into the eyes of the man sitting beside me, the more I believed I was okay. Yet all I kept waiting for was that tiny irrational thought to come back, telling me I wasn't.

When I turned away, I saw the Minit Mart ahead, and a small dose of panic shot through my nerves. That's when reality quickly settled back into my mind. "C-Can you park at the end? In the last spot?" I said, catching his peculiar expression. Every bit of me expected him to question my reasoning, but instead he remained silent and pulled the truck into the last empty space. He cleared his throat as if he was about to speak but instead just sat there for a long moment.

"So, um, I'll be back in a jiff, okay? I'll leave the A/C on, but feel free to roll down the window if you need it."

"Okay."

He nodded and glanced over at me, hesitant, before hastily climbing out and shutting the door. I sat upright in the seat and looked at the entrance, then back at him. The lock flicked back and forth three times.

Harley and I watched him jog down the strip of pavement and as he held open the door for an elderly man, before walking into the store. I sat back, anxiously biting my bottom lip as people came and went. A little girl with pigtails and a yellow dress, holding an orange creamsicle in her hand, left the store. Harley's ears perked. Whenever I saw a child with a bright smile on her face, I still asked myself if I was a bad person for keeping this baby. Would I be keeping her from a happier life? The child skipped down the sidewalk and pointed at Harley, gasping, "Granny, look! A doggy!"

The older woman by her side turned her head my direction. Mrs. Anderson's brows raised, and I sank into the seat as deep and as fast as I could. Once the little girl's voice became faint, I slowly raised myself in the seat and checked for any sign of them nearby. My chest deflated. I peered over the dashboard, seeing the top of my neighbor's head as he finally walked out of the store. He opened the driver's side door, setting the shopping bag down on his seat. Harley sniffed the bag, wagging his tail.

"I didn't know what you liked, so I kinda got you a little of everything," he muttered, reaching into the bag. I leaned over the console as far as I could to sneak a peek in the bag just as Harley did. "There's some Greek yogurt, some trail mix, and a granola bar. All good things to eat when you're pregnant. Also, some apple juice. I-I tried to find one that's not loaded with sugar, 'cause the insulin production to the baby and all that can go up. It's not something you want." He spared an awkward half- smile, rubbing the back of his left ear. I looked at the bag, then at the juice box he had set down in the cup holder, unsure of how to express my gratitude. Even with just a simple thank you.

"Anyway, um, I hope one of those things tickles your fancy. If not I—"

"Tickles my fancy?"

"Yeah, my . . . my pop used to say that a lot. But, um, you're fine with these things, right? If not, I could run back in and find somethin' else."

"No, these are fine. Thank you. You didn't have to do all that." I took the bag, resting it on my lap.

"Yeah, no problem," he said, suddenly bashful. He climbed into his seat, shutting the door.

I plunged the straw into the top of the juice box, taking a sip. The crisp taste cooled my body, and I relaxed into the seat. The engine accelerated as we turned back onto the road. Despite the inevitable silence, this time I didn't mind it. If anything, I finally understood what my mama had told me years ago. That there are times when we're more ourselves around strangers who don't know our stories than with the ones we see every day. If he didn't ask, I wouldn't tell. It was peaceful. I ripped open the bag of trail mix, realizing just how hungry I was. Each salt-coated nut settled the nausea as I chewed.

"So, um," he began and cleared his throat. I looked over at him, surprised. Harley even perked his ears, directing his attention away from the bag of food in my lap. "What's that you got there? You were lookin' at it earlier." He gestured to the folded piece of paper that had slipped off my lap and onto the seat. I looked to where he pointed and reached down.

"Oh, it's just some list of names I got from this baby magazine," I said. "They're my top two."

"Top two?"

"You making fun of me?"

His right brow quirked. "No . . . no, what are they?" he asked, his voice full of hesitation and curiosity.

His question momentarily caught me off guard. I sat there, unsure of how to answer. There was something different about the way he asked me than when Mason did. Like it was an obligation to do it, and Mason never wanted or liked to be expected to do anything. He liked doing things when he wanted to in his own time. But this was entirely different. This man simply wanted to know.

I hesitated at first. "You really wanna know?"

"Yeah."

"Why?"

"I wanna know."

"Daisy and Faye."

He glanced at me with his usual expression, but this time his eyes were unexpectedly gentle.

"Daisy and Faye. I like it."

I placed the list safely back in my bag and closed the clasp. "Can I ask you somethin'?"

"Sure, I guess," he said gently but guarded.

"How'd you know that it was Braxton Hicks? And that thing about the baby's insulin. I didn't think you'd . . ."

"Think I what?"

"Know that," I muttered, but I knew he heard it loud and clear. "And I know that's a bad thing to say, I know, but not a lotta men do. At least the men I know. It just took me by surprise is all," I admitted. Looking over at him, I caught his glance, expecting him to be offended. But before I had a chance to figure out if he was or not, he had already returned his attention to the road, his fingers tapping on the wheel every few seconds.

"Well, after I got back home, I got married. So . . ." He went quiet and shook his head in disbelief. "That was years ago now." Catching my stunned expression, he then asked, "What, you thought I was younger or somethin'?"

"No."

"Oh." He turned back to the road. "I guess it doesn't really help that most men in my family start graying by the time they're pushin' thirty. And I bet my beard doesn't help either. Anyway, uh, since I was a kid, I knew I wanted to be a father and . . ." He went quiet again as if to process the fact he was speaking out loud about it to someone he didn't even know. "My wife and I tried for a while, but after we lost . . ." He cleared his throat with an unsure look in his eyes, afraid to expose himself even more. "It—It just wasn't in the cards for us, so I signed up for another tour. End of story," he replied short and quick, scratching his beard. "You never know where life's gonna take you, that's for sure." He exhaled and focused on the road harder as if it would empty his mind of unpleasant memories.

I stayed quiet and watched his eyes darken in sadness. And though he didn't say anything further, his words had begun to click into place one by one in my mind like a puzzle.

I looked at my lap.

"I think any child would be lucky to have you as their father."

His eyes snapped at me, and I immediately expected a cheap shot about how I shouldn't say such things. Things I wouldn't understand. Yet it was anything but. His eyes were soft, tender, and even relieved, like a part of him had been yearning to hear those words for so long. I looked at the bag of trail mix as the silence grew. Harley rested his chin on the console, watching me pick out another cashew, hopeful.

"How . . ." His voice broke. "And how would you know that?" he asked, facing forward.

"Well, you said you'd wanted a child since you were a kid. That says a lot about you. Don't you think?"

"That's . . ." He paused, and his eyes swept my face so fast that I only had about a second to fully catch it.

Even though it was brief, there was something in his eyes that told me he was trying to figure out the real me. He averted his attention back to the road. His cheeks flushed red and he let the silence build again; his eyes still soft, despite their intensity. While a part of me had become accustomed to these awkward silences, it had also given me that chance to witness the light of the sun reveal each emotion in his eyes. And although we stayed quiet for the remainder of the drive home, every several seconds, we found ourselves catching each other's glances. As we drove up the dirt road, I kept my arm propped on the windowsill and my hand by my face to avoid another run-in like I'd had with Mrs. Anderson.

He parked the truck in front of my trailer, but before I could step out, he had already made his way around and opened the door.

"You know, you don't have to do that."

A faint smile spread across his face, and he scratched his beard, saying, "Well, my pop may not have been the best parent out there, but he did raise me right in some ways. Here let me take that." He took the bag from my lap.

"Oh, thank you." I carefully stepped down and faced him, tucking a strand of hair behind my ear. "And thank you for the um . . ."

"The ride?"

"Yeah."

"Yeah, no problem. So, um, just take it easy for the rest of the day. Okay?"

He handed me the bag of food and walked past me, shutting the passenger door.

I turned to leave but stopped, looking back at him. "Hey."

He halted in his tracks and regarded me, lowering his hand from his left ear. "Yeah?"

I hesitated. "Can I at least pay you back? I wanna pay you while I still have the money." I opened my bag, digging through it. "My mama always taught me to have cash on hand in case you're in a sticky situation or needin' to repay someone for a favor," I said as I found the last several dollar bills, counting them out loud. He propped his arm on the frame of the driver side door and stared at me, strangely curious. "What?"

"You're in sticky situations often?"

"Well, as my mama said, you never know."

"Uh-huh."

"Let me just run inside and get another five for you. I'm sure that will be enough then, right?"

"Look, kid, you don't need to pay me."

"I'm not a kid," I stated firmly.

The same peculiar expression formed on his face, his brows pinching together. His mouth slightly opened to speak, but I continued.

"And I told you to stop calling me that." I turned away. Halfway up the porch, I looked back as he was about to climb into the truck. "Also," I called out. He paused and lifted his head. "I'm not some charity case either. So, stop it."

I walked up to the door just as the truck's tires churned the dirt. Unable to help myself, I glanced over my shoulder one last time to watch the rear of his truck leave down the road. And for the first time in seven months, a small pang of guilt weighed on my chest. Old habits really do die hard. Even pride.

# 6

Sitting on the porch, I watched Mrs. Taylor's grandkids play a game of hopscotch before the daytime ended. And I couldn't help but smile. Though they knew it would end, it didn't lessen their joy. Nothing ever seemed to lessen a child's joy. That's why whenever I could, I looked up at the sky to find mine. Its serene, pastel horizon took away the need to cry, and my mind was almost quiet again. It was the little bit of peace I always carried with me.

Mrs. Taylor stepped out from her trailer. Though I couldn't hear what she said, I reckoned from the two boys and the girl moving closer to the side of the road that I knew what it was. She turned to leave, but before doing so she gave me a quick wave, hardly giving me the chance to return the gesture. And then, like nothing had happened, the kids returned to their game. A soft but fast *thump thump* caused me to pull my attention away. Harley was running toward me, all bright-eyed, barking.

"Well, good evenin' to you, too," I said, just as eager to see him as he was to lick my whole face. I wiped each cheek. "Yes, yes, I love ya, too." He whined and barked. "What, boy?" He rolled onto his back, exposing his belly. "Do you want a belly rub? I think you want a belly rub." His back leg started to shake as I scratched. "You're such a good boy. Yes, you are. Yes, you are. You're such a good and handsome boy."

Harley yowled as my fingers continued working his belly.

"So that's where you ran off to."

Harley sat upright as I did, and I tried my best to not look as that pair of dirty Timberlands got closer.

"Oh, don't give me that look. You know you shouldn't be runnin' around here."

Harley whined.

"No, don't give me that."

I bit my bottom lip to stifle a laugh, but a small snort escaped. Then, unable to resist it any longer, I looked up at him, still in disbelief that he had walked over. It was the closest we'd ever been outside of the confining space of his truck. And I wanted to take this chance to ask at least one of the dozen questions I had. There were, however, limitations in place. Limitations to what I could ask him. A man was different from a boy like Mason. Yet I couldn't pass up this moment to talk with him again and to perhaps let go of the guilt weighing on my chest since yesterday.

"Hi."

"Hi. Sorry about him, he can be . . ."

"No, no, it's fine."

He cleared his throat, and as I expected, his fingers reached for his left ear. "So how—"

Harley yowled.

"Harley, I'm tryin' to talk here," he said, and I held back another laugh. "So, how you doin'? You feelin' any better? I heard they can last a while. The Braxton Hicks, I mean. Are they as bad as they were yesterday?"

"I'm doin' better."

"Good, good." He nodded and looked at his boots as he placed one hand in the pocket of his jeans.

"So, how—"

"How was, um——"

"Sorry, you go."

"No, no, you go."

"How was your day?" I asked.

"It . . . it was a good day," he replied, looking off into the distance, as he reached for the back of his ear again.

It was like an itch he could never scratch. And if it wasn't for my close proximity, able to take in every detail of him, I wouldn't have been able to notice the way his brown eyes reminded me of the rich dark soils of the earth. Much like Harley's. Full of wisdom. They even stood the same way. Tall and strong. And though both of them looked rough from a distance, there was a certain gentleness up close, and a part of me was curious to know what was really lurking beneath the surface.

I looked up at him one last time and then to my feet, saying, "Well, that's good to hear."

"What?" he asked, and I could hear the smile. "Did I do somethin' funny? You're smilin'."

Before I could say anything, Harley yowled in protest, now standing in front of me, his tongue hanging lopsided at the corner of his mouth.

"What? Do you want more belly scratches?" I asked in a high-pitched, playful voice.

"You know, you're the only one who he lets pet him."

"Really?" I faced Harley. "Am I the only one? Yes, I am. Yes, I am," I said in the same playful voice. "I don't know why I'm talking like this, but I gotta stop. Yes, I do. You're just so adorable." I scratched Harley's cheeks and kissed his nose. "Yes, you are."

"Yeah, I think he really likes you."

"Well, good. Cause I like you, too," I said to Harley, who howled loudly in agreement.

"Grace, what did I tell ya about that yapping dog?" Mr. Emerson stepped out from his trailer with a bottle of beer. "Hey! Don't you dare roll them eyes at me, Grace! I saw that!"

I slapped my knees and stood. "Oh, just stuff it where it don't shine, Earl!" I exclaimed.

"I know ya hear me!"

"I hear ya!" I shouted. He huffed and shut the trailer door with more force than normal.

Just as I was about to sit back down, I looked over at Harley's owner. His face was incredulous, but something lit in his eyes, golden flecks dancing in delight. And he smiled just enough to show the beginning crevice of a right dimple. But before it could possibly blossom into a full smile, he shook his head, turning away with a soft, breathless laugh.

"I'm thinking the people around here don't like dogs, huh?"

I lowered myself back on the step. "No, not even Tico."

"Tico?"

"He's the chihuahua who lives a few homes down. By the way, about yesterday, I just wanna say I'm—"

The sound of Pa's approaching truck caused me to quickly pull my hand away from Harley and stand up just as he parked in the driveway. It had suddenly become difficult to swallow or even breathe. The engine died and the door creaked open as Pa stepped out, clocking the new neighbor. As their attention fell upon each other, the air grew heavy. It wasn't so much rage flickering in Pa's eyes. It was more annoyance. As if he had just come face to face with the pesky bug that had been causing him sleepless nights and that deserved to be squished. And to my surprise, the neighbor's eyes never left Pa. Though he never allowed much to show, there was something in his eyes that reminded me of the times Ray would look at Pa. Aloof but aware, and not in the least bit hesitant to act upon an instinct.

Pa shut the door and, with a mouthful of gum, said, "Nice to see ya again. Don't know if I introduced myself last time, but name's Bill." Pa held out his hand. The neighbor glanced at it and extended his own hand to give a firm shake. I glimpsed between them. "Nice dog you got there by the way." Pa jerked his head to Harley who was now by the neighbor's side at attention. Pa then spat the gum onto the ground, saying, "That's, uh, a Malinois, right? You don't see 'em a lot around here."

"Yeah," the neighbor answered in a steady tone.

Pa nodded and said, "Well, just keep the dog on your side, and we'll get along just fine, alright?" He walked past me onto the porch. "Mason still picking you up at nine, Grace? For that county fair?"

"Yeah," I replied.

"And you have money?" Pa asked.

"Yeah, I have some," I said. Pa nodded and observed both the neighbor and me one last time before slamming the screen door behind him.

"I should git goin'. I have some stuff to do," I lied with a quick smile, taking a step up the porch. Harley whined.

"Yeah, right, of course. Don't wanna keep ya. Come on, Harley." He cleared his throat and turned away but stopped, saying, "Hey, that county fair he was talkin' about. Did he mean the one in Pima County?"

"Yeah. You going?"

"Uh, maybe. Not big on crowds, though. And this one," he gestured to Harley, "doesn't like being alone too long."

"Well, you should. It's fun. And I don't know what you like, but they have these pretzels that you can dip—"

"Grace!" Pa yelled from inside, and I flinched as the screen door swung open. "Get your ass in here. Now."

I hesitated and looked at the neighbor one last time, saying, "I gotta go. See ya around. Bye, Harley."

Holding the door open, Pa watched the neighbor leave, a cigarette hanging between his lips. Only when I stepped inside did Pa slam the door shut. I tensed. "It really goes in one ear and out the other with you. Just like your Ma," Pa spat, taking out the cigarette. Apprehensively, my eyes followed him as he made his way to the kitchen. He flicked the ash into the sink.

"Pa—"

"Why can't you just listen to me for once? I didn't want you talkin' to him. And what do I see you doin'? Talkin'. You're still just a stupid kid, Grace. Eighteen don't mean nothin'. You know nothin'." He took another drag. "Every kid thinks they know somethin', but they don't."

There it was again. The courage, stirring in my throat to finally say what I'd been wanting to say since I was nine years old. But instead I breathed through my nose and settled the anger brewing inside me, knowing it wouldn't change anything. That's when I learned to appreciate the little things in life. Like now. He could be yelling.

But he wasn't.

"You're under my roof. That means you follow my rules. You treat me with respect, you got that, Grace?"

"I'm sorry, Pa."

"And this time keep your legs closed when you see that boy," Pa spat. My heart sank. Wetness pooled at the corners of my eyes. I blinked it away and fought off the desire to cry. Pa stopped halfway down the hall and turned back, opening his mouth to speak, as if regretful. Yet he didn't say a word. He just continued his way to the bedroom.

***

Other than watching the last light of day slide down the wall, there wasn't much to keep myself occupied. And by the time I had fallen asleep on the couch and woke up, it was a quarter to nine. The promise of a hot pretzel and popcorn willed my feet to stand and begin freshening up. Taking one final look in the mirror, I tied the strings of the dress together above my belly. I smoothed out the white floral fabric and then pulled two front strands of hair to the back with a scrunchie. Slipping on a pair of flats, I quickly grabbed my bag and cardigan.

"I'm leavin', Pa!"

When there was no answer, I peeked into the bedroom. Pa was sprawled across the bed in a deep sleep. Quietly shutting the door, I headed outside. Stepping off the porch, I looked over to see the neighbor's empty driveway. I then spotted Ray, who was sitting in a fold-out chair with his feet on display and a glass of his homemade Long Island iced tea. I smiled and walked over.

"Hi, Ray."

"Well, howdy, Grace."

"That your new chair?"

"Yes, it is. Got two cup holders now. Fancy, huh? And don't you look pretty. Where you headed off to?"

"To the county fair."

"Oh, yeah? Got a date?"

"You could say that."

"Well, whoever he is, he's one lucky boy. And he better know it. Unlike Mason. It still bothers the heck outta me, what he did. Even thought about pushin' that big Jeep of his down into the arroyo a few times. Hey, ain't it supposed to rain next week?" Ray asked, unsure.

"Ray, don't even think about it. I mean it. I know what he did was bad, but he doesn't deserve that."

He rolled his eyes and set down his glass. "Dagnabbit, Grace. You're going out with him again, aren't you? Are you kiddin' me? After what he did to you? Somethin' like that isn't easy to let go."

"I don't know. He wants to try. So, can't hurt, can it?"

Ray exhaled deeply and muttered. "Well, at least you're getting out and having some fun."

"Well, hi, Grace!" Arlene stepped out from the trailer, holding a veggie platter. "You goin' somewhere?" she asked, setting the platter down on her chair next to Ray. "Ain't seen you all dressed up like this in a while. You're even wearing the shoes with the little flowers on 'em."

"She's off to the county fair," Ray said.

"Why'd you say it like that?" Arlene asked.

"I'm not happy about it."

"Why—"

"I'm goin' with Mason. That's why he ain't happy about it," I said to Arlene, who nodded.

"Well, as long as you have fun, then that's all that matters. You're overdue for some fun."

A loud bass in the distance caused us to look over. "That must be him," I said. Ray rolled his eyes.

"Okay, well, before you go, gimme a hug." Arlene walked over and hugged me tightly. "Have fun, okay? And then when you get back, you can tell us all about it. Alright?" She leaned back, fixing a strand of my hair. "There. Gotta git that away from your pretty face now. Don't want anythin' covering it up."

"Arlene," I said, flustered.

"What, I can't help it. You're beautiful. You gotta start believing that, too, sweetie." She patted my cheek. "And hey, listen. Don't let Ray make you feel bad for doing what you're doing. He's just a grump."

"Hey," Ray exclaimed.

Mason's Jeep pulled up alongside my trailer. The passenger window rolled down, and he waved across from the driver's seat to Arlene and Ray. "Howdy, Mr. and Mrs. Johnson! How are you doin' this evenin'?"

"Hi, Mason!" Arlene smiled. "We're doin' just fine. How's your daddy doing after his new promotion? I heard he finally got it."

"Very busy, as always," Mason answered. "Let's get going, Grace. The lines are probably gittin' longer."

"Alrighty, I'm comin'. Bye, Arlene." I gave her another side hug, and she kissed the top of my head.

"The boy gonna get out or what? Does he have a broken leg?" Ray said in a hushed tone, sneering.

"Quiet, Ray," Arlene warned.

"Bye, Ray." I smiled and gave him a quick peck on the top of his head before rushing over to the Jeep.

I opened the passenger door, climbing up into the seat. Mason tapped the wheel and gave me a quick once-over as I sat down with a sigh. The smell of beer and stale food hung in the air. Fast food containers littered the floor. Giving Arlene and Ray a reassuring smile, I buckled in and looked at Mason.

"What?"

"Nothing, you just look pretty is all," Mason said with one of his charming smiles. And like all the times before, he twisted his baseball cap backwards before we took off down the road.

As much as it reminded me of Pa, all I wanted to take away from this night was an escape. That it was possible to be a teenager again. I couldn't remember the last time I laughed with no thought for the past or the future. To laugh without inhibition. And though I was sitting beside one of the most sought-after boys in school, it didn't feel any different. I know I should let it go. But Mama once said to me: *It's a sin, a sin of omission to not be there presently for someone.* I knew she was talking about Pa and maybe even herself.

Mason was focused on the road ahead, and I took note of his bare forearms as they gripped the steering wheel. He scratched at his clean-shaven jaw and stole a sideways glance at me, smiling. That smile . . . the same smile that used to make my stomach flutter. My heart ached at the recognition. Without thinking, I smiled back. His smile grew brighter, almost emboldened. Though he said he wanted to try, some part of me knew the outcome would be no different. If there was one thing I'd learned from this life so far, it was that what seemed to be destined to last forever, didn't.

Nothing ever did.

Nothing could ever outlast the desert.

Resting my head against the window, I fiddled with the end of my reddish brown curl. The desert always seemed different at night. A certain unpredictability existed in its blackness. A blackness that surrounded the expanse of any vehicle that dared to drive alongside it. Like an empty void. That no matter how far my fingers would reach out to touch it, I'd never find the end. And somehow, even after living here all these years, I still had never gotten used to that. And I reckoned I never would.

"You really haven't changed, you know that?"

I regarded him. "Whaddya mean?"

"Your hair."

For some reason, the tone in his voice awakened the butterflies in my stomach. "Oh, right." I lowered my hand.

Mason reached forward and pushed in a cassette tape. "Hey, you still like Elvis Presley?"

"Is the world still round?"

He grinned. "Point taken."

As the soft and smooth familiar beat of "Money Honey" started, my muscles relaxed into the seat. The next hour passed by, and though a few more looks and smiles were exchanged, we still never said a word. I spent the time playing with the ends of my hair and staring out at the darkness. My face lit up as we neared Exit 255 for Houghton Road and turned off Highway 10. Just a little longer and straight up on Brekke Road. It was there in the distance; bright colorful lights danced and flashed and reflected the tops of dozens of cars parked in the lot nearby. Mason pulled in, and I unbuckled my seatbelt, stepping down from the Jeep. Even from far away, the red and blue lights of the Ferris wheel glimmered brightly. Mason walked up to me, sticking his hands into the pocket of his jeans.

"You know, it's gonna be pretty loud. And I know you don't like that. You get all weird."

I rolled my eyes and shut the door. "I think I'll be fine."

"Alright, let's go and get the tickets." Mason jerked his head toward the dozen people waiting in line by the entrance and grabbed my hand. "I think Grady and everyone else are already there."

The monsoon rains from this afternoon had not allowed the mud to completely dry the eager footprints of passersby. Beyond the ticket booth lay tents of livestock and carts full of games and prizes. I gazed at the tall Ferris wheel in excitement. As we made our way through the crowd, the smell of popcorn and sweets made my feet pick up their pace in anticipation. Over to the right was a clearing with ponies, endlessly circling a white fence with their heads down as kids urged them to go faster. Mason's group of friends were huddled by the bean bag toss with their dates beside them, laughing. My eyes fell to the girls' exposed flat stomachs, and I reached down, adjusting the hem of my dress. As we made our way over, Grady's face lit up, and he raised his arm in the air, high fiving Mason.

"Big M! Glad you made it, buddy. We've been waiting for you," Grady said. The girls directed their attention to my belly, their eyes as big as white gumballs. Two of the three gazed a little longer than usual at my legs. It's then I noticed they were staring at the yellow spandex shorts underneath my short, white dress. They covered their mouths as if to stifle their laughs.

"Hey, Grace. You gonna go on any rides with us?" Grady asked. "There's a new one that goes upside down four times. We're all gonna make bets on if Nick's gonna hurl or not." He laughed.

"That ain't funny, Grady," Nick said.

"I think I'd rather stay down here. Those things aren't exactly the safest thing around here, you know? I actually read in *Reader's Digest* that a pregnant woman went on a ride, and due to the forces of the turns, it caused separation of the placenta from her uterus," I said. Grady and Mason shared a look as the group fell silent. "It-It's called placental abruption. It doesn't happen often, but . . . ." I stammered. "It can happen."

The girls' faces and Nick's twisted in disgust.

"You really haven't changed, you know that, Grace?" Grady laughed, shaking his head. "She knows such weird shit. Oh, by the way, Joanne's here, Mason. She's been asking about you."

"Who's Joanne?" I asked.

"No one important," Mason assured me. "I'm gonna go get one of those pretzels you like. There's no line right now. I'll get a second cup of that cheese you like with it," Mason said into my ear and shared a glance with Grady before rushing over to the vendors of food, disappearing into the crowds. One of the girls conducted a quick sweep of my body, and her upper lip curled in disdain.

"So, Grace, you gonna—"

"You know, my momma said that that baby's an abomination and proof of what sin does to nice girls like you. She says the day you die, she hopes God is as forgiving as he claims to be."

"Mary!" Grady exclaimed.

"What? I was gonna say, I hope so, too," Mary proclaimed. "I ain't that mean, Grady."

"Well, I'm sorry your momma feels that way," I said as politely as I could. "Tell her I'm sorry."

Mason returned, saying, "Hey, I'm back." He looked at the others, who were still silent. "Did I miss something?"

"Nah, man. Let's go find a ride," Grady reassured him. He wrapped his arm around Mary, walking away.

"A kiddy ride," Nick snickered.

Mason waited for an explanation, but instead I gave him a smile, saying, "That mine?"

"Yep, here you go."

I took the hot pretzel, ripping off a piece of the salty dough. "So, who's Joanne?" I asked, taking a bite with the cheese as we followed behind the group. "She a new friend of yours?"

Mason shrugged. "Just some girl."

For the next hour and a half, we gorged on greasy food until our stomachs couldn't hold any more and wasted half our tickets on rigged games. While I was eager to keep going, pushed by the gleeful screams and smiling faces, a ringing grew in my ears. Like a dead phone line that I couldn't hang up on. And if it wasn't for the throbbing pain of my feet and the infernal noise stabbing each nerve in my body, I'd be just as eager as them to swing high. As all of us stood in line for the ride, the taste of popcorn and the vanilla milkshake slowly but surely inched its way up my throat.

A cold sweat spread across my forehead and palms. I bolted for the nearest restroom. After losing an entire day's worth of food, my knees ached more than ever, and the burn of heaving stung my throat. I glanced around for Mason and his group of friends, but the line to the swing carousel was no longer in sight. They were gone. And the thought of walking in circles to find them made my shoulders deflate in exhaustion. After rewarding myself with a few minutes of rest on a nearby bench, I slowly stood up to begin the search. I sighed heavily and began to walk away.

"Grace?"

Looking back, I halted as I saw *him* standing just a few feet away. I stood there and stared.

"Sorry, I didn't mean to . . . I just, I sort of saw you run into the restroom a while back." He gestured behind him and lowered his hand from his left ear. "And thought I'd check up on ya. You alright?"

The speckles of honey in his brown eyes seemed to dance even more than usual from the lights around us, exposing the tenderness and sincerity behind them. My heart swelled, and something filled it that I couldn't place. Though he still looked rough at first glance, he didn't reek with sweat as he usually did. Even his clothes were cleaner. All the things I'd been curious to see.

"Um," I began faintly, becoming lost in every detail of him. "Y-yeah . . . where's Harley?"

"Oh, I had to leave him home." He cleared his throat as he scratched the side of his jaw. "By the way—"

"Peter, our food's ready! Come on. Milo's waiting for us!" a woman called out, causing his head to turn back.

"Just gimme a minute!"

At that moment, I never felt so grateful to know a name. Finally. A name to the man who I had grown so curious about. It was a silly thing, since it was just a name. But to me, it wasn't. It was a simple name, and he was anything but. I spotted the young woman who stood fifteen feet away holding a tray of food. Between her bright red lips and the black bouncy curls, she held herself with such confidence. A confidence I hoped to have one day. I regarded him just as he returned his attention to me.

"Okay, I should, uh, head on back or she's gonna get louder," Peter said and turned away but stopped, glancing around for a moment. "Hey, didn't you say you were gonna be here with someone?"

"Yeah, he went to get me something to drink," I reassured him with a feigned smile. "I was just on my way over to him."

He nodded, doubtful, but he didn't pry as I expected him to. Instead, he remained silent, and I wondered if he had seen through my lie. A dozen thoughts seemed to run through his mind as his doleful eyes swept my face, deeply considering one of them. Just as he took a step forward and opened his mouth to speak, the woman called out, this time with more urgency and impatience, "Peter! Come on!" And I believed if she hadn't, he would've told me that very thought that seemed of great importance.

He glanced back.

"Okay, she's gonna blow a gasket. It was nice runnin' into you, Grace. Have a good night." Peter turned and stumbled over a discarded soda can, quickly catching himself. "Whew, that was close."

"You alright?"

"Oh yeah, I'm fine. I'm fine," he said, his cheeks turning red, and he left but not before flashing a toothy grin.

With each of our encounters, an awkwardness and a shyness filled his brown eyes, and if I was lucky enough to see it, his cheeks would turn red. Almost like a boy experiencing his first crush again. Or was he just that uncomfortable talking to me? I watched him walk away. Peter's mouth moved. The woman smacked his shoulder, disappearing into the crowd by his side. What was he like with a woman? Though I knew there was no chance, would he ever see me that way? Would there be any man who would see me that way, and not just as a girl who got knocked up?

"There you are!" Mason's frantic voice interrupted my thoughts, and I saw him come to a halt. "I've been looking all over for you. Jesus Christ. You just took off. You really do move fast," he said, out of breath. "Come on, let's go. We're gonna go on the Ferris wheel. You can ride that, right?"

"Why? Cause I'm fat?"

"I mean . . ." He paused, realizing there was no such thing as a good answer. "So who was that guy talkin' to ya?"

"Nobody."

# 7

I hadn't given a second thought to what time it was, but as we waited in line for food, the aches had started to become unbearable. The exhaustion weaved its way through my body as pain shot up my legs and lower back. I rubbed my chest with my palm in a back-and-forth motion, applying more pressure each time. Everything had become unbearable. The noise. Them. Mason and Grady cracked some jokes, laughing boisterously along with the girls. The second time I called Mason's name with no response killed the last of my patience, and I grabbed his arm, pulling him to the side.

"Jesus Christ! What?" he asked, yanking his arm back. "You hungry or somethin'?"

"I'm tired, Mason. That's what."

"Last time I checked it was only eleven-thirty. We have one more ride, and Grady wants—"

"Mason, I wanna go. So, you're either gonna take me home, or I'm gonna go on my own." I turned away.

"Oh, yeah, 'cause you're gonna find some good Samaritan willing to drive you an hour back home?"

"I'll figure it out. Either way, I'm goin'. I can't keep up. My feet are tired, and it's loud here."

"God, that's so like you, Grace," Mason said, exasperated, following behind my quick steps. "You say you'll be fine. Then you get all bent outta shape. And you get all whiny. You get all—"

I stopped and looked back at him. "I get all what? Tell me. Tell me how I'm supposed to be feelin' when you're so self-centered and so oblivious to how goddamn tired I am! I'm exhausted! I'm so exhausted I can't even look at your stupid face right now! This is your baby, too! Or did you forget that already?"

"Man, when did you become so high strung?" he asked. "I liked you better when—"

"You wanna know when? The moment your lousy dick got me pregnant! That's when!"

A few people close by glanced over with wide eyes, covering their mouths to muffle their snickers.

"You know what? Fine. Go ahead! Go fucking hitchhike! I don't care!" Mason threw his arms up in the air and stormed off.

By the time I had come to regret my outburst with Mason, I was sitting outside a small security trailer. Maybe I already had come to regret it the moment I walked away from him. If it wasn't for my pride, I would still have a ride home. If it wasn't for many things—things I could easily blame my baby girl for that brought me to this very moment. Though I was regretful, I was also relieved. To be away from the crowd. Away from all the noise. Away from them. A shiny red glimmer of light prompted me to look away from my belly and to the little girl by my left side. Her red shoes swung back and forth as she played with the ends of her strawberry blonde pigtails. Every few seconds she'd glance around and scratch her rosy freckled cheeks. I smiled and looked ahead, only to catch her big green eyes now watching me, full of life and curiosity. She smiled brightly.

"Hi."

"Hi, there."

"That a baby in your belly?" She pointed.

My hand slipped over my stomach. "Yeah, it is."

"A boy or a girl?"

"Girl."

"Good. Boys have cooties."

"Lulu!" a woman called out, running over. "What did we tell you about running ahead like that? I'm sorry if she bothered you," the woman said apologetically, grabbing the girl's hand before I had a chance to speak.

Lulu glanced back and then up at her mother. "But . . . but she looked sad, Momma. I just—"

"Lulu, be quiet. I'm so sorry," the mother said sincerely just as the father standing beside her picked Lulu up.

As I watched them walk away, it felt as if someone had punched me in the gut, the same way my mama must have felt when I asked her why she was so sad. It hit deep. So deep I knew it left a mark. Reminding me of the many wounds that were left open and fermenting. That led me to wonder if I'd ever been good at hiding my pain with a smile. The last thing I'd ever want was for my own child to see me in pain. To know it was easy to fake a smile. A shuffle and a gruff voice made me turn my head, seeing Owen, the other security officer, step out from the trailer. I sat upright.

"Found the kid's parents, John?" Owen asked.

"Yep, third one tonight. Crazy." John stepped back into the crowd, surveying the grounds.

"Also, Grace, I got a hold of your father. He's on his way," Owen said, wiping the sweat from his forehead before placing his hands on his sides. "Sounds like he's had one too many if you ask me."

"I'll be just fine, Owen. Don't worry." I grabbed my bag and sweater. "Have a good night."

"You sure you don't wanna wait here? You got a baby and all. Heck,

I'll drive you home. I live out that way anyway."

"Owen, I'm fine."

"Well, just take this, will ya? Make me feel better," he insisted and stepped back inside the trailer. He returned, holding out a bottle of water. "Dehydration is no little matter. And if you need anything, I'll be right here."

I took the bottle. "Thank you," I said. He smiled at me warmly and walked back inside.

Finding an empty bench just outside the entrance, I sighed in relief. I don't know for how long I sat out there, but long enough for the mud to start cracking along the heel of my shoes. Taking the last sip from the bottle of water, I set it beside me. Every so often, I found myself hoping to see Mason's group of friends leaving or hoping some kind family would take pity on me and ask if I needed a ride. But soon enough, the sounds grew faint, and hundreds of muddy footsteps from people returning to their cars were now imprinted on the concrete. My knee bounced in place.

Hearing the timbre of a familiar voice, I turned my head. And there he was, twenty-five feet away, talking with the same young woman from before. As a large group of teenagers made their way past me, I saw the perfect opportunity to slip beside them, but just as I stood from the bench, he did a double take and his face fell. My feet stopped. The look in his eyes branded itself in my memory. Never have I witnessed such care and worry in a person's eyes. And strangely enough, I found myself wanting to run into his arms.

"Grace?" Peter's concerned voice made me walk briskly in the other direction. "Hey! Hey, what are you—" He quickly caught up to me. "Grace, what are you doing out here alone? You okay?"

I stopped.

"Pete!" the young woman exclaimed and raised her arms. "We're about to leave! Milo—"

Peter turned back to her and called out, "Just give me a second. Grace, what are you—"

"Just go. I'm fine. I'm just waitin' for my date to come around with the truck is all," I said.

He didn't move but looked toward the parking lot, glancing right and left before facing me. His brows drew together, a hard line forming between them, like he was trying to lift the truth from my head. It was then I wondered: Was he able to see it? Was he able to see the same thing just like Lulu?

"And just how long have you been waiting out here, Grace?" he asked, his voice soft.

I hesitated by the forwardness of his question, uncertain of how to answer and sound convincing. His eyes swept my face, and it was then I knew my silence had answered for me. Knowing there wasn't a chance to convince him otherwise, I brought my attention back to my swollen feet.

"You and Milo go on ahead," Peter told the woman. "I'm gonna take her back home."

I lifted my head.

"Pete, are you kiddin' me?" the young woman said, irritated, keeping her arms folded. Peter opened his mouth to speak, but she cut him off. "You always do this. You always find a reason to ditch us. We were gonna go listen to some music. And you said you were gonna go. You know how upset Milo will be?"

Though he was standing a few feet away, I recognized the caution in his face, reconsidering his own decision. "Just go. I'm fine waitin' out here," I said, catching the sudden flicker of disapproval in Peter's eyes.

"I don't like that idea, kid." He didn't sound angry. In fact, he sounded uneasy. "It's past midnight—"

"How many times do I have to tell you to stop callin' me that before it gets through your thick head?" I snapped. His face fell. "I'm not some charity case you can use to give yourself a nice ego boost. Now go, will ya?"

His expression softened ever so slightly, but his face remained blatantly shocked. "Look, I—"

"Pete!" a man's voice called out. "What are you doing over there, man? Let's get going."

From afar, I could only catch his friend's scraggly, unkempt beard, dark blue T-shirt, and faded jeans that no doubt reeked of sweat given the heat that still hadn't broken. He nodded his head at me in place of a wave. Peter turned back at me, all the more hesitant. His Adam's apple bobbed in his throat, and the longer his eyes lingered, the more they deepened with pain. A pain brought by the wrangling of mind and heart.

"Pete," the man repeated, causing Peter to reluctantly glance over his shoulder once again.

"I'm fine. Just go," I reassured him, unable to muster the courage to just say it. *Take me home.* If I did, I'd be allowing him to see the one thing that most people take advantage of.

"Grace—"

"I said I'm fine," I said as his friend walked up to us.

"Pete."

Peter looked at his friend and returned his focus to me one last time before striding off without another word. His friends quickly caught up to him. Once they were more than twenty feet away, Peter unexpectedly looked back over his shoulder, catching my stare. I walked away and sat down on the bench with an exhausted sigh. A part of me wanted to go, and that's what frightened me the most. Pa's truck backfired in the distance. The urgency and recklessness in which he accelerated told me all I needed to know. It was never the big things that made Pa snap.

It was the little things.

The brakes squeaked to a halt as the tire caught the curb. He climbed out and slammed the door shut; his hair was just as tousled as his clothing. "Get your ass in the truck," Pa demanded, every step fueled with anger.

Though the voice inside told me to run, I stood there. I saw it. I felt it. He wanted to hurt me. Every bit of me prayed he wouldn't. Yet that hope vanished just as quickly as I had thought it when he snatched my arm, dragging me with him to the truck. A few pedestrians turned, but no one found the courage or interest to intervene. Using all my strength to fight against him, I planted my feet.

"God damn it, stop fighting me, Grace. I said stop it!"

He backhanded me, but before I could tumble to the ground, Pa grabbed me by the scruff of my dress. His fingers pulled with such force that I cried out from the pressure. He shoved me inside, and I flinched as he slammed the door. Fallen strands of sweaty hair hung over my face, moving with each tremble of my unsteady breath as I watched Pa storm around the front of the truck. He clambered into his seat, and I pressed myself as far as I could against the passenger door, protectively sliding my hands around my belly. It was then, in the side-view mirror, I caught sight of Owen coming to a running stop as we took off. Seeing the lights of the Ferris wheel become dimmer and dimmer, I never wanted to cry more than I did now. Never had I been more regretful of my pride.

The headlights cast a spotlight on the dust floating in the air as the dark and empty highway stretched out before us. But something else lingered in the midst of the thick heat, something causing the little hairs on the back of my neck to stand and my gut to twist. Like the time I picked up something shiny, thinking it was a penny, but instead, it was a piece of glass that cut my finger.

I glanced over. Pa's wide, frenzied eyes remained fixed on the windshield. Though the thought of walking alone in the middle of night made my feet ache, anything would be better than being stuck with my pa. Nothing was more frightening than an unpredictable man. As the truck's tires began to settle on the road, so did the dust, disappearing into the blackness. I wished it was just as easy for me. I wished for many things. Like how I wished to never feel the burn of Pa's hand on my cheek. Now I truly was my mama, and I despised it with every bit of my soul.

"Pa—"

"Don't. Don't say nothin'. You think you could pull a fast one on your old man, huh? You think I wouldn't ever find out? I know about your little joyride the other day in that neighbor's truck. Mrs. Anderson told me all about it. You're just like your goddamn mother. A dirty fucking liar."

As painful as his words were, I knew there wasn't anything I could say to change his mind. Not even the truth could help me at this point. Turning away, I faced the windshield, holding back tears.

"I hate you."

"Guess what, kid, I don't like you much either, but I'm your goddamn father, so you're gonna listen to me."

"I wanna get out," I faintly pleaded.

"What?"

"I wanna get out."

Pa snorted. "And where you gonna go? You think you can make it without me? You think you're an adult now? You think you know everything? You don't have a fucking clue what it takes to be a parent. I do!" he seethed and pointed to his chest. "I do everything! I get up in the middle of the night and drive an hour to pick your sorry ass up! You should be thanking me! You don't have a fucking clue! I did everything for your mother, and look at how that bitch thanked me! She left us!"

"I wanna get out!!" I yelled.

"Shut up! Just shut up!"

He returned his attention back to the road, his chest heaving. My eyes drifted to the steering wheel. Pa drew a cigarette from the carton and fiddled with his lighter, giving me all the courage and opportunity I needed to grab the wheel and swerve the truck off the highway. The tail end of the truck whipped around as Pa fought to control the wheel. I clenched the sides of my seat and braced myself for the worst possible outcome. Regaining control, he pulled off the road. Hastily unbuckling my seatbelt, I reached for the handle.

"Where you goin'? Hey!"

My body reacted, and I hit him anywhere I could, struggling to push him away as I screamed. Our hands flailed against each other. Pa smacked me across the face. "You don't fucking run from me!"

An arm suddenly appeared through the open driver's side window, grabbing the collar of Pa's shirt and slamming his face back and forth into the steering wheel. His head flung back, splatters of blood lining the dashboard. The door then swung open, and Pa was dragged out of the truck. He pushed himself up from the dirt and stumbled to catch his balance, holding his bloody nose. It wasn't until the tall, broad-shouldered man stepped in front of the headlights that I realized who it was. I climbed out and rushed over, my frantic eyes going from Peter to Pa. Peter's face and body trembled with such burning rage it whipped my breath away. So tangible. Like a wildfire.

"I'll kill you if you ever hit her again, you got that?" Peter threatened in a low voice, his eyes blazing with fury but also promise, making it clear to Pa he meant every word. "You got that?"

Though he had just vowed to kill my pa, a warmth expanded in my belly. Each nook and cranny of my body filled with it. It was something I hadn't ever experienced with a man. But it was the most exhilarating mix of conflicting but reassuring emotions all at once, and I savored each moment of it because I knew it was real. By the time I remembered to take a breath, my throat had gone dry, and I hadn't taken my eyes off him. Peter turned toward me but stopped as Pa started to reach behind his back.

"Pa!"

In one quick motion, just as Pa drew his weapon, Peter's left arm came down on Pa's hand, and his right hand struck Pa's throat. I winced and watched Pa go down. Peter picked up Pa's gun and tucked it underneath the waistline of his jeans, pulling down his white T-shirt. Pa strained to push himself up, wheezing like a javelina who had been walking the desert for days without any water. Peter stepped closer, and Pa reached into his pocket, taking out his switchblade. With one click it snapped open, and he swung his arm forward. Peter swiftly moved his upper body to the side to avoid the blade and caught Pa's hand. Pa lurched his head forward, headbutting Peter who stumbled back. That split second was all that Pa needed to strike Peter. I stood wide-eyed as he fell to the ground. He turned onto his stomach and started to push himself upright until Pa's boot swung itself into his gut.

"Like you're any better?" Pa spat out a line of blood before swinging his foot into Peter's stomach again.

"Pa, stop it!" I cried out.

"Going after my kid!"

Pa's leg went back, readying for another kick, but just as quickly, Peter's leg swept forward and knocked Pa off his feet, causing him to fall. Peter scrambled on top of him and grabbed Pa's shirt, bringing his upper body off the ground. He raised his arm and swung his fist into Pa's face. Fury fueled each strike of his arm, becoming only more powerful. And I felt no fear watching him as he continued to hit my pa again and again. I somehow found peace in his violence. It was raw. Like picking at a scab until the bloody red and pink flesh exposed itself. His face was like that of a mad man. Peter struck one last time, causing Pa's head to drop onto the dirt. And that's when I heard it.

It was guttural, something coming from the depths of his being. Peter yelled in blind rage, baring his teeth over my pa like a wild animal.

It was magnificent. Pa's eyes were full of terror as Peter slowly stood upright. Small droplets of blood scattered the side of Peter's face. I knew it wasn't his.

But I didn't care.

Peter turned toward me and halted, strands of hair hanging in front of his face. He remained quiet, his eyes careful, like he was expecting me to scream but also ashamed for ever allowing me to see such a thing. A part of me searched for that scream. To be scared. To be uneasy. But I found nothing. I only found a dozen emotions and a strange sense of safety as we stood there.

A nervous swallow passed through his throat, hesitating. "You okay?" he asked gently.

I nodded, and when I didn't take a step back as he stepped forward, he seemed relieved. A pair of headlights in the distance caused Peter to look back and then at me. He put his hand on the small of my back and led me to his truck, glancing right and left. Peter's pace quickened and I stumbled, unable to keep up with his long strides. He opened the door, and I hastily climbed in.

He shut the door and jogged around the truck, sliding in beside me. The engine revved to life and the tires squealed. My back was thrown into the seat as he sped toward the exit and took a sharp left. The truck raced forward as we merged onto Highway 10. And like the truck, my heart raced just as fast. Adrenaline at full force. I looked over. He stared ahead, but every few seconds he'd glance right and left as if he was patrolling, on guard. I then noticed how badly his knuckles were bruised and the thin layer of dirt on his clothes and face. The little specks of blood again.

"Peter—"

His cautious eyes flickered over, and he stayed quiet, returning his attention to the road. As much as I wanted to say something, there was an inexplicable feeling that I needed to stay quiet. Not from fear. But for him. Sometimes, in the midst of chaos, people needed silence, to know that they still have some control. All I knew was that no matter how calm and controlled he seemed to be, no matter the words we had ceased to share with each other, he was just as worried and scared as I was.

"By the way, it's . . . it's Pete. Not Peter. No one calls me Peter," he said quietly, still facing the windshield.

# 8

In the short time it took for us to arrive back in Catalina, we had found some semblance of calm. Keeping my head propped on the windowsill, I admired the pitch-black desert. It was just a void of darkness outside. Everything seemed to cease to exist. Sometimes it wasn't as easy to hide the unpleasant things like the desert did. It never mattered how deep I dug the problem into the farthest corner of my mind, it still had a way of coming back to me. Each time in a new way. I sat up, as we were moments away from turning left down the street towards the trailer park, but Peter flew by the exit.

"Hey, you missed it."

"What?" He glanced back and exhaled in exhaustion. "Sorry. I-I'll try to find some place to turn around."

He kept his sights on the white lines. Though he didn't really say much or let his mask slip away, there were moments when I believed he was just as exhausted with life as I was. A kind of exhaustion I knew all too well. I looked away. Other than a few fleeting headlights, nothing else seemed to lay ahead on the dark road.

"Hey, uh," Peter began. "I-I don't know if you're hungry or not, but um . . . I think eating some food would be good right now. Could take the edge off, you know? Ray told me that Sunny Side Cafe was pretty good."

"Ray? Ray Johnson?"

"Yeah, he was tellin' me about it the other day. It's close by, I think. I've passed by it a few times. I-If you don't want to, I don't mind goin' back and dropping you off. Really. Whatever you wanna do."

I knew with all my heart that if I said it, he wouldn't think twice about turning around to appease me, but there was another want. A want I never thought I'd have. It wasn't a want born out of obligation for what he had done, but from the look in his eyes right now. A look I never wanted to see again. And I knew it would be my biggest regret if I didn't take this chance to take it away. Even if it was for a brief time.

"Alright."

For the remainder of the drive, we didn't utter a word. He seemed relieved he didn't have to say anything further. In less than fifteen minutes, the letters of Sunny Side Cafe glowed red in the distance. After letting the engine sputter to a silence, Peter climbed out slower than usual, holding his lower back. A heavy ache weighed on my chest like the time I held my breath too long underwater. I'd always wondered what Pa was doing to Mama as I hid in the closet down the hall. I wasn't unfamiliar with the violence that people were capable of, and yet, all I cared about at that moment was Peter. As he made his way around the truck, his limp more noticeable than before, I pulled down the visor and ran my fingers through my hair. That's when I saw the few bruises along my right arm and the beginning of another around the side of my eye. Just as he opened the door, I shut the visor.

"You need any help gittin' down?"

I shook my head and unbuckled my seatbelt, slowly sliding off the seat as I stifled a whine.

Peter stepped forward. "Grace—"

"I'm fine. Really, I'm fine." I set my feet on the pavement. He shut the door and then locked and unlocked the truck three times before walking up beside me. I slipped each arm through the sleeves of my cardigan.

"Can I ask why you do that?"

"Do what?"

"Lock the truck three times."

"It's an old habit of mine is all."

Peter jogged ahead of me and caught the door just as a man left, holding it open. The walls were just as yellow as I remembered them. Windows framed the rugged beauty of the Catalina Mountains during the day. A row of black and white pictures displayed the history of Tucson. Redbone's "Come and Get your Love" softly played on the radio. The smells of nicotine and beer hung in the air from the half dozen night workers drinking their coffee. A few burly men at the counter and a waitress conducted full body sweeps as they watched Peter follow behind me. Their gazes and the suspicious murmurs traveled through the cafe like dust on a windy day. Spotting the sign for the restroom, I started to make my way there but stopped when a hand grabbed my arm, and I looked over my shoulder. Peter had that same look from the fair when he saw me all alone.

His cheeks flushed red, and he immediately pulled away his hand. "Sorry, I didn't mean . . ." he stammered. "I'll, uh, let you do your thing . . ." He stepped back, looking over at the waitress who stared at him. "S-she's with me." He cleared his throat. The woman's eyes swept over me from top to bottom.

"I am," I reassured her and regarded Peter, who still hadn't moved. "I'm just gonna go to the bathroom real quick. I'm comin' right back. I promise," I said calmly in hopes to comfort him. "Alright?"

He nodded. "I'll be at a table if you need me. Okay?" He hesitated and then walked over to a booth.

I turned and rushed down the hall, rattling the doorknob to the women's bathroom. Holding my legs tight, I urgently knocked on the door and bounced in place. I tried the doorknob to the men's and quickly slipped inside. The smell alone made me gag. After relieving my bladder,

I washed my hands and splashed water on my face and on the back of my neck. Taking a deep breath, I finally looked at myself in the mirror and gently touched the bruise with my fingertips. It almost looked like my mama's. Just as purple. Just as red. Though its swell would heal, the memory of its sting would forever hold the hate I held for my pa. After taking one last breath, I left to find Peter already seated, his foot tapping anxiously. I sat down in relief and set my bag beside me, still unable to shake the feeling of curious eyes. Looking back, I caught their heads whipping away.

"Everything alright?" he asked.

"Yeah." I reached into the basket, took out a menu, and sat back in the booth. "You'd just think their mommas would've taught them that starin' is rude." I lowered my focus to the foggy, plastic cover and flipped it open but not without peeking up at Peter. His brows were pinched together like they always were whenever he'd heard something strange. Almost skeptical, but this time the apple of his cheek was lifted ever so slightly. Like he was smiling. And if it wasn't for his face leaning into his hand, with his fingers splayed across that very cheek, I would've seen that smile.

"What? Why you lookin' at me like that?" I asked.

"Nothin'." He let out a quiet chuckle. "No reason," he said and reached into the basket for a menu of his own.

Whatever it was that I'd said or done, it didn't matter as it brought that smile and light to his face again. Even if it was for only a brief moment. Biting my bottom lip, I returned my gaze to the choices of food. I flipped through the menu.

"You know what you're gonna get? I haven't been here in years, so I don't know what's good anymore," I said. "Now that I am here, I don't think I am all that hungry."

"Not even for a good burger and fries? Maybe even a milkshake? You're eating for two, aren't you?"

"You know that's a myth, right? You can eat what you normally would eat during the first trimester but by the second I had to up my calories by three hundred fifty, and by the third—" I paused, catching his full attention. He didn't say a word and just waited, keen to know more. "And right now, it's four hundred and fifty calories." I fumbled over my words and tucked a strand of hair behind my ear. "I-I read it in a magazine."

"Huh." He nodded, offering little reaction as he scratched his beard. "You learn something new every day."

A hand then set down two sets of cutlery in front of us. "Welcome to Sunny's. I'll be your waitress tonight. Name's Martha." A woman in her mid sixties had walked up to our table. She had gray, kinky curls atop her head and smelled of overripe fruit. Martha reached into the pocket of her white apron, taking out a notepad and a red pen. "Can I get you two anything to drink? We're having a special tonight. Buy one—Good Lord Almighty, what happened to you?" She gaped at Peter. Even her downturned eyes were now full and wide. Then they fell upon me, then to my stomach, and then back at Peter, who stopped scratching his jaw. "You alright there?" she asked.

"Oh, I'm fine, ma'am. I'll be fine." He cleared his throat, fiddling with the back of his ear.

"Uh-huh." Only after giving Peter another once over did Martha look away and say, "We're havin' a special tonight. Buy one entree and get the next one half off. The buttermilk pancakes are my favorite, and they'll fill you right up, honey, since you're eating for two." She smiled. I bit the tip of my tongue, resisting the urge to explain the myth once again, and offered a smile in return. "You two know what you'd like, or do you need more time to look over the menu?"

"Uh, I'm gonna have a black coffee. And the Sunny's burger with extra bacon. No cheese. Medium well. And is there any chance you could also add another patty on the side?" Peter asked.

"Sure." Martha regarded me once again. "And you, honey? What would you and the baby like?"

"I'll get the same thing. Well done, please. With two patties and two slices of cheese. And make sure they add 'em, or I'll know. Also, is there any way they can not add salt to the fries?"

"I can ask," Martha said.

"If they can't, it's fine. I'll just get the salad then. And I'm gonna have a glass of apple juice. With a straw. No ice," I said with a smile until I noticed the stillness of her pen and the thinning of her red lips.

"You want the dressin' on the side with that?"

"No, it's fine."

"You sure about that?"

"Yeah."

"Alright." Martha took our menus and walked away, shaking her head.

When I looked at Peter, he was staring at me, strangely intrigued.

"What? I know what I like. Nothing wrong with that. More people should know what they want. Especially when it comes to food."

"You've got a bit of a temper, don't you?" he stated, a subtle tone of humor laced through his voice.

"Got it from my mama. Never really liked it," I unthinkingly admitted. Peter slowly nodded and looked over to the window with a big yawn. Bit by bit, his tired eyes slowly began to close.

Unable to resist it any longer, I slipped my swollen feet from my sandals. I couldn't hold back an "mmm" of relief as I propped them up on the seat across from me, stretching my achy legs and feet. Using my right toes, I pressed them on top of the others and bent them till I heard a satisfying crack. Switching to the other foot to do the same thing, it was then I realized Peter was intently watching my feet. I expected a sneer or a comment of disgust. Instead, he turned to the window but not without glancing at my feet one last time, holding back a smile.

"You know, you should take a picture. It'll last longer."

"I don't like cameras."

"Why?"

"You ask a lot of questions, you know that?"

"There's always a reason why someone doesn't like somethin'. So why don't you like them?"

"Are you one of those people who needs to find the answers no matter what in order to satisfy their curiosity?"

"Yeah. How'd you know?"

"Just a hunch."

Ten minutes had passed without any further explanation. When he closed his eyes again, his head began to bob and droop, but he quickly caught himself and patted his cheek. Another yawn escaped him. Martha returned with our drinks, looking between Peter and me with pursed lips.

"Thank you," I said.

"Yes, thank you." Peter gave her a sincere but tired smile, and Martha left without a word. He sighed, reaching for two packets of sugar, muttering, "I really hope she didn't spit in my coffee."

I leaned forward, searching for any spit particles floating in my drink. "She didn't in mine."

"Then I'll keep havin' hope."

I bit my bottom lip and smiled, watching him empty the packets of sugar. Gently setting the glass on my belly, I took a much-needed sip. My shoulders relaxed. The heavenly aroma of greasy burgers and sizzling bacon emanated from the kitchen, and my stomach growled in anticipation. Peter looked up, his brows raised. A grin stretched from one side of my face to the other, showing every tooth. He lowered his head and let out a breathy chuckle before taking a sip of his coffee. Martha walked over with a tray and set down our plates of food. I sat upright in excitement and set the glass of apple juice to the side.

I smiled. "Thank you."

"Thank you, ma'am."

"Uh-huh." Martha turned away.

I looked at my unsalted fries and double cheeseburger, plucking off the red onions. The sound of chewing and a low soft "hmm" made me raise my head as Peter took a large bite of his burger. He picked up a piece of soggy lettuce that slipped out from the bun, and once he was satisfied with its placement, assured no condiments would drop and dampen the enjoyment of his meal, only then did he take another bite.

The way he fixed his meal reminded me of the times my mama used to take care of her Portulacas. Everything had to be in its place, with the soil gently patted to perfection before she could pull herself away from the masterpiece that she took great pride in tending. I never thought I'd be envious of a flower. I didn't even know what envious meant at the time. I only longed for the day she'd look at me the same way.

The few men from the bar turned their heads, hearing the low hum of Peter's throat as he ate. Peter stopped chewing, and his finger paused from swirling the fry in the ketchup, as he finally realized I had been staring. He raised his head and regarded me, slowly beginning to chew again. After swallowing his food and wiping his mouth with a napkin, he spoke. "Somethin' wrong?"

"No."

"Then why aren't you eating?" he asked. "Did they not cook it all the way through? Cause I could—"

"No. No, they did," I reassured him, tucking a strand of hair behind my ear. The humming started again until I placed six fries on the cheeseburger and caught him staring at me with a mouthful of food. "What? Don't knock it till you try it," I said and picked up my burger, taking a bite. I groaned in delight, shutting my eyes.

We lapsed back into silence as Peter downed his burger in less than ten minutes. Setting down my half-eaten burger, I placed my hand over my belly. Peter wrapped the second patty in a napkin like a safety blanket and carefully tucked it in his back pocket.

Taking the last sip of apple juice, I leaned back and said, "I didn't think I'd be that hungry."

Martha appeared from the corner, saying, "Can I get you two anything else? Any more coffee?"

"No, thank you, ma'am. We'll just take the check." Peter stood from the booth. "Unless you want somethin' else," he said to me.

I shook my head. "No. I'm full."

"Alright, I'll be back in a jiff," he said. "Just gonna use the bathroom real quick before we go." He walked past Martha, giving her an affable smile. "Thanks again, ma'am. Have a good night."

"You, too."

I slipped my feet through my sandals and wiggled my toes one last time. Martha slipped her notepad into her apron and glanced back one last time before placing her hand on my shoulder.

"Honey, you okay? You want me to call the cops?"

"What? Oh no, ma'am. You got it all wrong. It's-it's not what it looks like. Really. He—"

"Honey, I've heard every excuse there is. It's not my first time comin' across a girl like you."

"Ma'am, it's not what you think. Really. You got it all wrong. He wouldn't ever hurt me."

She placed her hands on her hips and shifted her weight, sighing heavily once she realized I wasn't going to say another word. "Well, the last thing I'm gonna say is that you and your baby don't deserve to go through that. Shouldn't even have gone through it to begin with," Martha said, setting down the check. "There's no shame in leavin', honey," she said and walked away with our dirty dishes.

Though I wondered how many times Mama had been questioned like this, I also wondered how many times she said no. And how many times she reassured them with a smile. At five years old, I remember making a wish for my mama. That maybe, one day, someone big and strong would take away my pa.

A pair of heavy boots scraping against the floor made me look up to see Peter, who had stopped three feet away, his expression soft. My tears blurred his face, and I hastily swiped my hand across my cheek, giving him a quick smile. He reached into his back pocket, taking out his wallet.

"You alright? You look sick. Was it the meat?" he asked. "It was a bit pink in the middle."

"I'm okay."

"Well, I'll get you a bottle of water when we get to my truck. Okay?" He began to count the dollar bills. "Hey, I know it's not far, but do you need to use the bathroom before we go?"

"No, I'll be fine." I stood up with a grunt of effort. "You know, I read today in *Reader's Digest* that a food critic in Minnesota didn't check to see if his meat was cooked all the way and almost died of E. coli," I said. Peter stopped counting and lifted his eyes momentarily to the wall and then to me.

"What? It's just funny. Not him almost dying. That ain't funny at all. Just that I read that today and then I had a burger. Which is what he ate. You know? Cause I ate the same thing."

After another second, his attention returned to the dollar bills. He let out a breathy chuckle, shaking his head. I caught the hint of a small smile. As he slipped the bills underneath his cup of coffee, I couldn't help but stare at the total. My first instinct was to reach for my chest. He placed his wallet back into the pocket of his jeans.

"What is it?" he asked. I regarded him. "What, you don't like odd numbers or somethin'?"

"No."

"Huh," he muttered, his brows pulling together as if he had an inkling to what the reason could be. "Do you think even numbers are good luck?" He asked and walked unusually close by my side as we made our way across the diner, sticking his hands into the pockets of his jeans.

"Yeah."

"Why?" he asked and held open the door.

When I glanced up, I caught his curious waiting gaze. "You know, you don't have to do this."

"Uh . . . do what?"

"I really don't need people trying to make conversation with me just to make me . . . feel better. I've had enough of that these past seven months," I said, expecting him to call me the one thing I hate the most.

"I know I don't need to. It's just . . . I never really know how to go about this," he admitted in a soft tone. Even though his eyes were conflicted, the vulnerability in his voice struck me hard in the chest. "I know I haven't . . ." he paused, unsure of how to continue. "I've just never really been good at talkin'."

I stepped outside. "You're not that bad."

"Really?"

"Yeah."

He nodded, following by my side. "So, why do you not like them? The uh, numbers."

"It's a long story."

A couple turned their heads toward us before they walked in whispering to each other.

We headed down the ramp, making our way toward the truck. "Well," he began and stopped in his tracks to look at me, opening the passenger side door. "Nine is divisible by three. So that's good luck in my book."

I smiled and climbed into the truck. Peter shut the door and jogged around, sitting down beside me. The engine revved to life, and I shifted, pressing my knees together, struggling to find a comfortable position. He looked over and lifted a brow, watching me slump back into the seat.

"You okay there?"

I blew a strand of hair from my face. "I think that second apple juice was a bad idea."

"Do you wanna run back inside, or do you think you can hold it until I get you home?"

"No, I'm good."

"You sure? Cause if you need to go, you should go," he insisted sincerely. I looked at him.

"I'm good."

He nodded, saying, "Alright," and glanced over at me one last time before reversing out of the parking lot.

At first, I did mind the mixed smell of Harley and Peter's sweat. But now, I didn't so much. In fact, it had become a bit peaceful. Rearranging myself in the seat again, I stretched each leg outward and sighed in relief. I then caught his head turning back to center. Though it was pitch black, the dashboard lights were enough for me to trace the slope of his nose and chin. His tired eyes focused on the road, but what caught my attention was the tapping of his pointer and middle finger. Every several seconds he'd tap the wheel three times, then pause, and tap three times again. Like Ray who always had to tuck in his shirt one last time before leaving or Arlene who always had to file her nails on Wednesdays. I always wondered why, but I never mustered up the courage to ask them.

"Why do you do that?"

His fingers stopped tapping.

"Do what?"

"That. With the wheel . . . Is that just another old habit of yours, or is it somethin' else?"

"Yeah, it's—it's a few things. What about you? What's your thing with the even numbers?"

"Why do you wanna know so bad?"

"Cause I wanna know."

I looked away.

"You know, you're not like many people. Not a lot of people would care to know somethin' like that. Even if they'd ask me, I'd think they were just tryin' to be nice. I don't think my pa has ever asked me that. About my thing with the numbers," I thought out loud. "I think he'd just make fun of it, like he did with a lot of things. That's why I said you'd be a great father. Cause the day I told him that I was pregnant, he said, 'Well, guess you're gonna get fat. No boy is gonna take you to the prom now.'" I let out a small laugh and looked back at Peter. He stared ahead, seeming to dwell on my words.

There was a glint of fury building in his eyes, like a sandstorm about to break free. The second his eyes landed back on my face, his expression immediately softened, and the storm settled. I sat there unsure of whether to continue or not. "I just . . . I always wanted a baby of my own. Since I was little, I knew I wanted to be a momma. To be a different mama than mine was. I just thought I would've been married when it happened. I thought of a lot of things . . . that's why I said what I said the other day," I admitted, unsure of why this suddenly surfaced. Was it because of what had happened? Or was it just because I could? That for some inexplicable reason, I had a feeling he wouldn't ever repeat these words outside of this truck. I looked down at my round stomach. "I know my pa isn't the greatest man, but I'd like to think he was. I think he just . . . I don't think he ever reckoned on being such a young parent. Not a lot of people do."

"Huh."

"What?"

"Nothing, you're just . . ." He paused. "H-How old are you again? Twenty?"

"Eighteen."

Both his brows raised, and he nodded, saying, "Well, you certainly don't talk or hold yourself like an eighteen-year-old. That's for sure."

"My mama said I'm an old soul."

He quickly laughed, catching me off guard. I caught a glimpse of a smile just as the truck came to a harsh stop, throwing us forward. His face and body became still, eyes wide, as the headlights cast a glow upon the animal. Its pig-like nose twitched, and its teeth clacked. Peter exhaled, watching the family of javelinas safely cross the road. That's when I felt the warm and protective embrace around my hand. I looked down at my fingers, which were tightly woven with his.

"Peter, can I have my hand back?"

He glanced down at our hands and quickly released his grip. I stretched out my fingers, relieved.

"Sorry." A crooked, almost boyish grin spread across his face. He turned to the road, his ears fully red in realization. "I think . . . I'm still a bit on edge. Sorry. I-I didn't hurt your hand, did I?"

"N-no, you didn't."

He nodded and hesitated as if he were about to speak, but instead he lifted his foot off the brake, letting the truck move forward.

The redness began to fade across my left hand where just moments ago his fingers were wrapped around mine. And I'd bet all the money I had stashed away in the Pampers box that that would be the only time he'd ever touch me. Though it didn't take long for him to return to his usual stoic self, it was still plain as day on his face. The regret. The regret of what he did to my pa. I was the reason he had unleashed that side of himself. But the little girl in me wasn't scared. In fact, she was relieved. Grateful, even. And at the same time, mad at herself for letting such a thing happen to her pa.

I now had a pain wrangling my own mind and heart. A kind of pain I reckoned would take a toll on me that would last for days. And I fought with all my strength to keep my eyes open. But inevitably, the temptation of sleep won. A gentle rock and a small thud woke me up. I blinked a few times, letting my eyes adjust to the glare of the trailer's porch lights. Slowly sitting upright, I winced, catching Peter's glance.

"You alright?"

"I'm fine. I'm just tired," I said. "Thank you again for . . . for driving me home. And the food."

He nodded. "No problem. I hope it, uh, made you feel better."

I turned ahead and sat there, uncertain of what else to say or do. Bringing my attention up from my lap, I stared at the trailer. As tired as I was, no part of me wanted to step inside. If I did, it would then mean I'd willingly welcome this new day. And the day after that, just waiting for the repercussions of my choices. Waiting to feel regretful of them. About what Peter did to my pa. I looked at him. He was still facing forward. Unable to take the silence any longer, I reached for the handle just as he spoke.

"Look, I—I'd feel a lot better if we—"

"I said I'm fine, Peter."

He turned away, and his lips thinned into a scowl. "If you say fine one more time, Grace, I swear I'm gonna turn this truck around and start driving again till you tell me the truth. I'm—"

"You really want the truth? You wouldn't be asking me this right now if I didn't have a baby. You wouldn't be doin' all this. No people like to help just 'cause they can. I'm fine. So lay off."

As quick as I was to open the door, his hand was just as quick to close it. "You think I regret it?" he asked harshly, the intensity of his voice taking me aback. "The only thing I regret, Grace, is that I didn't get there quick enough. Cause if I had, you wouldn't have gotten hurt," he said, his distraught voice striking a twinge of guilt in my chest. "And you wanna know another thing? You're better off without that sad excuse of a father. I've been around long enough to know what kind of man he is. And I regret saying such a thing, but my point stands. There would be one less woman abused in this already godforsaken world. You got it? So, before you put words in my mouth, maybe stop and think. I wouldn't have done anything differently. Pregnant or not. You're still trying to survive in this world as much as I am."

There was no shroud of doubt on his face. Nothing but a solid certainty that I knew couldn't be breached. Never had I heard someone say those words aloud before. The very words that my soul had been crying out for. Words that made me feel so guilty. I did love my pa, but only because the little girl inside still wanted that pa who held me on his shoulders and bought me a root beer float every Friday. With our eyes locked on each other, the impulse to cry rose, and I hastily climbed out of my seat.

"Grace, wait. Grace, I'm sorry." He jumped out of the truck, catching up to me as I made a beeline to the trailer. "Grace. I'm sorry. That might've been a bit harsh. I just . . . I'm not—"

I turned back to him and cried out, "Just go away!"

He stopped. His sorrowful, gentle expression did something to my stomach; it made me want to run into his arms. And for some reason, standing here, right now, across from him, I believed he could see it on my face, even through the tears. I quickly walked away, retreating inside.

# 9

Growing up, I never saw what Pa did to Mama. It was the bad sounds that stayed with me. But this time was different. Shouldn't I feel a certain way? That I stood there, doing nothing, watching Peter beat my pa to a pulp. Shouldn't I be afraid of him? As much as it unsettled me to admit, his violence was the violence I had yearned for. To scream and hit my pa with abandon, just as Pa had done to my mama. It's funny how one man's violence could be just what another person needed. Maybe if it was only my own safety on the line, I would have done something worse by now. Maybe I would have left already. All I knew was, if and when Pa came home, I was more frightened now than ever.

At least I still had this. The fiery light rising in the east. The one constant. Something that would always be there to greet me in the morning. Even if only for a short time. Nonetheless, I sat there until the air became thick with heat, and those lingering questions returned. A dull throb spread itself across my lower back and I shifted, stretching my sunburned legs across the steps of the porch. Not even the healing warmth of a sun's hug could take away the aches, reminding me of the events that had taken place the night before. And though it was quiet, a part of me waited for Uncle Wayne's loud truck to rumble the trailer park to life and awaken the dogs in a unison of howls and barks.

I pushed myself up and walked back inside the trailer. Opening the trash can, the smell of overripe fruit wafted upward into my nose, causing me to gag. I twisted the red ties together and slipped on my sandals and lugged the trash outside to the metal bin by the side of the road. The sound of an engine caused me to lift my head. To shield the sun's glare from my eyes, I raised my hand and squinted to make out the vehicle from afar. A dark green Ford Explorer sped up the road, parking behind Peter's truck. For a split second, my mind readied itself to see those black voluminous curls again. The driver's door shut, and a familiar man in a baseball cap stepped out. His scraggly beard helped me place him as Peter's friend from last night. He looked over at me and halted, giving me a brief wave. I threw the bag of spoiled food inside the bin. Unable to help myself, I then watched him knock on Peter's front door.

"Pete!" he called out. "Pete, come on. I know you're in there. Your truck's outside, man."

Any normal woman, after witnessing what he was capable of, wouldn't allow herself to still be this curious. Let alone stand here. Mama once said that even the kindest men are capable of doing unspeakable things. However, no matter how many times I had told myself nothing good would come of it, I allowed myself to be this way. It was safe, because he would never see me as a real woman.

Just as I convinced myself to leave, Peter's friend banged on the door again. "Pete, I swear, I'm gittin' really sick and tired of this fucking attitude . . . Pete! I'm gonna keep standing here! You know I will! I've got all day!"

The screen door swung open, and Pete's friend stumbled back.

"What are you doin?" Peter asked.

"What am I doin'? I'm here to check up on you. And good thing I did, 'cause you look like shit. What the hell happened to you?"

"I'm fine. You can go."

Peter's friend caught the frame of the door. "Now just wait a dang second. You're the one who left us to go off doing God knows what. And I come up here, and you look like this? What the heck did you do? The—"

"I said I'm fine. Now go, will you?" Peter spit the words out, stepping closer, standing just a few inches taller than his friend. "I got enough . . ." He paused, and his eyes flickered over to me as he became quiet. In that second, Harley had already shimmied his way between the frame and Peter's leg, bolting out the door. I hesitated, unsure of what to do, but I couldn't walk away and deny Harley.

He came to a running stop in front of me and readied himself into a play position. "Harley, go," I urged, stepping back. He yowled in protest, wagging his tail. "I'll play with ya later. Okay? But you gotta go," I pleaded. "You gotta go, okay?" Harley whined. "Yes, I know. I love you, too."

I looked over.

Peter and his friend spoke in hushed tones, but their eyes were intense and wide. His friend's thumb jerked toward me, leaning further into Peter's face, who pushed his hand down. Their mouths moved, but I couldn't hear what they said. "Just let it go. I don't need you checkin' up on me. I said I'm fine," Peter spat and turned back inside, shutting the door behind him with more force than normal.

His friend rolled his eyes and walked away, but stopped, yelling, "You know what, that's the last time I'm inviting you out, Pete! If you wanna talk, you're gonna be the one to call! It's about damn time you stepped up! I'm sick and tired of being the one carrying this friendship! Dick." He jumped the last step of the porch and stopped in his tracks just several feet away from me. Looking back at Peter's trailer and then at me, he asked, "You're that girl from last night, aren't you? Name's Grace, right?"

I stood upright. "Yeah."

"Right, I figured. You're kinda hard to miss. Name's Milo, by the way. Nice to meet ya. Can I ask how long you've known Pete? Cause, his dog, Harley, doesn't run over like that to just anyone."

I glanced over at Harley, who whined, sitting by my side. "Really? It ain't been that long."

"Huh. Well, Harley must really like ya, then," Milo said in disbelief, jangling the keys in his hand. He brought his attention to Peter's trailer for a brief moment. "You really haven't known Pete long? Cause last night, I've never seen him act that way. And I've known him for a while. He was a stone cold sonuvabitch in the Marines. It wasn't until they assigned him Harley that he started to soften up. He's never been big on people. But I think you already know that, living next door to him."

"Harley was with him?" I asked and looked at Harley, who had laid down on the ground, panting.

"Yeah, Harley was one of the best IED dogs out there. Pete would die for that dog." Milo stared at Harley and then back at me. "So, just recently, huh?"

"Yeah."

"Well, I should head back. Nice meetin' ya, Grace." Milo caught the keys in his hand and walked away.

"How long were you with him?" I called out.

Milo halted, saying, "In the Marines?" He leaned against the car, crossing his arms with a shrug. "Four years, give or take. Would've been longer if he hadn't been honorably discharged. Shrapnel to the right knee and loss of hearing. But let me tell you, even with the limp, he can still run like nobody's business."

"And you?"

"Me?"

"Are you still in the Marines?"

"About ten years now. We miss him and Harley. Pete was good. Reliable. Both of them were." Milo was about to continue but stopped as his attention fell over to the kitchen window of Peter's trailer. I looked and saw the blinds snapping shut. Harley's ears perked. Milo shook his head and walked around the vehicle. "Think that's my cue. Nice meet'n you again, Grace."

"Nice meeting you, too."

He climbed into the driver's seat and reversed the large hunk of metal to face the road. But before taking off, he rolled down the passenger side window and stuck his head out. "By the way . . ." He hesitated. "I don't know if this is my place or not to tell you, but while it may seem like Pete has everything together, he's anything but. So, would you keep an eye on him for me?"

"Okay."

"And take care of that cut." He gestured with a brief flick of his hand before taking off.

With Harley by my side, we watched Milo speed down the road. As the dust and dirt settled, I looked over at him, and his big ears perked in anticipation.

"I gotta go buddy. I'll see you again, okay?"

He whined and ran back to Peter's porch, slipping inside just as the door quickly opened and snapped closed. My mind raced with questions. Assumptions. If only it was as easy to be rid of these thoughts as it was to clean the crumbs and stains off this very table. The ache of my body became heavier as I sat down at the kitchen table and propped up my feet, watching the time go by. If only I didn't need to be so curious. Slowly but surely, the heat lulled me into a deep sleep until I heard the sound of a loud bass and dogs howling. I opened my eyes and stood to look out the kitchen window. The back of Uncle Wayne's red truck disappeared down the road as the front door creaked open. Pa stepped inside. A line of bruises spread like a rash across the side of his face. Between a swollen-shut eye, day-old clothes, greasy tousled hair, and the nick by his lower lip, he reminded me of my mama.

"Pa," I said softly as he shut the door. "Pa, I—"

He suddenly turned on the heel of his boot, and my body winced, readying myself for the worst. The bedroom door slammed shut, and I opened my eyes toward the hall. It was as if there was a storm brewing in there, and only I could feel its heavy presence. For the first time, his silence was more frightening than his words and the promise of his fist. I didn't know what was more unsettling. The little girl in me wanted to try and calm him down. But deep down, I knew this wasn't one of those times.

✳

Sitting on the porch the next morning, I stared at the jagged lines of the Catalina Mountains. A part of me hoped that some force in the universe would turn back time for me to witness the sunrise. It only made me realize just how fragile and precious a routine was. For the first time in seven months, I had missed the harmonious view of the rising sun and was instead awakened by the infernal sound of Uncle Wayne's truck. The odds were not in my favor today. Uncle Wayne leaned against the front fender with his arms crossed, smelling of his usual morning cigarettes and grilled cheese sandwich. Uncle Wayne held the stick of death between his index finger and thumb and, after taking a long drag and exhaling, expelled two streams of smoke from his nostrils. My nose scrunched. He flicked the excess ash onto the dirt, and I wondered to myself how I was related to such a man.

He sighed heavily, checking his watch. "How long does it take for the man to shit? We're burning daylight here. I could've driven to Oracle and back by now." Uncle Wayne took another long drag, shaking his head.

As the cloud of death left his nose, the nicotine stung my eyes, traveling to my lungs to start the first stage of decay. My first memory of tobacco was when I was seven years old with my Uncle Wayne. We were inside, windows closed. I was on the floor playing with my dolls.

He was sitting in Pa's chair, drinking a beer. Then he lit a cigarette. I remember being fascinated at how the smoke rose and formed a cloud near the ceiling. Then, there was a foul odor. It was so strong, and I thought of the time my pa caught a dead cat underneath our trailer. Soon, my nose ran, and my eyes watered. At that age, I didn't know how to put my misery into words. Instead, I cried and waved my arms at the cigarette. Uncle Wayne expelled another puff of smoke and looked over.

"What? What's that look for? Is it morning sickness or somethin'?" he asked. "Or is that just your face nowadays?"

"You know you can die from those things, right? Remember what Tina said to you? At the rate you're smokin', one of your lungs is gonna dry up and die. I'm startin' to believe her," I said.

He snorted. "And what does Tina know, huh? What does any woman know? If you were dealin' with the shit I got going on, you'd want a hit. God will know when it's my time. Until then, Grace, I'm gonna smoke."

"Yeah, you have fun with that, Uncle Wayne."

I stood to go back inside the trailer, wrapping my cardigan across my waist, but his next words stopped me. "Hey, hey, now, just wait a second. You gonna tell me what happened to that pretty face of yours or not?"

"What do you care?"

"You're my niece, that's what."

"You didn't care when it was my mama."

Uncle Wayne didn't say a word and slicked his tongue across his teeth, looking off in the distance as he took a drag. He threw the cigarette to the ground and put it out with the sole of his boot. "I'm gonna go wait in the truck. And tell your father to hurry the hell up." He leaned off the front fender just as a door creaked open. He paused and lifted his chin as a gesture, saying, "Hey, that your neighbor?"

I looked and saw Peter.

He still walked slower than usual, but his limp was less noticeable. Peter regarded me for only a moment, all the more hesitant to make eye contact but his attention quickly fell to Uncle Wayne, his face becoming cold and stark—as if he was staring down the barrel of a gun and Uncle Wayne was his target. I'd never considered my Uncle Wayne to be skittish, but from the look in his eyes right now, anyone might think he did have a gun pointed at him. Giving me one last glance, Peter then strode over to his truck and climbed inside. All the while, Uncle Wayne never allowed his gaze to waver as Peter took off down the road. When the dust settled, a sneer pulled the corners of Uncle Wayne's mouth tight.

"I really don't like the look of that guy."

"You don't like the look of anyone."

"Hey, you know what his kind are like, Gracie? I'd even bet that guy was dishonorably discharged. I don't understand why your dad won't do nothin'. He's lucky he's still walkin'." Uncle Wayne jerked his head to the trailer. "Where there's blame, there's always a claim. That's what I live by."

"Don't go spoutin' what you don't know, Uncle Wayne," I said bitterly. "You know nothin' about him."

"Haven't you ever read a story about them in that little book of yours you always carry 'round? What is it called? Reader's something or other. PTSD is a real thing, Gracie. You best be careful," Uncle Wayne said just as the door swung open. I looked back. "'Bout time. What the heck were you doin' in there?"

"You know what, Wayne, you try wiping your ass with a bad neck and three bruised ribs." Pa grimaced and slammed the screen door shut. "Can we git going now? I wanna get my truck. If it's even still there."

Pa walked past me. Though he still hadn't spoken a word to me since the fair, his silence proved just how much anger was brewing inside him. Uncle Wayne glanced between us, all the more curious as to what had happened. Just as I was about to leave, I heard Arlene's jubilant voice.

"Morning, Bill! It's a sight to see you up and at 'em this early!" she exclaimed in delight, eagerly walking over with a casserole dish wrapped in tin foil. Uncle Wayne eyed her bright pink capris and bedazzled T-shirt. "Grace, I tried this recipe with your—oh my, Bill." Her wedged sandals came to a stop as she noticed the state of Pa's face, bringing one hand up to cover her mouth. "I'm really surprised you're up and walkin' around lookin' like that." She stifled a laugh and looked at Uncle Wayne. "Good golly, Wayne, that you? You certainly bulked up since the last time I saw ya."

Uncle Wayne crossed his arms. "Yeah, it pays off to lug limestone for a livin'. How's Ray?"

"Twenty pounds heavier. And where you two off to? The hospital? Cause, I gotta tell ya, Bill, that's one nasty lookin' eye."

Pa rolled his one good eye, and he opened the passenger door with more force than normal.

"Don't trip on your way up," Arlene said.

Pa looked back at her. "Yeah, you'd enjoy that, wouldn't ya, Arlene?"

Uncle Wayne bit his bottom lip, a tell he had when he was holding back a smile and a laugh of his own.

"I'd have witnessed two miracles today if that happened," she replied with a sweet smile.

Uncle Wayne walked away, saying, "Well, nice seeing you again, Arlene. Say hi to Ray for me, alright?" He opened the driver's side door. But before climbing up into the seat, he looked back at me and said, "And Gracie, try some saltines and ginger ale for that morning sickness. Okay? It worked wonders for my ex." Uncle Wayne shut the door, and the truck revved to life.

A unison of howls and barks filled the air.

As they reversed, I watched Pa's one dark, soulless eye peering directly at Arlene. His upper lip curled into another sneer, and I glanced over to Arlene for her reaction. She simply smiled and wiggled her fingers goodbye as they left.

"You gotta tell me who did that to your daddy so I can thank them.

Lord, forgive me. And you can tell me all about it over this casserole. I think I finally found the recipe this time. Three cheeses, can you believe it? I'm gonna be on the toilet after this. But it'll be worth it. I know it will."

"Three cheeses? I thought you said I needed to watch my dairy intake. And my sodium."

"We can live on the edge. Won't that be fun? Sweetie, aren't you hot in that thing? You're gonna drop dead from heat exhaustion."

"I'm fine."

"Grace—"

"I said I'm fine, Arlene."

She grabbed my right sleeve, yanking it down my arm, giving no second thought to the tumbled casserole on the ground. Her eyes were wide and the color of her face drained as she stared at the bruises. I yanked my arm back and pulled the sleeve up. When her fingers reached for the side of my face, I smacked her hand away and faced her. A glassy sheen had overtaken her blue eyes. A look I recognized all too well crossed her face, and a wave of nausea hit me. Not from morning sickness, but from the absolute fact that I had no excuses. Nothing to convince her otherwise.

"Your dad did this, didn't he?"

"I fell." I turned, walking up to the door.

"Don't you dare give me that load of hooey, Grace. You fell? Grace, tell me right now if that man hit you—"

"That man is my father!" I cried out, causing Arlene to halt in her tracks. "He's my father!"

"A father doesn't do that to his little girl, Grace! When are you gonna get that through your head?!"

"When are you gonna do something?" I yelled.

Her breath caught in her throat.

"You never did anything! Not even for my mama!"

"You don't think I did somethin'? You can only help a person so much before they gotta' help themselves. Your mama—"

"My mama ain't here anymore, Arlene!"

I rushed into the trailer. The ground spun beneath me. I stumbled my way to the sink, waiting. It wanted to come up, but my body wouldn't allow it. I stifled my sobs, sliding down in the corner, resting my sweaty forehead against the cabinet. My feet ached in relief to have the weight lifted off them. Just as the tears were ready to spill over, the door slowly creaked open.

"Grace?"

Arlene peeked her head in.

"Oh, sweetie." She quickly stepped inside and shut the door, squishing herself beside me.

Arlene lifted her arm and I rested my cheek on her breast. My nose twitched. Though her perfume was overwhelming, and I had to close my eyes each time to make the smell a bit more tolerable, I didn't find myself wanting to leave her arms. Especially when she would start to rub my back. Like right now. The gentle pressure of her knuckles and the relaxing scratch of her nails moving up and down my back restored all the balance I needed. The world slowly but surely stopped spinning. Everything seemed okay again. There was something surreal about having my back scratched. As if each scratch literally scratched away the worries and bad moments from the day, leaving me inevitably calmer and more serene. It was like the times I watched my mama sweeping the dirt off the porch after every fight with my pa. She wouldn't stop until each inch of that porch was clean. I shut my eyes and leaned further into her, letting out my first easy breath.

Arlene kissed my head, resting her cheek on top.

"I'm right here, sweetie."

After nine years, Arlene knew words wouldn't do me any good, but sometimes she just couldn't help herself. I didn't know how long we stayed on the kitchen floor, but long enough till our backs started to ache and the afternoon heat had started to warm the linoleum. Only after the twelfth time reassuring her I was okay did she leave the trailer. Patting my face with a wet paper towel, I looked outside to see her picking up the food and broken pieces of the casserole dish. She dropped a piece and covered her mouth, holding her head down. A heavy ache settled in my chest as her shoulders begin to shake. There had only been two times I'd seen Arlene cry. The first was the day she heard she was going to be a grandmother, and the second was the day she first saw the bruises on my mama. After her shoulders relaxed, she patted her cheeks. Closing the curtain, I lowered myself back down in the corner between the cabinet and fridge.

I shut my eyes tight, hoping some force would quiet my mind.

There were times like this when I wish I could turn to my mama. Have her arms around me instead of Arlene's. After she left, Pa became that person for a while, and then Arlene, then Ray, and Sam. Yet, in these past seven months, I finally understood what my mama was preaching all along: *There's no one but you to fill up that loneliness in your chest. Some can for a bit. But at the end of the day, it's up to you.* It was like choosing a pair of shoes. Pa was the sparkly red shoes that I knew deep down wouldn't ever hold up for more than six months. Arlene and Ray were the pair of sturdy brown shoes that would last me for the rest of my life but never fully satisfy me. No matter how much I wanted them to. Was that why Mama left? Was that the answer? To leave all the people in her world? That way, the only person who disappointed her was herself?

No one else.

# 10

By the time I opened my eyes, the golden hour had settled in. Hazy streams of light peeked through the blinds, touching everything it could. Just as my eyelids started to become heavy again, the sound of an engine woke me, and I rose from the couch. I peeked outside and flinched in surprise as I saw Pa fall onto the ground. A six pack of beer tumbled from under his arm, causing a group of dogs to bark. I rushed outside. His hand splayed itself on the first step of the porch, attempting to push himself up. I quickly headed down the steps as he struggled to stand. I stepped closer to assist him but stopped when he said, "Don't. Don't fucking help me. Just don't."

"Pa—"

"When are those mutts gonna shut their fucking trap? I'm sick and tired of it." Pa stood, and started to pick up the bottles of beer, but he stopped to hold his left side and groan. "Gosh dang it. My ribs are killin' me."

"Pa, stop. You need to sit down." I reached to touch his arm, but he smacked my hand away.

"Don't fucking touch me." Pa spat and looked over, spotting Arlene standing outside. "What are you looking at, bitch? What? You wish you could've done this?" he gestured to his whole face. "Get your butt over here and see what will happen! I dare ya! Let's see what ya got, Arlene!"

"Pa—"

"Shut up!" He whipped around and faced me, his glazed eyes wide and furious. "You keep that mouth of yours shut, I swear, or I'll shut it for you." Pa hit my shoulder as he stormed past me and into the trailer.

I looked at Arlene and turned away.

Shutting the door behind me, I saw that Pa had already begun ransacking the fridge. Containers of leftovers hit the floor as he struggled to reach all the way in the back, straining his already sore muscles. I knew it was painful for him to move, but it was as if that pain somehow only fueled his anger even more. Seeing him this way had brought me back to the times when he would always pop open a cold one after hitting my mama. Propping his feet on the coffee table in his favorite chair with a beer beside him always made him feel better. As if the alcohol itself had burned away the sins he had just committed. And as I stood here, I no longer saw my pa. The happy memories that had kept me going didn't matter anymore. All I saw was a man who was just as tormented as me. But the ache of my own body made me realize his pain was different. The kind of pain he could only live with if he took it out on my mama and now me. Tears welled in my eyes watching this sad, pained soul, unraveling as he tried to make sense of his world.

Pa pulled himself out of the fridge and slammed the door. "Your ma come here and take all the beer? Or what?"

"No, Pa, she didn't."

"Oh yeah? What makes you think I'd believe anything that comes out of your fucking mouth?" Pa pointed, looking back at me with wild and crazed eyes. "You gonna tell me you weren't the girl in that man's truck now? I told you to not do one thing. One thing, Grace!"

"He was just helping me!"

"Yeah, sure he was. Cause all men just want to help a pretty girl," Pa slurred. "That man has been wanting that thing between your legs since the second he rolled up in here and saw ya. And we know how easy it is for you to spread your legs. Hell, it's easy for all of you Callaway women."

"I haven't done anything!"

"Yeah, and your mother wasn't a liar or a whore."

"Pa, I'm not lying," I pleaded, standing with my arms hanging by my sides. "I'm not, Pa." I stepped closer but stopped as he looked at me. "Pa, please. I didn't mean—I didn't mean—"

"I-I didn't," Pa mocked. "What? You didn't do what, Grace? You just stood there watching him beat me up! And then you ran off with that fucker! A goddamn stranger had to drop me off at the hospital! A fucking stranger, Grace! They didn't even ask what happened! They all just assumed it was my fault! Again! That I finally got what I deserve! That's what that fat fucker of a doctor said to me!" His words came at me with such an intensity that I winced. "So just spit it out, Grace! Tell me what I did wrong now. Tell me. Gimme another reason to believe how much of a screw up I am!"

I swallowed, surprised my stare did not waver from him. What was worse was that I had nothing to say. He was right about everything, and the little girl in me didn't care anymore. "What did I ever do to you, Pa?"

"You wanna know what you did, Grace?" Pa walked straight up to me, but this time I didn't move. "You happened! That's what! You're the kid who keeps ruining my fucking life! I had dreams! I wanted to be something! But nooo. I kept that on hold for you and your stupid mother!"

"I never asked you for anything! I never expected anything more than what a child expects from their father!" I yelled.

He raised his brows, surprised, some shame gleaming in his eyes.

"You let Mama push you around! That wasn't my fault! I was just a child! It wasn't my fault your dreams were put on hold! You figure it out! That's what you do! You don't blame your kid!"

His eyes flared, and the flicker of sadness was quickly replaced with fury once again. "Oh, fuck you, Grace! Fuck you!" Pa exclaimed as he paced back and forth. "Fuck you! You know nothin'! Nothin'!"

"You didn't need to stay. If you were that unhappy, you should've left. Mama and I would've been fine without you."

"Are you kidding me? You don't know the first thing about your mother. You think she'd show up for you? Especially now? You're the one who couldn't keep her legs fucking shut! Now you're knocked up just like your mother was! Not even your Granny wanted ya! You needed me! I stepped up, and look at what that got me. You're just a fucking, ungrateful child, Grace. You always have been. I step up every day for you, and you just sit around doing fucking nothing! I'm the one who showed up! Not your mama! Not Arlene! Me! All me!" Pa yelled in my face and stepped back, catching his breath. "And you wanna know somethin' else, Grace?" His voice went almost soft. "You're gonna mess that kid up, too. Because that's all you Callaway women do."

I slapped him. He slowly turned his head. Tears swelled behind my eyes like a tidal wave, and my throat tightened as I realized I had just crossed a line I could never step back from. There was no time to avoid his powerful backhand. Pain exploded through my head the second I hit the chair and tumbled to the floor. I cried out and tentatively touched the side of my temple. My vision blurred only for a moment as I focused on my red fingertips. Pa turned down the hall and shut the bedroom door. A sharp ache pinched my chest. The same one I felt when I watched my mama leave. When I heard the shoe boxes falling from the top shelf in the bedroom closet, I knew I had done what my mama had not.

Still stifling my cries, I called out, "Pa." When there was no answer but just the sounds of drawers opening and closing, I did it again. "Pa. I'm sorry. Pa, please," I pleaded between shaky breaths.

Pa appeared from the bedroom holding the straps of a large duffle bag. I managed to pull myself up as quickly as I could just as his shoulder brushed past me and toward the door. My fingers grabbed the sleeve of his shirt, but he yanked his arm away without so much as a glance at me.

"Pa!" I ran outside as he was opening the driver's side door of his truck. "Pa! Stop! Please!"

My feet came to a stop as I watched him climb into the driver's seat without a second thought. As I heard the engine come to life, the sensation of loss was replaced with something I hadn't ever felt before. Or maybe it was there all along. Dormant. I held in my breath, fearful of the sounds scrambling up my throat, longing for release. The rage was so overwhelming that at first no sounds escaped me. I just stood there. Every bit of me yearned to see the brake lights, because then I would know that this was just as hard for him. By the time my words found release, there was no one to hear it but me.

"Fine! Leave!" I screamed.

I took off my sandals, throwing each one at the back of the truck as he drove away.

"Leave just like Mama!"

Be it the pain from my head or my heart, the ground seemed to spin. I hunched over as my knees buckled. Rapid footsteps crunched on the gravel.

"Grace!" Arlene cried out, rushing over to my side. "Oh gosh, your head! You're gonna be okay. Ray! Ray, get the keys!"

That's when everything that had been holding me together fell apart. Tears started to cloud my vision as the weight of it all came crashing down on me. Pa. Mama. My grandparents. My baby. Me. My entire body shook from the violent sobs that could no longer be contained. I could hear the concerned voice of Arlene urging me to move. Yet even as the scorching dirt burned my feet, all I could do was just cry and completely lean my full weight into Arlene's side as she tried to shuffle us over to the car.

"Sweetie, you gotta work with me. I can't drag you. Ray! Hurry up!" she yelled, keeping her arm around me.

I then saw the familiar outline of a blurry figure running over towards us.

"Grace!" Peter said, frantic. When I blinked away the tears and saw his clear expression, it only deepened the guilt inside me. "Grace, what happened? Why's she bleeding?" he asked Arlene, coming to a running stop.

"I-I don't know. I think she fell. Ray! Get out here!" Arlene shouted, struggling to keep me upright. "Sweetie, you gotta help me here. I can't keep holding you up like this. Will you help her into the car for me?"

"Yeah, let me—"

"No! Just stop helping me!" I cried out at Peter and hit his chest. "I don't need it!" On the second hit, he stepped back, calmly. "I didn't need it then! I don't need it now! So just stop it!"

"Grace—" Peter began.

"This is all your fault! If you hadn't done anything, my pa wouldn't have left! Why did you have to care?"

"Grace, listen to me."

He placed his hands on the sides of my arms, and with his touch, my cries became louder as the loneliness cemented itself deeper into my chest. I was all alone. My baby and me. We're all alone. The wall had started to crack the day I woke up nine years ago and didn't smell Mama's chocolate chip pancakes. Now, it was completely gone. Every support I'd ever had, had now crumbled.

"Why couldn't you have left me alone? I didn't need your help. This is all my fault. I—"

"It's not your fault that he left. Do you hear me, Grace? It's not your fault," Peter said.

I shook my head, yanking myself away from him.

"Hey." He grabbed my shoulders tighter this time. "You need to get yourself together and think of your baby right now. You hear me? You—"

I protested through incoherent sobs, struggling to free myself from his strong hold. A hold that made me feel calm and safe, something I didn't feel I should deserve. His grip became stronger, and my cries became louder as I withered in his arms. My hands tried to slap him away in a feeble attempt. He turned me around and locked his arms around my chest, keeping my arms pinned to my sides. My legs kicked until my mind and body gave up fighting, leaving him to support me. I shut my eyes, failing to stifle a broken cry as the shock finally began to subside. The steady rise and fall of his chest against my back and the tightness of his arms around me soothed every frazzled nerve. He didn't say a word, allowing me to cool down at my own pace. The security of his arms and body caused my anxiety to slowly fall away. Right then, I knew I wanted to be in these arms anytime I cried for the rest of my life. The ground disappeared from beneath me. Peter lifted me into his arms, as if I were a baby, and I was far too tired to fight back.

"Where's the closest hospital?" he asked.

"Northwest. We'll go with you," Arlene answered as she climbed into the car with Ray.

※

My head rested against the seat, staring into the darkness as we drove home. It almost gave me the sensation of floating. The only sources of light were the high beams of Peter's truck and Ray's car traveling behind us. In some ways it was peaceful. In other ways it wasn't. I looked at Peter just as he reached over to take a sip of his black coffee to keep him focused on the white lines. Though it was dark, I could see the subtle purplish hue surrounding the side of his eye, reminding me of the guilt that was still present in my chest. And even though he acted stoic, there were fleeting moments when his guard was down just long enough to catch a glimpse of what he might be thinking. Like right now. A part of me wanted to ask. But instead, I looked back outside and watched the few glimpses of lights speed by.

*Pop. Thud.*

Harley shot straight up from the backseat. We safely pulled off to the side of the highway. Ray followed and parked behind us. "I think we popped a tire. I'll be right back," Peter said, catching Harley's panicked eyes. "Hey, I'll be right outside, buddy. Okay?" He climbed out of the truck and shut the door. Harley whined and circled around three times, resting his chin on the center console. His stomach rose and fell at a fast pace, looking around with big, frantic eyes.

"It's okay. He'll be right back." I placed my hand on Harley to scratch behind his ears.

Slowly but surely, Harley's breathing fell to a normal pace, and he began to doze off. My fingers continued to gently scratch the middle of his ear. I then heard muffled chatter between Ray and Peter outside. Leaning over, I checked the side mirror and spotted them inspecting the rear right tire. Arlene walked over and knocked on the window. Harley's ears perked, but his eyes didn't open.

I rolled the window down. "How bad is it?"

"Not too bad," Arlene said and folded her arms. "You gonna be okay if Ray and I go on ahead? He's gonna wanna change the tire, and you know his back. He'll throw it out again."

"Yeah, I'll be fine."

"Alright. And when you get home, promise me you'll go to bed. The doctor said to take it easy."

"I know, Arlene."

She exhaled and smiled, saying, "I know you know. I just say it so many times because I love you." If it wasn't for the headlights reflecting the tears in her eyes, it would have been the hitch in her voice that told me she was resisting the impulse to cry. She reached in and cupped my cheek tenderly. "Alright. We'll see you back at home. Be safe," she said and walked away. "Ray! Get up. Come on."

"What?"

"We're goin'."

I settled back against the seat, resting my tired eyes. A *creak* and a loud *thud* abruptly woke me up. Harley whined and looked toward the bed of the truck. I saw the clock. Only five minutes had gone by. I opened the door and carefully lowered myself onto the ground. Harley stuck his head outside and watched me make my way to the end of the truck. Peter had jumped into the back to grab the spare tire. He held a small flashlight between his teeth, inspecting the tire's tread. After doing so, he then took the light from his mouth and examined the other side, muttering to himself.

"You need any help with that?"

He flinched and turned around, bringing the light with him. I squinted, holding up my hand in an attempt to shield the light from my face. "Grace? What are you doin' out here? It's not safe. There's snakes out here. And scorpions. I really don't need something else happening to you right now."

"I've grown up here all my life, and I've never been bitten. Not once. And damn it if I do tonight, so hand me the flashlight before you break a tooth," I said, holding out my hand.

"Grace—"

"I'm not asking for the spare tire, Peter. It will take half the time if I help you," I insisted.

He looked at the large tire and then at me with a sigh. He extended his arm and I reached up, taking the flashlight. I stepped closer, keeping the beam of light centered to where he stood until he jumped down onto the ground. He centered the jack underneath the frame and locked it into place. For the next ten minutes, I kept my hand on top of the spare tire and the light on his hands as he began to remove the lug nuts. Every few seconds I'd glance to make sure the jack was secured when he started to remove the flat tire from the hub. And as he did, I found myself becoming fascinated by his hands. I had forgotten how rough they appeared at first glance. I had even forgotten the little scars across his palm. But most of all, I remembered that night. When he had unintentionally grabbed my hand. It was anything but coarse. Much like his hands, his voice had a funny way of melting all my bad thoughts away. They didn't completely disappear, but they were darn close to it. Close enough to make my mind quiet. His eyes turned upward, landing on my face, and I averted mine, flustered.

He held out his palm with a few lug nuts. "Mind holding these?"

"Sure."

"Thank you," he said and grabbed the spare tire, securing it to the hub. One by one, Peter plucked each lug nut from my hand and reinstalled them. He then lowered the jack and removed it from underneath the frame, standing upright. He wiped the dirt off his knees and exhaled. Sweat was slicked across his forehead. He kicked the side of the tire, double checking its stability.

"Sorry I couldn't help more."

"Hey, you kept the tire from rolling down the road, that's more than I could've asked for."

I watched as he put away the jack and lug wrench into the utility box. His shoulder brushed past me as he carried the box in his hand, sliding it into the bed of the truck before hopping up. Peter stood and let out a sigh of exhaustion. I carefully lifted myself onto the tailgate, allowing my feet to dangle, and observed him standing there. Like with my mama and pa, I've learned better to not ask or say anything. If and when he wants to, he will tell me. Only after he wiped the sweat from his forehead and let out another breath did he push the heavy box back towards the corner with his boot. I looked away and turned my attention to the overflowing clusters of stars and constellations.

I let out my first easy breath.

It wasn't until I was five that I knew this existed. It was breathtaking. It was moments like this when the little girl in me remembered the few times Mama and I would stargaze in the back of Pa's truck. Admiring the vast sky and stars one night, my mama had turned to me and said: *Every choice you'll make, sweet pea, may seem big, but if you step back just enough, you'll realize just how small it is in the grand scheme of things.* I stared upwards, hoping that some shooting star would appear and point me in the right direction. A creak made me turn my head. Peter jumped onto the ground.

"We should git goin'. It's late. I'm not a big fan of driving at night, kid. Ray and Arlene—"

"Would you stop calling me a kid? I'm sick and tired of it." I turned back to the sky. "I'm about to be a mom. And I'd rather be stuck out here than at home. I just need . . . a second. Alright?"

Though I couldn't see it, I knew he scratched the back of his left ear. He cleared his throat. Our eyes met, and he halted in his tracks as if he expected me to protest. When I said nothing, he continued to sit down next to me. He exhaled, rubbed the back of his neck, and then dropped his hands to his lap. He seemed to scan the perimeter; his legs set at a wide stance, readying himself to stand at any moment. I drifted my attention to my pink hospital slippers. A few moments passed until we heard the cries of coyotes in the distance. His head turned in the direction of the sound.

"They're not gonna hurt you," I said. "They're more afraid of you than you are of them. My mama actually used to say hearing a coyote's howl meant good things were on their way. I think of that whenever I hear them. Like there's something bigger than me, living out there. Helps me forget all the wrong choices I've made. It's funny, because every bad thing that has happened to me has happened on a day with an odd number," I thought out loud. "Just an hour ago it was still August 23rd. The day my pa left . . . I was nine when my mama left. It's why I've always liked even numbers. Cause maybe it means some good is on its way . . . I know I can't go on living life like that, but don't you think it all means somethin'?" I stared at the sky. "What we do? No matter how little it is?"

Peter expressed no indication that he had heard me, and yet I felt his weight shift. When I looked over, his eyes settled onto my face and then turned to the horizon. "Maybe," he said, doubtful. "What makes you ask that?"

"I don't know. Like every choice I've made has led me to this very moment, sitting here, on my birthday. Every time there was a chance to do the right thing, I somehow always wound up doing the thing that made it even more horrible. Like what happened with my pa," I answered and let out another soft breath. "I just thought I would have graduated and left by now, but here I am . . . I don't know, maybe I do deserve to have all this happen to me. I hated my mama for having me when she couldn't even take care of herself, and now look at me . . . I'm just like her. Stuck here. I'm two years older now than she was when she had me, and yet I still feel like a poster child for teenage pregnancy." I shook my head and laughed. "I really am a joke."

"Hey, don't ever say that. You hear me?" Peter declared. "You really think this is what you deserve?"

"I don't know. The things I want haven't happened."

"Things take time, Grace. That I know for certain."

"Have they for you?"

He didn't say anything for several seconds but soon followed with a somber, "Well, things don't work out for many reasons, Grace. You just make a new plan when that happens. That's what I've done all this time," he replied. I couldn't tell if he was just simply agreeing with me to put an end to this conversation or being genuine.

"So, what, am I just being punished?" I asked, finally admitting the one question that had been weighing on my mind.

He looked at me, taken aback. "Bad stuff happens to good people, Grace. That's just part of life. I should know that. I've seen enough bad things to last a lifetime. Things I can't repress," he said and lowered his gaze to the ground. A dark thought had taken over, and he hesitated

155

to speak. "After Kuwait, I've seen things most men my age won't ever see, things that would give anyone gray hair." His words hit me hard, seeing the grief behind those dark brown eyes. "So, no, you're not being punished, Grace." He scratched at his beard, letting out a breath. "You're not."

"Why not, though? I'm about to have a baby out of wedlock. There's plenty of reasons why God would punish me. I mean, I don't really love my pa anymore. I don't care if I never see him again. Is that horrible to say?"

"No, I know that feeling all too well with my pop," he said in a softer tone.

"But when I saw him leaving, it was like . . ." I paused, afraid my voice would break.

"You were scared."

"And it's okay to be scared?"

"Of course it is."

"And you . . . you're okay?"

"Yeah. What makes you think I'm not okay? I don't panic unless I need to. Wastes energy."

"How you've been acting these past few days makes it seem like you're not," I said, looking at him.

He said nothing as his brows drew together, two hard lines forming between them. But there was something else lingering behind those surprised brown eyes, like he wasn't expecting his own response. Something he had locked away for years, and it was now out there in the open space. Peter turned away and said, "Grace, I may not be a firm believer in God, but I know for a fact He's not punishing you. God doesn't do that. Not to you, or anyone. People already punish themselves enough. God is just watchin'. That's all He does."

Other than Arlene, Ray, and Sam, I believed no one else would ever speak to me that way. Like a good and kind person. Flaws and all. Even the way he was looking at me right this second. The promise in his face alone would make anyone trust his words. And I did. He turned away, regret burning in his eyes. Like the night of the fair.

"I know . . . I know I haven't given you much reason to think I'm a good guy, Grace. But I am very sorry for what I did to your father."

He didn't say another word as he kept his eyes on the ground. Seeing him like this reminded me of the times when my mama would stand on the porch. She never moved much. All she did was smoke her cigarette, hoping the nicotine would burn away the remains of her tears and bad memories. Those were the moments when all I wanted to do was ask her what was wrong, but I knew she would play it off and smile at me like there was no one else in the world but the two of us. Peter leaned his head back toward the stars. Like he was searching for a shooting star of his own to point him in the right direction. Though he only closed his eyes for a moment, it was the first time he seemed truly calm. At peace. Yet when he opened his eyes and released a breath, reality had returned.

"Look we should really get goin'. It's late. We've both had a long night," he said and slipped off the tailgate. "I think both of us could use some sleep, so come on." Peter held out his hand. I hesitated at first but took it. He helped me down and walked ahead to the passenger door and held it open, waiting for me to climb in.

Just as I was about to, he spoke. "Hey look . . . you better not say that kind of thing again. Alright? I don't want you thinking that way. Okay? It's not good." He gave me an awkward pat on the side of my arm. "Alright, let's, uh, we should get going. It's gittin' pretty late." He cleared his throat and hastily turned away. His face flushed red in the headlights as he walked around the front of the truck.

No other words were said for the remainder of the drive. And like all the other times I had arrived back home, there was nothing I wanted more than to leave. Even with the emptiness that now awaited me. My body ached for rest, but before I could make my way to the bedroom a wave of nausea hit me. I raced into the bathroom. Knowing I wouldn't make it to the toilet, I heaved into the sink and gripped the counter. I shut my eyes and rested my hot forehead against the cool mirror. Turning on the faucet, I gently patted water on the back of my neck. Taking a breath, I braved the sight of my reflection.

My hair was a tangled mess. Two dark shadows cast a half moon underneath each sunken red eye. Reaching up, my fingers touched the purplish hue surrounding my temple. I leaned back and looked at Mama's compact concealer in the basket of old makeup she had long forgotten. She'd always smear some on to forget. I wondered if it would do the same for me. But I didn't want to forget. Nothing could make me forget.

Nothing could take away the pain. Even the scattered clothes across the bedroom floor was a sight I knew I couldn't forget. They were like Mama's. And just like her, it was a sign that he had been in an obvious rush to leave.

I lay on the bed and stared at the white popcorn ceiling. Tears started to push their way up, but I squeezed my eyes shut, forcing them away. Taking a breath, I held it and listened for any sign of Pa. Silence. Like the times Pa had stayed the nights at Uncle Wayne's, I always enjoyed the quiet. Every noise I had heard since I was little was clearer. So clear, like I had discovered it all over again. Even the soft *thump thump* of my feet hitting the floor. Yet this wasn't the same. This was a different kind of silence. A silence of loneliness that would bring only one of two things. Peace or torture. But for now, in this moment, it was peaceful. It was just me and my baby girl. That's all that mattered. I exhaled as the numbness slowly lulled me into a deep sleep.

＊

Rays of sun streamed through the blinds, and I was hit with the sudden realization and disappointment that I had missed the sunrise again. A part of me wanted to go outside, hoping the Arizona heat would somehow melt the pain and heaviness in my chest. Yet like the day I found out I had a baby growing inside me, I wanted to bury myself underneath a blanket and let all the bad thoughts torture me. They had a way of slipping into the crevices of mind and heart. Never leaving. Just hiding. In the nooks and crannies. Making room for the other little hardships to come and settle. And as much as I wanted to stay in bed and succumb to the mental exhaustion from the past twelve hours, I sat up, let out a breath, and placed my feet onto the floor. I was like Mama in every way now. Bruises and all. Even on the bad days, Mama brushed herself off, pulled back the tears, and got up. Cause like me, she knew if she didn't, she would never move again.

The sound of an engine quickened my pace, and I ran into the kitchen, looking out the window in hopes of seeing Pa, only to catch the sight of Peter's truck leaving down the road. I pulled myself back from the counter and set my feet on the floor. On days like today, when the bad thoughts did torture me, all I could do was sit down and ride it out till it was okay again. Like a monsoon. Whenever a heat wave broke, the floods came. Staring at the two empty chairs across from me at the kitchen table, I remembered learning from the time I was five years old a monsoon could exist in everything and in everyone.

*"Whaddya mean I gotta go out to get her a new cake? This one's fine. It has—"*

*"She doesn't like cakes with colored frosting. She only eats vanilla. Remember?"*

*"She's a kid. They like frosting."*

*"Not your kid, Bill."*

*"Uh-huh."*

*"Just get your daughter what she—"*

*"She's a kid! She's not gonna care! Can't you just shut up?!"*

A knock at the door made me flinch. I stood and crossed the kitchen to peek out the curtain only to quickly duck. "Grace?" Arlene asked. "Grace, I know you're in there. I just wanted to check in on you and to tell you that Ray's gonna put up the awning for you tomorrow. Storm's a comin'.''

Hearing her departing footsteps, I pulled back the curtain, watching her leave. Though I had convinced myself I was fine alone, every sound made me jump, preparing for the worst. After a much-needed shower, I wandered to the couch and kept myself occupied rereading my old editions of *Reader's Digest* and listening to the few cassette tapes I had of Elvis Presley. Other than Arlene stopping by again and dropping off a dish of her baked macaroni and cheese, there weren't any other interruptions.

The light flashed from my Polaroid, and I pulled back the camera, taking out the printed photo, waving it dry. As it developed and the curve of my belly became more prominent, I couldn't help but smile. I slid the picture underneath the plastic cover in its precise place in the scrapbook, cutting out shapes and glueing pink ribbon to adorn the page. I flipped through the many empty pages, waiting to be used for happier days. As silly as I had felt accepting this gift from Arlene, a part of me hoped that one day this book would be filled to the brim with those happy moments.

The next morning I opened my eyes to the sound of a clatter, and I swung my legs off the couch. Giving myself a moment longer to refocus and clear the haze of a deep sleep, I stood to open the door. There was Ray on a step stool, struggling to secure the awning to the frame of the trailer. Sweat slicked across his forehead and his armpits. He fiddled with one of the screws and muttered expletives to himself before he finally turned his head.

"Oh, howdy, Grace. Just give me another few minutes and I'll be done in a jiff. Okay?"

I folded my arms and leaned against the door frame, watching him wrangle with the screw. "You want any help?"

"No, I got it," he said.

Looking over, I saw Arlene carrying an overnight bag to the car.

"Where you guys goin'?"

Ray stepped down from the stool. "Finally. Got that sucker to stick," he said, out of breath. "Oh, we're gonna head up to Flagstaff where Paul is for a few days. We're gonna try and leave before the rain hits. They have some big news. I reckon he knocked up his wife again. I swear that boy needs a vasectomy." He shook his head, moving to the other side of the awning. "Hey, Arlene!"

"What?" she called out and shut the trunk, making her way over with a packet. "You need the manual again?"

"No. I don't need the manual. Do we have any room for Grace in the back? You could hitch a ride with us."

"Ray, I'll be fine. We didn't get much flooding here last year. Besides, I have Sam right up the road."

"Grace, sweetie, it sounds like it's gonna get bad," Arlene said and walked up to the porch.

"Uncle Wayne laid a slab of foundation almost a year ago. If anything, I'll be safer," I replied.

Ray sighed and shared a meaningful look with Arlene before securing the other side of the awning. He stepped down and wiped the dirt off his hands. "You know, I never really liked that Wayne. Something about him always rubbed me the wrong way," he muttered. Arlene looked over at him.

"Everyone rubs you the wrong way, Ray," she said.

"Not everyone."

"Thank you, Ray. For the awnin'," I said with a smile. He gave a brief wave of his hand and grabbed the stepladder, heading back to their trailer. Arlene returned her attention to me and folded her arms.

"I don't like the thought of leaving you alone here for a few days, Grace. Especially after the other day. The doctor said to take it easy. I know you've lived here all your life, but drowning and valley fever are very real things."

"I'll be okay, Arlene. There's no arroyos around here. We're on flat land. I just have to ride it out."

Arlene briefly turned her sights on Peter's trailer before facing me. "You stocked up on food? Water?" she asked, but before I could answer, she continued. "Okay, before Ray and I take off tomorrow we'll drop you off at Sam's so you can get some things. He'll drive you back. And if anything happens, knock on wood, that one—" Arlene pointed to Peter's trailer— "will be over here faster than two shakes of a lamb's tail. Don't give me that look, girlie. You know I'm right."

"Mm-hmm."

"Oh, and before I forget." She took out a pink card from her back pocket, handing it to me. "It's a bit crinkled, but I was supposed to give this to ya yesterday. It ain't much. But we wanna get you a cake when we get back. And we're not taking no for an answer. You're nineteen now."

I smiled. "Thank you, Arlene."

She took the last step up the porch and gave me a quick peck on the head. "Happy birthday, sweetie." Arlene smiled and walked away but stopped halfway to her trailer, looking back at me. "And Grace, tomorrow afternoon, you got that? Don't go walking there on your own." She pointed at me with her finger.

"I got it, Arlene."

"Good."

# 11

Just as promised, Arlene and Ray dropped me off at the Minit Mart. But before I stepped out of the car, Ray slipped me a twenty. After giving them each a kiss on their cheek, I climbed out as a strong gust of wind hit my dress. I waved goodbye and raced inside the store as a bolt of lightning lit up the heavy, dark skies. The fluorescent lights flickered, and Sam appeared from the back room, carrying a big box. He hummed to the melody on his earbuds and set down the box. I wrapped the cardigan around me tighter, walking up to the counter. Leaning forward, I extended my finger as far as I could and touched Sam's shoulder, causing him to jump.

"Sweet baby Jesus!"

"Hey Sam."

He clutched his chest and exhaled. "Of course. It's you. The one person who doesn't shy away from a little storm. And where's your father? I swear, you better have not walked here, Grace. I—"

"I didn't walk here. Arlene and Ray dropped me off. And my pa won't be back until the rain lets up."

"Where are they goin'?"

"Up to Flagstaff."

"That's smart. Should've gone with them." Another bolt of light caused us to look up at the flickering lights and then outside, watching the first pelts of rainfall. Large dense clouds loomed above, promising drivers slippery roads ahead. The wind howled. "Get what you need, and we'll hightail it outta here," he said as the phone rang. "I bet that's my wife. She's worried sick. Hey, what happened to your eye? Did you fall?"

"Yeah, I slipped when I was walkin' up to my trailer. I'm fine, Sam. It doesn't really hurt."

"Uh-huh." Sam nodded, skeptical for a moment before turning away to pick up the phone.

Scouring each aisle, I grabbed the items I needed. The bell rang. Wet boots squeaked against the floor, causing me to look back, seeing Peter. He was almost soaked. Strands of hair lay flat against his forehead, and he bent down, grabbing the last two jugs of water. For the first time, my heart didn't quicken. I just looked at him, and the little knot in my chest went away. It was like I'd taken a deep breath. Sam hung up and looked at Peter incredulously as he set the jugs of water by his feet.

"You don't shy away from a little rain, either, huh?" Sam asked. "Just the water, today?"

"Just the water," Peter said and did a double take. His face fell. "Grace, what are you doing out?"

"That's what I said," Sam agreed.

"You have anyone to drive you back home? It's pouring out there right now," Peter asked.

"Sam's drivin' me home," I gestured.

Peter opened his mouth to speak but instead just nodded, scratching the back of his left ear.

"You're the one with the truck, right? The neighbor?" Sam asked, taking the ten-dollar bill Peter had given him.

"Yeah," Peter replied.

"You should go with him, Grace. He'll get you home faster," Sam suggested. "My wife will start listening for sirens if I don't make it home in the next twenty minutes. You okay with that?"

"If she is."

"Um, yeah. T-that's fine." I cleared my throat and tucked a strand of hair behind my ear.

"I'll wait outside. Alright?"

"Alright."

Peter grabbed the change and shoved it in his pocket before lugging the jugs of water to the truck. In the short time it took for Sam to ring up my items, sheaths of rain started to come down. After saying goodbye to Sam and giving him a quick side hug, I raced outside to where Peter was waiting under the awning. The temperature had significantly dropped, bringing a chill to the air. Streets collected puddles of rising water. After the next bolt of lightning hit, Peter's hand rested on the small of my back, and our feet fell into a quickened pace to the truck. Pelts of rain and hair whipped my face as the wind picked up. I climbed inside with my bags and buckled my seatbelt. Peter shut the door and ran around the truck. I brought my hair to one side of my shoulder, ringing out the excess water.

Heavy rain hit the windshield, giving the wipers hardly a fighting chance. Loud powerful wind whistled against the truck. Rapids of water raced for the storm drains and pummeled the hoods of cars. Whitewash crashed into the curbs before sinking down into the sewers. It was an orchestra of white noise. Even the southern drawl of the singer's voice on the radio was barely audible. Peter focused hard on the long stretch of Golder Ranch Road, not wavering in the least. I couldn't resist taking a long look at him, as he seemed to be mulling over something heavy. And though I might've taken my time wondering what it could be, the flushed hue of his cheeks and the dark circles under his eyes told me that these last few days had been just as tough for him as they had been for me. Droplets of water dripped off the strands of his hair, and he pushed them back. Rain began to strike the windshield faster and stronger. The visibility was nearly impossible. Harley sat upright, focused on the incessant noise.

"Man, it's really comin' down," Peter said, flicking the knob higher. The wipers went back and forth so fast that by the time I stopped watching them, I had to shut my eyes to refocus. "Hey, how's your head?"

"It's fine," I answered faintly. "It's just a bit sore, is all."

"No headache?"

"Peter, I'm . . ." I stopped myself, knowing what I'd say would only worry him more. "No. No headache."

He nodded. "Good."

I don't know if it was the way he said it or the way he looked, but something told me that a swell inside him was about to break. Like he had a monsoon of his very own. There's only so much a person can hold back before it all overflows. Even the crease in between his brows was more noticeable. He rolled back his stiff shoulder and then brought it forward, closing one eye in a grimace of pain.

"Your shoulder okay?"

"Yeah, I'll live."

He exhaled a breath through his nose and propped his elbow on the windowsill. I looked away as he made the final turn for the road home. Though I had become used to the silence, a part of me now had to fight off the impulse to speak. To speak about the little things. Sharing all those little things with him had made it all the easier to step inside that trailer again. He didn't need to care or say anything. All I needed was that escape. To know I still had the ability and desire to share myself with another soul was all that mattered to me. No matter how short it was. And though there wasn't any talking today, the quiet was enough for now. Peter pulled up in front of the trailer.

"You'll be fine from here, right?"

"Yeah, I'll be fine." I grabbed my bags, carefully opening the door. Harley whined. "Bye, Harley."

Wind and rain hit my face as I slowly stepped outside, shutting the door behind me. Just as I made my way up the porch, the sound of squelching mud caused me to turn around, and I saw Peter in front of the truck, standing there in the rain. A glassy sheen had overtaken his eyes as a pained expression twisted his face. It was a look I hadn't ever expected from him. Like the night at the fair. He hesitantly inched closer, acting as if he was about to say something, but instead he quickly stepped back and walked away. As he did, the sole of his right boot slipped on the mud and he fell back.

"Peter!"

I dropped my bags and ran to him. He pushed himself up and leaned against the side of the truck, hunched over, holding his knees as he tried to catch his breath. A heavy ache settled in my chest as I held back the urge to touch him, afraid of overstepping a boundary. He grabbed both my arms, agony and grief spreading across his face. I stood there, unsure of what to do, stunned by the feel of his hands. It was the first time in a long time I had allowed someone to touch me. And I knew that this must've been a risk for him, too. But I didn't pull away. He looked down, resting his forehead on the top of my belly.

"I'm sorry." His voice cracked, full of pain. "I'm so sorry, Grace." He started breathing heavier and faster, struggling to catch his breath. "I . . . I used to be better at this. Better at everything. Better at life."

"Peter." My voice broke. "I'm okay. I'm right here. I'm okay."

My fingers rested upon the side of his face and combed back the strands of his hair. I didn't know what made me do it. Maybe it's because I knew some part of him needed it, and it was the only thing I thought of at that moment. Because seeing him in pain had brought me pain. Much like the rain, my body had absorbed his suffering, and it seeped into the crevices of my heart. I never thought of myself as a refuge for someone else. Anyone important in my life had moved on, leaving me behind. But in my heart, I knew Peter was someone who wouldn't ever leave. Not on his own accord. And little by little, his breathing started to slow down.

"We need to go inside. It's really comin' down. Can you walk?"

He nodded, standing upright.

I let Harley out of the truck, and he raced to the door. Peter was about to take a step but winced in pain, hunching over again. I slipped my arm around his side, and we made our way to the trailer. Stepping inside, I carefully led him to the couch. The floors creaked underneath his heavy footsteps as we made our way across the room. Lowering him onto the cushion, I propped one of the pillows behind his neck. I slid his legs onto the blanket and untied his boots, slipping them off his feet. Harley shook the excess water from his coat and laid down on the floor. Peter shut his eyes, breathing shakily with strands of hair still stuck to his wet face. I checked his forehead.

"Grace—"

"You've got a fever." I turned away, but his hand grabbed my forearm.

He plopped his head back down on the pillow. "Where are you going?" he asked in a rough and unsteady voice.

"I'm not goin' anywhere. I promise. I just need to get you something for your fever, and you better not move."

He shut his eyes in agreement, nodding. Before leaving the room, I checked one last time to see if he had moved before heading to the bathroom. I shut the door and locked it, desperate to relieve myself. As I sat on the toilet, I slipped off my soaked cardigan. Goosebumps spread their way over my body as the air hit my chilled skin. Struggling at first, I managed to lift the wet, heavy, dress off my body, hanging it to dry on the shower rod. Opening the medicine cabinet, I quickly searched for the bottle with the red cap. After finding the Tylenol, I pulled on my pink-striped pajama set, desperate to have something dry and warm on my chilled skin. I returned to the couch with a glass of water and sat down on the coffee table. Peter opened his tired eyes.

"I'm sorry, Grace."

"For what?"

"Letting you see me like this."

"Don't be sorry. It's okay to not always be okay. I should know . . . You taught me that," I replied. His face softened. "Now, you need to take two of these. Alright? They'll help with the fever. And you should sit up," I said, holding out the glass of water in one hand and the two tablets in the other.

Peter sat upright, running a hand through his wet, tousled hair. He shut his eyes for a long moment and exhaled a deep breath. Finally opening his eyes, he reached over to take the tablets from me.

"Not exactly my day, is it?" He placed them in his mouth and gulped down half the glass, setting it on the table with a long sigh. "Then again, I haven't had one of those in a while," he said, propping his arms on the tops of his knees. "In a very long while." His eyes were focused on his hands, and I noticed the lingering bruises and scrapes across his knuckles. "You know what I've been wantin' to ask you, Grace, is why you're not afraid of me," he muttered. "You've seen me hurt someone. And not just anyone. Your father. You saw me do it. You saw me like that. And—"

"Peter—"

"A man you don't even know hurt your father in front of you, and you're not even a bit scared?"

"No," I said with the most absolute certainty. "And don't ask me why, because I still don't know myself, but my answer is no," I said again, expecting his shock, but his eyes were still low to the floor, almost ashamed.

"I don't like hurting people, Grace," he admitted gently. "I never have. I don't get off on it like some men do. Back then all I could think about was that I just took some mother's son away. A brother. A husband. Every man I killed was like killing a piece of myself, but when I saw your father . . ." His voice cracked. "And then hearing you scream, I just blacked out. I didn't care, and I know I would've killed him if I hadn't stopped myself."

His words were laced with such torment that it made me want to cry. He lifted his head, searching for any hesitation or uneasiness, but I knew he would find none. His brown eyes roamed my face, anxious for me to say something. Speaking with him this time felt different. It was raw, open, and vulnerable.

I scooted myself closer to the edge of the table. "Peter."

He dropped his head and breathed out, "I'm sorry. I'm sorry you had to see such a thing."

"Killing and protecting . . . those are two very different things," I said, my heart quickening the moment his eyes landed back on my face.

He sat still, at a loss for words. Finally acting upon the urge, I gently took his hands and placed them in my lap.

"I'm not scared of you. You're not a bad man. I know what a bad man is. And you're not one of 'em. You're more of a good man than you realize."

"Grace, I'm not. I'm not a good man. I know I would do it again if someone tried to hurt you and that baby," he continued in a deep hushed tone, as if just saying it aloud would awaken that side of him. At that moment I didn't care how tight his grip was around my hand. I watched his thumb swipe back and forth across the side of my palm. His body shook as he exhaled a deep breath. "I don't . . . I don't think I could ever live with myself if I let you and that baby get hurt." His voice sounded distraught. "I didn't get there fast enough, and you got hurt. You and—"

"Is that what you meant? That you used to be better at this?" I asked, unsure. He looked at me, and I wondered if I had pushed too far. "Sorry," I looked down. "You don't need to tell me right now, but I'd like to know. It's only fair. You know a lot about me. Things I don't really tell anyone."

We stared at each other in silence for a moment before he began speaking in a faint tone. "Well, anyone can lose touch when they've stopped living in the yellow zone," he said and brought his attention to Harley who had fallen asleep on the floor. "I was stronger and faster. Harley and I both were, but that was years ago. You know, if my pop was here now, I wonder what he would say." He chuckled dryly and shook his head, reaching for his left ear. "Probably something like, well, you let yourself go, whaddya expect?"

"I don't think he'd say that," I said. "I think he'd be proud of you for doin' somethin' that not a lot of people would do. I know I don't know him, but I'd like to think he would."

His doleful but tender gaze swept over my face, as if he had finally heard the words he'd been wanting to hear for a long time. "How do you do that? You always say what I wanna hear." He sighed deeply, letting his head fall and rest in the middle of my chest, between my breasts and the roundness of my belly. "It's like you're in my head . . . you say all the right things." His back rose and fell as he let out another breath. He didn't move. My fingertips combed the hair back from his face. With each pass of my hand, the tension in his muscles began to ease. I couldn't think of anything.

All I wanted was to stay like this forever.

※

A weight shifted against my stomach causing my arm to gently brush against something broad and strong. My tired eyes slowly opened, and I looked down, seeing Peter in a deep sleep with his head propped on my thigh. His nose was pressed against the curve of my belly and his chest rose and fell as it expanded with oxygen. With each heavy exhale, a soft snore escaped. Harley was on the floor, lying on his back, unbothered by the sound. A small groan rumbled from Peter's throat, and he shifted slightly but flinched the moment his right knee moved.

It was then the baby pressed down, urging me to make my way to the bathroom. I carefully slid myself out from underneath him and stepped over his foot that was draped off the couch. Harley rolled over and stood upright, stretching his legs.

"You need to go out, buddy?" I asked quietly, opening the door.

Harley ran outside, finding a mesquite tree to relieve himself under.

Yesterday's rainfall had left puddles across the whole trailer park. Not only that but the smell of petrichor hung heavy in the air. It was distinct. One that brought water and the desert together in the most heavenly way possible. A few neighbors up the road, and even Mr. Emerson, left their doors open to soak it in until the next storm.

Harley returned, and we headed inside. I shut the screen door. Peter jumped straight off the couch. I stood still as his frantic eyes searched around the room and landed back on me. He let out a sigh. "Sorry," he said, clearing his throat. "I hope I didn't scare ya at all. I just got a bit . . ."

"You didn't. My mama and pa had shotguns when I was growin' up, so . . ." I paused, unsure of where I was heading with that. He nodded, relieved, and slowly lowered himself back onto the couch, letting out a low grunt of pain. He shut his eyes and exhaled a deep breath, holding the side of his knee.

Harley barked and readied himself into a play position.

"I'll get to you in a minute, Harley, don't worry," Peter said.

"I already let him out."

"You did?"

"Yeah."

"Oh. Thank you."

"Well, I'm gonna go wash up."

"Alright."

"You need anythin'?"

"No. No, I'm fine. Thank you, though."

"Alright, just call out if you need anythin'."

After washing up, I fixed a few strands of hair to look somewhat presentable. I was just returning from the bathroom and tying the strings of my yellow dress above my belly when Peter got up from the couch with a grunt of effort. He wasn't smiling at first, but when his sights fell upon me, as I was slipping my arms through the sleeves of my cardigan, his expression lightened. I looked at him, catching his eyes. Clearing his throat, he turned away, the red undertone on his cheeks deepening.

"So, uh, I'm gonna head over to my place and change," he said, bashful, and lowered his hand from his ear.

"Alright."

He opened the door, and Harley bolted outside, barking. I followed him to the porch. "Also, I can pay you back for the dry cleaning. For the blanket," Peter offered, stepping down onto the muddy ground.

I smiled and stopped at the last step. "It's an old blanket. Don't worry about it," I reassured him.

He stopped in his tracks and faced me, saying, "By the way, I was gonna ask. Would it be okay if I left my truck here for a bit? I'd just like to take care of Harley here and my knee. I can move it though, if—"

"It's fine. I don't mind." I folded my arms, leaning against the post. "Leave it here as long as you need to."

Peter nodded, his eyes lingering a little longer than usual at my yellow dress. "Huh," he said as if he was baffled by some realization. He turned away but not before I witnessed the corner of his mouth lifting into a small smile. I watched him and Harley walk away. He looked back at me, still smiling.

"Thanks again."

"Yeah, no problem." I pushed myself off the post and headed inside the trailer.

For the rest of the morning, I cleaned till my elbows ached. Grabbing the blanket from the couch, I bundled it up in my arms and carried it outside to the trash can. The sound of an engine caused me to look up, expecting to see Ray and Arlene, but the smile disappeared upon seeing who it was. The tires came to a squelching stop as Mama parked behind Peter's truck. My mind raced with questions. Did she know about Pa? Was that why she was here? Did Uncle Wayne know? Would she finally take me this time? She climbed out, careful to not step in any puddles with her bright pink wedges. Not even a little rain would ever keep Mama from putting on a full face of makeup and doing her hair. Mama did a once over of Peter's truck before making her way over. I lifted the lid off the trash can and shoved the blanket in.

"Hey, sweet pea. Your daddy have company?" she asked, trying to sneak a peek in the trailer's kitchen window.

Shutting the lid, I said, "No. What are you doin' back here? Aren't you supposed to be in California or somethin'?"

"My, my, someone woke up on the wrong side of the bed this morning. The rain kept you up, baby?"

"No." I turned away.

"Grace, is your daddy here or not? I got a bone to pick with him. The man hasn't called me back and—"

"He's not here, Mama."

"Dagnabbit!"

I looked back and saw her pulling her wedge out from the mud, holding the side of Peter's truck. I reluctantly retraced my steps and helped her cross the mud till we arrived on the porch.

"Why do you wear those shoes, Mama?"

"Is it a crime for a woman to always look her best? Beauty is pain, sweet pea." She shook the bits and pieces of mud off the sole of her shoe, and we headed inside. Mama looked to the left and to the right, then left again, setting her bag on the counter. "So, what's that truck doin' there? Is it Uncle Wayne's? Did he finally git rid of that red beast and get a new one? He oughta. It's loud as all heck."

"No, he hasn't been here in a few days." I opened the fridge, carefully bending forward.

"Is it that neighbor's?" Mama asked. When I didn't answer, she continued. "So it is, isn't it? I'd reckon you two are gettin' along then since his truck's here. Is he still here?" She opened her bag and drew a cigarette from the carton.

I set down the pitcher of iced tea as Mama rummaged through her purse for the lighter. "Now, I may not be the brightest crayon in the box, sweet pea, but I do know a few things about men. Mostly from your daddy." Mama lit her cigarette and took her first puff, waving the smoke from her face. "There's only one reason why a man like that would be hangin' 'round a girl like you, Grace. Hell, any man. They all like the young ones. Everything's still in the right places. And I guess some of 'em don't even care if a woman's carrying another man's baby."

"Couldn't it be because he thinks I'm pretty or smart, Mama? Or 'cause he cares about me?"

"Sweet pea, no man wants trailer park trash. Remember what I said? Once trailer park trash, always trailer park trash. There's only one reason why a man his age goes after a young girl like you. And when you're knocked up. Just when I thought men couldn't get any worse. They're sick."

"He's actually real sweet, Mama," I said, taking out two glasses. Mama rolled her eyes.

"They all act sweet to get what they want, Grace. Take Mason. Look at what happened to you. And I bet you knew it, too. Boys can't hide it. Men can. You'd do best to learn that and not fall for that sweet act."

"You and Pa are like two peas in a pod, I swear."

"Speaking of your pa . . ." Mama flicked the ash into the sink. "When's he gonna be back?"

"Did Uncle Wayne not tell you? Your brother?" I asked, pouring the iced tea into each glass.

"Sweet pea, after you told me he got back with Tina, I said to myself: I ain't gonna bother him again till that man gets his ducks in a row."

"I don't think he's planning to let her go anytime soon."

"Give it another six months to a year. There'll always be someone younger for him." Mama expelled smoke through her pursed lips and then pointed with her manicured nail, saying, "By the way, what happened to your eye over there? You even got a little cut there," she said and gestured to her own brow. "And you got a bruise or two on your face. You didn't faint and fall, did you?"

"Whaddya think happened, Mama? You seem to know everything, so why don't you guess."

Mama slicked her tongue over her teeth and crossed one leg over the other. "Well, you must've done somethin' to make your daddy angry. Probably told you to not do somethin,' but you went and did it anyway."

This time when she went in for another drag, the cloud of smoke was more dense and packed a punch in its burn. My nose stung like the time I squirted lemon juice in my eye. The taste of nicotine spread across my tongue, leaving tiny, prickling needles in its wake.

"Why you lookin' at me like that?"

"Will you put it out?"

She glanced between me and her cigarette. "You want me to open the window for ya?"

"It's bad for the baby, Mama."

She cracked open the window before putting out the cigarette in the sink. "Grace. Sweet pea. You don't need to be so hung up on what and what not to do. I ate stuff I shouldn't have," Mama admitted.

I rolled my eyes and bent down, putting back the pitcher of sweet iced tea.

"I smoked. I'd have a beer here and there, but just a little bit. If it's a little bit, it's okay. And look at you, you—"

I slammed the door to the fridge and stood facing her. "I what, Mama? I turned out just fine?"

Mama's over-plucked brows raised. "Okay. Maybe not fine. You were a weird child. Always watching people. My point, sweet pea, is that no one can raise a baby right. Trust me, it's tiring. I had to do it. You think it was fun? No. I didn't git to be a teenager. So yeah, I sipped a beer and took a hit once in a while. Just 'cause you started being a goody two shoes, doesn't mean you know anything about raising a child. I've made mistakes, but I'm here now, Grace. That's gotta count for something, right?"

*I'm here now.*

The words she said with such conviction anytime I or anyone challenged her mothering. Her body may have been here but that was it. Just a body. Never a mother. It wasn't my pa who disappointed me first. It was Mama. The words were on the tip of my tongue, but I knew they didn't matter because she would just leave. Like always. Mama folded her arms tighter and leaned her hip against the counter.

"Oh, come on, Grace. Don't go all quiet on me. Whether you like it or not, that's the truth. You don't understand the responsibility yet of taking care of a child. I can't wait till that kid pops outta ya. You'll be beggin' for me to help. You think you won't now. But trust me, you will."

"What makes you think I'd ever want help from someone like you, Mama?" The harsh words flowed out of me freely, and I stood there appalled at how easily I could speak to my mama like that.

"Hey, that ain't nice of you to say that. It's not easy raisin' a child on your own. You'll be——"

"I did it already!" I yelled. "I raised myself and you! Who was the one who picked you up off the floor when you came home drunk? I did! You couldn't even take care of yourself, Mama! I was the one! I took care of you when you should've been taking care of me! Your child! Then you left me!" I exhaled a shaky breath. "With Pa! I was nine and you left me. I lost the one thing that should be permanent in this world! You're my mama, and you left me!" I screamed. "You left me all alone!"

"Oh, get over it! No one has the mother they really want, Grace! You think I had the momma I wanted? No! But I live with it! So, get over it!" she yelled. "That's what you do, Grace! You get over it!"

"I waited for you. For years!"

Mama's eyes were alive with anger. I thought she would wave off my accusations as another little annoyance in her life. Like she did with me. But without warning, the fury melted away in her face and was replaced with a pain I'd never seen. A sadness I had yearned to see since the day she left. Ruled by childish thoughts and fantasies, a part of me ached for her to hold me with those arms. Instead, Mama did what she did best. She grabbed her bag and left, but not before looking at me one last time. As silly as it was, the child in me held onto that because I knew a part of her didn't want to do it. Then *I* did what I always did best. Push the tears down and lock them deep inside.

*Knock. Knock.*

I raced to the door, only to find Peter standing there. Before he could say a word, I slammed the door closed.

"Grace. Grace, will you let me in? I want—"

"No."

"Open the door."

"Go away." I stood there, expecting an answer. Silence. "You're still there, aren't you?"

"Yeah, I'm not gonna go anywhere till you let me in," he insisted calmly. I remained silent, conflicted. "Grace . . ." He was quieter now, with a waver in his voice that said he was desperate to be let in. "Please."

Resting my forehead gently against the door, I closed my eyes. The sound of him calling my name was the second most wonderful sound I'd ever heard, the first being my child's heartbeat. I never knew hearing someone say my name could make me feel so at home. In a short amount of time, he had become the most important person in my life. My shaky fingers started to turn the lock, and I slowly opened the door. Peter lifted his head, facing me with those tender brown eyes and a look that conveyed so much relief. I inched back as he stepped inside, letting the screen door shut behind him.

I wrapped my arms around him and buried my face in his chest. He stood stiff for a few moments before I felt his strong arms slowly but surely wrap me in their protective embrace. I melted in exhaustion against his solid chest, not realizing there was a part of me longing for human touch. Even just a hug. His fingers slipped through the bottom of my hair, cradling the back of my head. All I could hear was our breathing and the steady beat of his pulse against my cheek. I wasn't alone. A sudden but little movement inside me nudged the front of my stomach and he stepped back.

"Whoa." He looked at my belly and back at me, then at my stomach again. "I-I forgot for a moment there's a little human in there," he admitted bashfully. "I wasn't squishing her, right?" he asked, suddenly worried.

"No, she's okay," I reassured him.

He nodded, and a swallow passed through his throat, seemingly hesitant to act upon something. He glanced at me and then back at my stomach again, his expression softening the longer he looked.

"You can touch, if you want. My belly. I don't mind." My heart quickened from saying the words aloud.

He regarded me and looked back at my stomach, cautious. I stepped forward and took his hand, gently placing it over my belly. He kept his hand and body incredibly still as if any sudden movement could hurt me or the baby.

"Peter," I said. His eyes quickly fell upon my face, not saying a word. "You're not gonna hurt her. Okay?"

"You sure?"

"Yes. I'm sure."

He slowly laid his palm flat against my stomach. Though he seemed to be at ease, his body was anything but. For some reason, seeing him this way, at a loss for words, brought a small smile to my face. His thumb then started caressing the side of my stomach, anxiously waiting. His eyes were soft and warm.

"It's a girl, right?"

"Yeah."

He looked down but not without smiling first. "A girl," he repeated to himself in a whisper. A small nudge hit his palm, and he went completely still. His expression changed, joy alighting his eyes. Full of love and sweetness. "She moved. She really just moved," he said in disbelief as tears welled in his eyes.

And that's when I first saw it. It started at the right corner of his mouth and made its way to the other end. His full smile nearly made my heart leap. A part of me didn't know what to do or say, but I knew I couldn't hide the red on my cheeks. Though his smile dipped ever so slightly at the left corner, I was able to see every inch of its brilliance. Mama once said no gift is more precious than a smile. Anyone can afford it. And just as she said it would, that smile left me with an equally pleasing smile on my face as I soaked up the effects of it, like a saguaro in the heat of the summer, having its first taste of water after weeks of dehydration.

Peter placed both hands on either side of my belly, wanting the full experience now. As I watched him anxiously awaiting another movement, that's when I felt it again. That glow. That warmth and the feeling of home. For a fleeting moment, I allowed myself to imagine what it would be like. If I were older. If I were his. And if he was the baby's father.

"Okay, now she's not moving. Maybe she doesn't like me," he said suddenly uneasy. "Or did I press too—"

"You just have to talk to her. That's all you have to do. A baby can remember your voice."

"Talk to her, huh? What do I even say?"

"Anything you want."

"Okay," he began, carefully choosing his words. "Hi, baby. Nice to meet you."

I bit my bottom lip, holding back a laugh. Peter shifted his stance and cleared his throat.

"Look, you better not plan to come out of there anytime soon. You gotta promise me that, okay? I'd rather not have your pretty mom here go into labor on the side of the road when she's on one of her walks. That would be a bumpy ride, let me tell you. And . . . I hope you know that I'm not gonna let anything bad happen to you or your mom," he continued, caressing the sides of my stomach with his thumbs. "So yeah, that's what I have to share. And the name's Peter by the way. Not Pete, because apparently your mom here doesn't like that. Why? I don't know. And I'll never know."

"It sounds better."

"Okay, but let's not tell anybody. Alright, baby?" he said to my belly, unenthusiastically.

A nudge hit my stomach, and his face lit up again. Another soft bump hit the side of his hand. I was trying to find words, but I found none. I could only stare at him as he stood there in contented silence.

"She's really moving in there. I didn't think . . . I didn't think she'd do that for me."

I looked down and ran my hand over the top of my belly, the swell of tears becoming difficult to resist. "I told you. If you talk to her enough, she'll remember. I've always had this feelin' that she's gonna be really smart. I don't know why, but I just do. I think she's gonna do great things in this life. And I really don't wanna mess it up for her. Like my mama did with me."

"Grace," Peter said, and I lifted my head, realizing a tear had spilled down my cheek. I sniffled, wiping it away.

"What if I do?" I said. "What if I mess it up for her? What if I was wrong? To think that she was all I needed. That she's gonna give me all the happiness I need. What if I was—"

"Grace, you're not supposed to know everything about raising a child yet. Even when you think you do, you don't. You think any mother knew what she was doing in the beginning? You're gonna have bad days. It's okay. It's normal. I should know. I've been having a lot of 'em."

"My mother didn't have bad days. She had bad years." I wiped my face again and sniffled. "What if that's me? What if I turn out just like her? She never asked for help, and I know I'm—"

He closed the space between us, saying, "Grace, you're not going to turn out like her."

"And how do you know that? I don't want to be. I don't ever want to be like my mama." I stifled a cry. Peter studied me intently with a slightly softer expression, not saying a word. My shoulders shook as the sobs finally broke free. "I really don't want to be like my mama. I really don't."

He brought me into his arms, and I continued to cry. I didn't mind the prickly stubble rubbing against my hair. Because at this moment, all I needed was the hold of his arms. My breathing and tears slowed, letting myself fully sink into him. We never uttered a word, nor did his grip ever loosen in the time we stood here. I'd forgotten how it felt to be held. I never wanted it to end. And I hoped that one day my baby girl would have someone to hold her like this.

Peter pulled back and placed both of his warm hands on my face. His thumbs carefully swept away the remaining tears.

For so long, I had imagined what it would be like for a man to hold my face. Not just any man. The one who would be the exception. All the times I spent daydreaming of what it would be like when and if it finally happened. That feeling of the tender brush of his lips pressing against my forehead. A feeling that felt so different than it had in my dreams. An act so simple and pure but a feeling so profound it had done the impossible. That little kiss on its own told me I was safe. That everything would be okay. It was a kiss that held a deep significance of something I hadn't figured out yet. Something I didn't want to let go of. My eyes opened. I looked to his face, to the rise and fall of his chest, and then his face again, unsure of whether to touch him. His hand then tucked a strand of hair behind my ear, his eyes still yet to meet mine.

"Peter," I said as steady as I could.

"Yeah?"

Our eyes stayed locked. I was completely enthralled by the way his gaze prevented me from pulling away. As if I was looking at a stranger I had always known. A thin line of fire danced just beneath the surface of my skin. Almost like laying in a bed of sand. Overwhelming me in the best possible way. There was a part of me that wondered if I should be terrified. But I remained still. Fluttery feelings tightened the muscles in the pit of my stomach.

"I-I need to use the bathroom."

"Oh, right." He stepped back. "S-sorry." He tore his eyes away as though to clear his mind.

I raced to the bathroom.

I shut the door and let out a much-needed breath. My knees were like jelly. I shut my eyes, trying to compose myself. The rush of blood had warmed my belly and parts of myself that I never knew could feel this way. I'd heard about it countless times from Arlene with the talks we shared after my breasts grew. It was something I wished I had experienced with Mason and even convinced myself I had. But this time, I didn't need any convincing to know it was real. I patted the back of my neck with a cool washcloth and closed my eyes one last time to recenter myself. Sometimes all it really took was a look, and the only way to cool the rising heat inside was to step away from the sun.

*Knock. Knock.*

I opened the door halfway and peeked my head between the crack. "Yeah?"

"Hey, I'm gonna git' goin'. I just wanted to check on you to see if you were feelin' okay."

"Yeah, I'm okay."

He nodded and scratched his chin, glancing down at his feet. "Good. Good." He cleared his throat. "Um, I was gonna ask you this the other day but . . . I-It's just an idea. You can say no. But I was gonna take a drive. Get away for a day or two, and I thought about ya and got to thinkin' if, maybe, you'd like to go with me. Like for your birthday or somethin'. I know it was a couple days ago, and I don't know if you got anything planned with Ray and Arlene, but I'd like to take you somewhere. Some place special to me. I think you'd like it. Again, y-you can say no." Peter hesitated with red cheeks. "I just—"

"When are you goin'?"

"The day after tomorrow. The weather isn't supposed to be bad that day. And I'd want to check the tires and whatnot."

"What time?"

He thought for a moment and stepped back, sticking his hands into the pockets of his jeans. "Eight-thirty?"

"Okay."

Peter stood still and nodded. "Alrighty, then. Well, I'm gonna head out and get some things ready," he said and gave me a lopsided smile. I stretched my neck further and watched him leave out the front door.

# 12

Though Mama always told me hearing a coyote's howl meant good things were on their way, I didn't believe it. Not until I woke up this morning, knowing I'd be away from here. Even if it was for only a short time. Peter loaded the duffle bag into the back of the truck, and after I slipped a note underneath Ray and Arlene's door, we set out for the open road. I watched the rugged and empty landscape in the side mirror fade into the distance. Whenever anything bad happened, I always wanted to run away. Even just for a day. But what I didn't ever expect would be wanting to share that with a man. A man who said all the right things. I never believed a man could be capable of that. And lately I found myself slipping into that fantasy again. The fantasy of what my life could be like with a man.

There were moments like when Peter held my stomach that made it difficult to not fantasize about that possibility. To me that was one of the few precious moments in my life. And when I first saw those two pink lines, heard my baby girl's heartbeat, and felt that first kick, I knew I'd have many more. Like the day I finally get to hold her in my arms. I thought I wanted to be alone on that day, but now a part of me wasn't so sure.

Turning my head, I saw Peter focusing on the road. He scratched his newly shaven jaw for the fifth time. Even he still wasn't used to it. He looked over at me and smiled before returning his attention to the highway. It was just us—no one else. No expectations. No interruptions. No chaos.

Was this what love should feel like?

The kind that feels like home?

Was this how Arlene felt with Ray?

The gentle hum of the truck had already lulled Harley to sleep. I pulled down the sun visor and patted my cheeks to bring some color, wiping the crust off near my eyes. Satisfied with my attempt to smooth down my hair, I shut the visor but not without catching Peter averting his eyes.

"What?"

His cheeks were red. "Nothin'."

"So, where we going?"

He grinned and looked at the road. "It just occurred to you to ask me that?" His voice was laced with humor. I rolled my eyes. "You ever been to the Grand Canyon? I know it's not everyone's cup of tea, but—" He paused, his eyes alight from the burst of excitement on my face. "What?"

"We're really goin' to the Grand Canyon?"

"Yeah. What, you've already been there?"

"No. I've only seen it in magazines."

"You've never seen the Grand Canyon in all the time you've lived here?"

"No, we only had one car, and my pa was always usin' it," I said and sat back against the seat. "We never really went anywhere, but it wasn't all that bad. Arlene and I used to play water tag with the hose every summer. I was luckier than most kids. I had a roof over my head and food on the table. Some kids had it worse," I continued, thinking out loud. And like the time my mama first took me stargazing, I turned and faced Peter with the same excitement. "Hey, can I ask you somethin'?"

"What?" he asked, with a broad smile.

"Why you smilin' like that?"

"Smiling like what?"

"Like you know something I don't."

"I just . . . never heard you talk so much with a smile on your face," he answered. "I like it."

I looked away and smiled at my belly.

"So, what is it you wanna ask me?"

"Why'd you come here?" I asked, looking over at him. "Didn't you wanna go anywhere else?"

"I kinda had to come here. It was either my mother or me. Someone needed to clean up her brother's trailer. And I have Harley, so I really don't mind where I go," he said. Just when I hoped he would continue, he stopped, as if he was still trying to decide what and what not to share with me.

Taking off my sandals, I stretched out my legs. "It must be nice to go wherever and whenever you wanna go. I feel like most people who live in trailer parks just wind up being stuck there, you know? My mama said I'd probably just marry the boy down a few trailers and have more kids than I could handle. Never really go anywhere. I remember what she told me a few days before she left. She said, 'Grace, when you meet a boy, don't spread your legs like Dawn down the road. We Callaway women have always been fertile. You'll end up just like her with four kids. Don't do what me and my own momma did.'"

"And you were nine?"

"Yeah, but my mama wasn't always bad. I think she just had bad stuff happen to her. It's like what you said. No one really knows how to take care of a kid. But she was right about one thing, I'm only gonna get fatter."

"You're not . . ." Peter hesitated. "You're not fat, Grace. If anything, you're growing the one thing that's still innocent and good in this world, and that's beautiful," he said with such sincerity and truth it brought tears to my eyes.

I searched his face for any dishonesty but found none, and for the first time in seven months, I felt seen. Like I mattered again. The same red hue had returned to his cheeks. I looked down at my white dress and couldn't help but smile again, as an unexpected weight lifted off my shoulders.

"Peter."

"Yeah?"

"If we're goin' to the Grand Canyon, does that mean we're gonna be eating Navajo tacos?"

"Why? Is that what you want when we get there? Tacos?"

"Tacos do sound good."

"Not fries with no salt?"

"That's not funny," I said.

He smiled and broke into a quiet laugh.

Even after chugging a whole water bottle and eating a granola bar, the morning sickness continued. The sound of Terri Gibbs' voice singing "Somebody's Knockin'" caused my eyes to droop. My body slumped into Peter's side, at peace knowing he was just a hand's reach from me. His scent alone had done what only the sunrise could do. The soft tang of musk and soap was something I could never grow tired of. Just like the steady rise and fall of his chest willing me deeper and deeper into sleep. I had forgotten what it was like. To be willingly vulnerable. To know that when I woke up, he would still be here. And I didn't want him going anywhere.

A bump in the road caused my eyes to open, meeting the sun's glare. I shifted in the seat and nestled my cheek into Peter's chest, shutting my eyes. "Why's it so hot?"

"Cause it's the summer," he replied, and I could hear the smile on his face. "We're only an hour and a half away now."

I slowly sat up.

He lifted his arm over my head and placed his hand back on the wheel. I leaned toward the window, staring at the barren and flat landscape. Wiping my sweaty forehead, I slumped into the seat. I adjusted the hem of my spandex shorts and sighed in frustration, throwing my head back.

"Want some more water?" He reached into the cooler behind my seat, passing me a bottle.

"Thank you." I twisted off the cap, taking a gulp.

I then carefully poured some water on my hand and spread the cool water across my thighs. Letting out a breath of relief, I rested my forehead against the dashboard to enjoy the soft gust of the A/C.

"Hang in there. We'll be there soon," Peter reassured me and gently rubbed my back before taking the water bottle. "Wanna stop and get something to eat? You ready for those tacos?"

I nodded.

"Alrighty, then."

After an hour on Highway 87, past Grand Canyon Junction, we pulled over. Harley and I anxiously waited in the parking lot for him to return from the store. Harley's ears raised as he saw Peter walking over with a plastic bag packed to the brim with Styrofoam boxes. In the same hand he carried two water bottles. He opened the driver's side door, and Harley jumped out to find the perfect spot to relieve himself. As Peter checked each box of food, I leaned forward.

"Are those the tacos?"

"Indeed they are."

"From the gas station?"

"Hey, don't knock it till you try these. I grew up eating these." He took a sip of water and set the bottle down, tying the handles of the plastic bag to secure the food. Peter looked back and watched Harley.

"What's it like?"

"The tacos?"

"Seeing the Grand Canyon. Is it just as pretty as they say, or is it just all hype?" I asked.

"It's a lot of rock."

"A lot of rock? That's the best answer you could come up with?" I said, causing a smile to spread across his face.

"I'm not gonna spoil it for you," he said and called for Harley, who came rushing over. He leaped with ease into the opened back window. Peter climbed in and shut the door. "You know, maybe tomorrow morning we can get Sonoran-style eggs in a tortilla bowl. Beef with black beans and roasted red peppers," he suggested. Harley stuck his head outside as we pulled out of the gas station.

"Sonoran-style eggs?"

He glanced at me, baffled. "Don't tell me. You've never had—"

"No. Are they good?"

"Are they good? You hear that, Harley?" he asked. Harley barked. "Are they good, she says." Peter shook his head.

"Well, are they?"

"Grace, you can't visit the Grand Canyon and not have some eggs with buckwheat pancakes. Which means we're not leavin' here until you do. Alright?" he insisted. I smiled. "Cause, you just can't do that."

"Alright."

For the remainder of the drive, I rested my head on the windowsill. It wasn't until I caught glimpses of stands on the side of the road, selling a variety of handmade Native American goods, that I sat upright in my seat. Knowing the destination ahead was close, my inner child gasped in delight. A dozen cars in front of us headed in the same direction. In just a few minutes, we were at the Desert View Entrance Station, and a park ranger was handing Peter our permit. He tipped his hat and bid us a farewell. My heart quickened as we followed behind the other vehicles. The breathtaking, panoramic view of the Grand Canyon was right outside my window. It was even more magnificent than on the cover of *National Geographic*. I shared a glance with Peter and returned my attention to the window to bask in its scenery. At Mile Marker 251, we turned into an extension lined with a parapet, overlooking the view.

Two cars had stopped as well, and a small family stood in front of their car, raising up their cameras. One young man had perched himself on the roof of his Jeep and lifted a heavy-duty camera to his face. My breath caught in my throat at the sight of the horizon, and I looked back at Peter, who smiled at my excited expression. I unbuckled myself and quickly opened the door, swinging my legs over. Just as I was about to lower myself down, Peter jogged over and held the door wider. When my feet landed on the ground, Harley jumped out to explore the patch of trees. My heart raced from the expansive landscape. I picked up the pace, my eagerness growing with each and every step.

The sun was still overhead, filling the cliffs and the Colorado River with a haze of sunshine. Pink and red hues reflected in the areas where it hit the tallest peaks. As I reached the edge, I placed my hands on the rail and leaned forward to inhale the fresh air and soak up the warmth. I stood awestruck by the never-ending extension of red rock and dramatic cliffs. It was perfect. She was the perfect testimony to how majestic the desert could be, terrifying in its mass but nonetheless beautiful. Every part of me wanted to take off my shoes and stand on the cliff with arms spread wide. To feel the earth's warm rocks soothing my soul. To be free, wild, and happy. That's all I needed.

"I can't believe something this big really exists. If I knew this was your special place, I would have brought my camera with me," I said, looking back at Peter. He glanced at the view and snorted, shaking his head as he lowered the tailgate. "What do you mean—" I mocked his snort "—by that?"

He looked surprised and amused at the same time before jerking his head toward the view, saying, "Trust me, Grace, that is something you won't ever forget. You don't need no picture." He set down the bag of food along with our drinks. I leaned against the tailgate, enjoying the breeze hitting my face. "And when my family and I would come here—Really, Harley? How many times do I have to tell you? Don't eat the grass." Peter kneeled down, shaking his head as he forced open Harley's jaw to grab the blades from his tongue. "Come on, up in the truck." He patted Harley's backside as he leaped up.

I smiled, admiring the horizon a little bit longer. "You would do what with your family?" I asked, curious, wanting him to continue as I lifted myself up onto the tailgate, providing him my full attention.

He stood and wiped Harley's saliva onto the side of his jeans. "Well, my family and I always took a trip out here every summer. I think I was around twelve years old when it really hit me how big this place was. My family and I would spend all day here. We'd hike over at the West Rim and see Eagle Rock. And there's no rails there like here. So, uh, it was basically natural selection at that point," he chuckled. I bit my bottom lip and smiled, letting out a small laugh. "This was also the one place where my pop and I didn't bicker at each other," he said and sat down, handing me the box of food.

Harley lay between us, watching with eager eyes.

"It brought me some peace of mind at the time, actually."

"What was on your mind?" I asked, unwrapping the foil from my taco.

A soft smile tugged at the corner of his mouth, and he popped the cap off a beer, using the corner of the tailgate. "That . . ." He took a small sip of his cold Guinness before continuing. ". . . if this kind of view was possible, a twelve-year-old kid wanting a family when he's all grown up didn't seem so impossible," Peter answered, setting down the bottle. "Right then I knew I wanted to bring my family here some day. But uh . . ." He paused and lowered his gaze to his boots. "You already know that part of the story. Like I told ya, life doesn't always go as planned."

"Twelve years old?"

"Yep. I wanted four kids. But now that I'm older and seeing how many gray hairs I gave my mother, I think one or two is a good number. I was sort of a spunky kid growing up," he admitted. "I guess I wanted to be the father that mine never was. I had to grovel for that man's respect. It was always hard to get a compliment from him or even a how are you. But my pop also taught me a lot of things. A lot of good things," he recalled, and I watched both his middle and pointer finger tap the neck of the bottle.

"Why do you tap three times?"

"Permanent nerve damage in the median nerve. A lot of guys can get it in the Marines. I was lucky it wasn't worse, though, like what some go through. Mine just spasms. But I have good days and bad days. Like we all do." Peter set down the bottle after taking a sip and leaned over. "See?" He pointed to the scar on his right wrist that faded up into his palm. "Doesn't look as bad as it used to. But it was my right knee that I couldn't really go back from. And Harley was getting tired."

"Is that another reason why you were honorably discharged?" I asked without thinking.

He looked at me and quirked a brow. "Just how much did my friend Milo tell you?"

"Enough."

"Enough, huh? I swear that man has always been a blabbermouth," he chuckled, shaking his head with a sigh and taking another swig of beer. "You know, if my pop was still around, I think he would've liked you."

"Really?"

"Yeah, I think so," he said, scratching the back of his left earlobe. "You just say what you want to say. My mother's like that. And I like that about her. It's something I wish I could do more of."

I smiled, listening to him. Whether it was the beer starting to lower his walls or the wide-open landscape, he was somehow answering all the questions I had without needing me to ask. Returning my gaze to the sky, I let out a soft breath.

"I think my mama would've liked this," I said, staring at the view. "She's always liked the desert. She liked that you could see everything and anything."

"Do you know where she is?" he asked hesitatingly.

"No. But that's okay. I think it's better for both of us. It's better for my baby, too. I don't want my baby anywhere near my mama," I said while picking out a packet of salsa from the bag.

"Whoa, whoa, hey. What are you doin' with that?" he asked. I looked over at him and then at my taco.

"What? I'm putting salsa on my taco."

"This is the one taco you do not put salsa on. Just try it, and if you don't like it, well, I'll think of something if we get to that point."

"Then why did they put it in the bag?"

He stared at me for a long moment and clicked his tongue, reaching into the bag. I smiled. Peter set down his food to rip open a packet of salsa with his teeth. He squeezed a line of salsa across my taco and then his, holding out the packet for Harley to lick off the excess. Making sure nothing would slip from the taco, I only then brought it to my mouth to take a bite. The cheese and sour cream combined with every known ingredient used on a taco created a satisfying mix for my tastebuds. I groaned and shut my eyes.

"Oh my God," I said with a mouthful. "That's really, really good."

Peter took a large bite of his, closing his eyes. His shoulders deflated and his whole body relaxed as he savored the moment. He topped it off with a swig of beer and finished chewing. "That's a damn good taco," he said, ripping a piece of the Indian frybread. "Even with the salsa."

I took another bite, noticing Harley's begging eyes. My finger plucked out a piece of ground beef and watched Harley gobble it up from my hand.

"So, where are you from?" I asked.

"Well, I never really stayed in one place long enough for me to answer that. 'Cause of my pop, we were always movin' around. And after my wife and I split, he died, and then I packed up my bags and took Harley with me to Montana," he explained, taking a bite and chasing it with another sip of beer.

"I'm sorry to hear that. Losing someone is never easy. No matter how much you might think you hate 'em," I said. Peter looked over. "But you have Harley with you. And not many people have that. A lot of people spend all their lives searching for a friend like that. My mama did, but that didn't go well for her. Like a lot of things . . . But I wish it had. I think she would've been happier."

He returned his focus to the horizon. "You don't know that, Grace. A person can't always make someone else happy. Cause we're always changing and wanting different things. That's why you gotta' find someone who can grow and change with you. Want the same things as you. Talk with you. My wife and I never really talked when I was away," he continued. "Maybe a few letters here and there. But the only times we really ever talked was when I would come back to visit her for a couple days. Then I'd have to go back. It's not easy. I don't blame her anymore for wanting to leave. I get it now."

"Because . . ." I hesitated. ". . . you were gone so much?"

"That . . ." He exhaled. "And I think it mostly had to do with the fact that there was a very big possibility I wouldn't come back."

A heavy ache settled in my chest, the weight of his words hitting me harder than I expected.

"After that, I found a new respect for my mother. She didn't have it easy with my pop and me."

"And where is your mother?"

"Montana. She's stayed there through everything. Never had the heart to leave."

"You close to her?"

He took a sip of beer and said, "Not really. Not anymore." He paused, and regarded me, leaning forward. "You see my mother used to say my pop was the peanut butter and she was the jelly. And you can't have a peanut butter sandwich with just jelly. It's just no good."

Watching my feet swing back and forth, I said, "I hope I have a peanut butter and jelly sandwich to call my own someday."

"Who's to say that you won't? You have your whole life ahead of you. Anything can happen."

"I don't know."

"Exactly. You don't know, Grace."

"And you don't know, either. Who's to say that you won't find someone to build a life with? You're still young, too. It's not just me."

His eyes drifted over but softened as they roamed my face.

"If you really want something, you gotta' take that leap of faith," I said. "No matter how big or scary the jump is."

"And do you, Grace Callaway, know what you want?"

"I've known what I wanted since I was ten years old. I never liked Catalina. And maybe I'm crazy, but I feel like it hates me, too. Even though I didn't plan for this to happen . . ." I looked at my stomach. "I like to think someday I'll get to have that white picket fence with the table and yellow umbrella on the front porch. Holding my baby girl and drinking a glass of my iced tea, just enjoying life," I answered, realizing I hadn't ever shared this with someone before. Even Arlene.

Peeking over apprehensively, I expected him to tell me to stop making wishes on dreams that weren't ever going to happen, but he didn't say anything. His eyes were gentle and even wistful as he continued to focus on the view. And that little light of hope glimmered in my chest again. Reassuring me that maybe, just maybe, it was possible. He didn't look at me, but I knew he was soaking up every word I said.

"And you?"

He looked at me, surprised. "Me?"

"Yeah, you. What do you want?" I asked, hesitant as to whether or not I should've asked.

"I don't know," he confessed. "I'm fine with it just being me and Harley. I had a plan, but now I don't know so much."

"What did you want to do before the Marines? Be a stay-at-home dad?" I joked, attempting to lighten the mood.

A smile spread across his face. "Pretty much, yeah. Not sure if that's in the cards for me anymore, though."

"Why? You're not old."

"Old enough to be set in my ways. At least that's what I thought at the time," Peter muttered, seeming to dwell on his words. "Either way, age may not be a factor for me but I'm not exactly a smooth talker, you know? I ain't good at all that stuff. I've never been," he said for a matter of fact and looked at the bottle in his lap, still tapping it with his finger. "I'm like my pop in that way."

"All that stuff?"

"Uh," he paused and lifted his head, deep in thought. "What do they call it these days? 'Goin' out?'"

I let out a small snort. "No, they don't call it that." I took a bite of my taco. Covering my mouth, I continued, "And it really doesn't matter what age a man is, like it is for a woman. They can still have a child if they want to before they bite the dust. And if they don't like their kid, they can make another one."

His shoulders started to shake as he threw his head back and laughed. It was a laugh that fit him perfectly, deep and hearty. And it wasn't just the baritone of his voice pulling me in. It was his smile. His eyes and now his laugh. It was everything. I never thought a laugh could bring me so much joy. Even after all the pain. After all the heartache. He'd shown me that it was possible to laugh again. And just like all the times I've been by Peter's side, the pain didn't feel so bad anymore. Because I knew I'd smile and laugh again. He caught his breath and let out a

197

carefree sigh, still smiling. A warmth built up inside me, and like the sunrise every morning, the heat first touched my tippy toes, then my legs, and then my belly, completely surrounding me in its light.

"Wow, I haven't laughed like that in ages," Peter said as he caught his breath and took a sip of beer. "I can't remember the last time I laughed like that. I think I'm still out of breath."

"Really?"

"Hey, after time in the Marines, it's kinda hard to find something that will make you laugh. My friend, Milo? He wasn't the guy he is now when I first met him. After you come back from something like that, you sort of lose your purpose. And you gotta' find a new one. I don't know how he can keep going back. I think in his mind it's the only thing he knows how to do. And I was like that for a while. Thinkin' I was doin' some good, but . . ." He exhaled deeply. "I guess what I'm trying to say is that I feel old. And that plays a big role in planning these days."

"You can't plan life."

"Coming from the girl who knew what she wanted since she was ten."

"That's different."

"How's that different?"

"Cause, you can only plan so much until something happens. And who knows, maybe, wherever you end up will be even better than that plan of yours. You never know."

"H-how old are you again?"

"Nineteen. Why?"

His brows raised, facing the horizon as he said, "Why? Cause a nineteen-year-old doesn't just say that, that's why."

"Well, that's no nineteen-year-old I ever wanna meet," I claimed. His face alighted with humor the moment he saw how serious I was. He shook his head, looking away, and he quietly laughed.

"It's not funny. It's true."

"I know. That's why it's so funny."

"Do you know how irritating it was to sit in a class all day with a bunch of kids who didn't know what they wanted in life? Or even what they wanted to eat the next day? Or where they hoped to be in five years?"

He smiled, saying, "Alright. Alright. Well, is there anything else you want? I know you gotta have more."

"A back scratch."

"A back scratch, huh?"

"Yeah. A back scratch. It's always nice to wake up with a back scratch."

"Alright, then, a back scratch." He returned his attention to the view, still smiling, shaking his head.

For the next few hours, we sat there watching the mighty sun lower itself closer and closer to the horizon where the sky met the canyon. Blues, pinks, and purples combined into a symphony of watercolors, signaling the end of the day. There was something wistful about witnessing something so powerful and bright moving behind a mass of rock that's only purpose was to be still. Mama told me that when the sun sets, it's ending its journey with us and beginning a new one somewhere else. It all brought a smile to my face. Not only from the masterpiece unfolding in front of my eyes but in sharing it with someone. Feeling the tears begin to rise as the last light of day began to melt away, I reached over. My fingers slipped between Peter's, bringing his hand to my lap.

"Thank you for bringing me here."

Though it was only the second time we had held hands, there was something about the way our fingers entwined that felt as if they belonged together. I expected him to pull away, but his hand stayed there for as long as it took the sun to completely vanish. And for the first time, he seemed as at peace as the wide-open space of rock that lay before him. Like he was finally letting go of all the bad. Maybe that's what I was doing, too.

When the sun had fully disappeared, our hands untangled, and we climbed into the truck. It didn't take long before I fell into a light sleep. The fleeting lights of passing cars and a gentle bump in the road caused my eyes to open, and I found myself resting against Peter's right shoulder. I slowly sat up and groaned, placing my hand over my belly, and leaned back.

"You alright?"

"I think you were right. I shouldn't have had that third taco."

"I'm sure you'll be okay."

"Tell that to the baby," I said, catching him rubbing behind his ear. "Why do you do that?"

"Do what?"

"Rub your ear."

"I do that?"

"Yeah. I think you do it when you're thinking real hard about somethin'. Kinda like a tell."

A smile grew on his face as he focused on the road.

"What? Am I right? I am right, aren't I?"

"It's just . . . you really do surprise me every day, Grace. You really do," he said, his voice soft. He glanced over and scratched the back of his neck as the red hue on his cheeks deepened.

"I do?"

"Yeah. Is that so hard to believe?"

"You just didn't strike me as someone who could be easily surprised."

"Me, either."

I smiled and looked away. We continued down the frontage road, two and a half miles from the highway, until I spotted the Motel 6 in the distance. The exterior was plain and simple, living up to its unpretentious reputation. Only five cars had taken up the dozen or so empty spots in front of the poorly maintained entrance, lowering my expectations for a clean room. A gated pool was off to the right. To any insect with a milky exoskeleton this place would be a paradise to harvest and build their nest. I leaned forward and eyed the flickering M above the roof, the rusty sidings, and then looked back at the M. We parked in the last spot near the front of the office.

"Do we really need to stay here?"

"Do you wanna sleep in the truck?" he asked, unbuckling his seatbelt. "You comin' in?"

I shook my head.

"Alright, I'll be back in a jiffy."

Harley stood on the center console, watching Peter head into the office. An older woman sat behind the desk, and she turned her attention to him, smiling. Harley whined. "He'll be back." I dove my hand into the plastic bag. Harley's ears perked, sniffing. His tail wagged as I took out the bag of liver treats. "You want a treat?" I opened the bag, and he sat down before gobbling the treat out of my hand.

Looking over, I saw Peter walking outside, putting the room key safely in his back pocket. He opened the passenger door, and I carefully started to lower myself down. Every part of my body ached, and the bottoms of my feet stung in defiance from the extra weight of my belly.

"Hey, how are your feet doing?"

"They hurt."

"Here, put your arm around me," he insisted, and I did just that as he lifted me with ease. Though it was short-lived, the relief of having the weight off my feet was great. He set me down on the pavement.

"When we get into the room, you should prop them up on a pillow. Okay?" Peter stepped further back to take a closer look at my complexion. "You fine to walk?" he asked. I nodded.

"Alrighty, I'm gonna get the bags."

"You need any help?"

"No, I got it. How about you just take care of you right now? Your feet hurt. I'll be fine."

Harley jumped outside and patiently waited by my side as we watched Peter throw the duffle bag and my backpack over his shoulder, yawning.

He stepped onto the sidewalk, still somehow managing to take out the motel key from his back pocket. "Room three. I like those odds," he said, catching the key mid air. I smiled. He wrapped his left arm around me, bringing me to his side as he gently kissed the top of my head. I looked up at him, stunned, and his cheeks flushed red in realization, swiftly pulling back his arm. He flashed me a toothy, awkward grin and shoved one hand in the pockets of his jeans, clearing his throat. "Sorry, uh, I think the room is down here."

With Harley between us, we started walking. Peter looked over his shoulder every few seconds. At the end of the sidewalk, he took out the room key and unlocked the door, but it didn't budge when he tried to open it. He exhaled and set down our belongings. A loud thud shook through the air as he barged straight into it with the side of his shoulder. He stepped back, impressed, and slinged the straps of our bags over his shoulder.

"Huh, still got the touch."

I bit my bottom lip to stifle a laugh.

A neighbor's door swung open, and a petite old lady stuck her face out, standing there in her pink floral nightgown with rollers in her hair.

"*Oi, guero, cálmate! Más tranquilo*, okay?"

"*Lo siento, señora, no volverá a pasar*," Peter replied politely. "*La puerta estaba atascada*."

The woman's brows raised, and she seemed just as stunned as I was. She hesitated before heading back into her room, muttering, "*Sabelotodo*," and slammed the door shut. I looked at Peter.

"What did she say?"

"Well, she doesn't like me that much, I can tell ya."

I snorted and laughed, walking past him into the room, desperate to rest my feet. Harley trotted inside and explored his new surroundings before finding a spot on the queen-size bed. Peter shut the door behind me and turned the lock. I willed my mind to not think of the dirty corners of the bathtub or the lifting baseboards, welcoming any small critter with open arms. The sound of Peter turning the lock again caused me to look back. After the third time, he finally was able to pull himself away, setting the duffle bag on the chair beside the entertainment center. I stared at the painted beige walls, red shag carpeting, and a TV so old I was certain if I tried plugging it in, I would be electrocuted.

"So, um . . ."

"I'll take the chair or floor. You can have the bed." He sat down at the small kitchen table alongside the single-paned window.

"But it's . . . dirty. And I don't think that chair has been cleaned since this hotel was built."

"I'll be fine. I've slept in worse places."

I looked at him. He regarded me, seeming to wait for the inevitable question. Choosing to ignore it, I set my backpack on the duvet. Peter began to untie his boots but cautiously glanced at me every several seconds. The awkward silence was entirely different this time from what I had experienced that night with Mason. We never uttered a word, and if our eyes did catch each other's, Mason would always shyly smile before stuffing his face with another greasy drumstick. But this. This was intense. As if we were both treading in new territory. Peter kicked off the second boot and cleared his throat, fiddling with his left ear.

"Grace."

"Yeah?"

"You alright?"

"I think I'm gonna get some ice," I said. "It will help me cool off." I grabbed the ice bucket from the side table.

"Want me to go with you?"

"I'll be fine. It's just down the sidewalk."

"Alright, I guess I'll just take a shower then."

"Okay."

We stood there in the middle of the room, staring at each other.

A thick swallow passed through his throat, and his eyes set on my face. My heart raced in anticipation. For what, though?

"Peter."

"Right, yeah."

He hastily stepped to the side, and I opened the door to head outside, but not before catching a glimpse of the bathroom door shutting. The cool air was just what I needed to empty my mind. I headed down the hall to the ice machine. Laughter bounced off the walls. It was then I saw three teenage boys in swim trunks racing to the pool. I opened the bin and scooped the ice cubes into the bucket.

"Hey, did you just git here? Haven't seen a pretty girl like you around," a boy said. I looked over and saw a tall lanky boy with kind blue eyes. "My buddy just turned the big two-one. We're gonna swim. Drink some beer. You wanna join?"

"No. Thanks, though."

I shut the bin, facing him. His face fell the moment he lowered his attention to my belly, and his eyes bulged like big white gumballs. He stammered and quickly walked away, scratching the back of his neck.

Harley greeted me with excited eyes when I returned to the room. I set the ice bucket on the table and found myself standing at the bathroom door, listening to the running water. It felt as if I had regressed to the times I would wait outside Mama's bedroom door, pleading for her to listen about my day. I wanted to tell Peter about what had just happened. I wanted to tell him many things. A rush of air escaped from me at the realization. Though my mama never took my words to heart, I knew, in every way, no matter how big or small, that Peter always listened. That I would never have to ask for his permission to tell him anything. And that's what frightened me the most about him.

"Peter," I blurted.

"Yeah? You okay?"

My lungs finally inhaled a much-needed breath. What was I about to do? What do I even say now?

"Yeah, I'm okay." I rested my head on the door, shutting my eyes. "I just wanted to say thank you again for today."

There were moments when I could hear the hesitance behind his strong voice. See the uncertainty flashing through his eyes whenever he found me looking at him. Even now I could feel all those things despite the hollow wood door between us. Though I wished for it, I knew deep down it was just a childish fantasy. Wetness pooled at the corners of my eyes. I blinked it away, allowing the feeling to seep into me.

"You're welcome."

# 13

Dawn officially cast a grayish hue, still dark but just light enough to see the outline of hills in the distance. My feet dangled off the tailgate, and I stared at the sky, anxiously waiting. I'd seen many sunrises, but today this one felt different. Maybe because for the first time, I was with someone. The sound of footsteps caused me to look over, seeing Peter return from the store with a plastic bag filled with two boxes of food. He yawned and set down the bag, taking a sip of black coffee. Harley stretched his neck as far as he could to sniff inside the boxes without moving from the spot beside me.

"Ready to go?"

"In a minute. Is that okay?" I asked and turned back to the sky. "I just need to see this."

"Yeah, sure," he said and took another sip of coffee, leaning against the right taillight.

I sat there, waiting for the light to emerge from the horizon, like a flame growing in size, expanding its warmth upon the earth. It had never taken this long before. Was it because I was waiting for it this time? A weight sank in my chest as the dozen thoughts that I had put on hold began to play again. One thought stuck. Pa. Where was he? As desperate as I was to not think about him, I couldn't help but wonder.

Though I knew it was better this way, there would always be some part of me connected to him. I was still his daughter. He was still my pa. Nothing could ever change that. As silly as it was, I always thought that the love from a family would never let me down. An unconditional kind of love. That no matter my imperfections, I'd still be loved. And that no matter their imperfections, I'd still love them. But the longer I sat on the edge of this truck, an achiness took over, and I wondered if the only love that hadn't let Peter down was Harley's love.

"Peter?"

"Yeah?"

"Do you ever miss your father?"

He let out a soft breath, propping his elbow on the back of the truck. "Sometimes, but he died after my wife and I split. I had to get away for a while. And it was nice, I'm not gonna lie. Out in the middle of nowhere. It was peaceful. It was just me and Harley," he explained and looked down at his cup of coffee.

The urge to hold his hand grew, and I hesitated about whether or not to act upon it. He cleared his throat, composing himself, and lifted his head. "My pop and I were never close. I never wanted to be a Marine. It was sort of expected in my family. So I was angry for a while about that. But, as my pop used to say, anger is like a wildfire. If you don't contain it, it will spread and destroy everything in its path. But you can only contain it so much until it starts to suffocate you."

"So what happened?"

"After he died, it sort of went with him. I didn't have anyone to be angry at anymore." He took another sip. "You know . . ."

I listened, stunned by how he was still talking. "I'd never wish for a kid to keep a house together. Kids should be playing house, not picking up after their parents, but we wouldn't be who we are. I know I wouldn't be. And I know you wouldn't be."

"I guess so." I looked back at the sky, catching only a smidge of light beginning to reveal itself. He reached into the bag and took out a second cup of coffee, pouring the rest of the first one into it.

He secured the lid back on top, catching my gaze.

"Hey, you may be a morning person, but I need a few cups of coffee to get me going."

"No, it's just . . . I can't imagine what your insides look like with the mix of beer and caffeine. You know drinking can damage the cells in the stomach, induce inflammation, and cause lesions, right?"

He regarded me with the cup of coffee paused mere inches from his mouth. "You read that in your *Reader's Digest* this morning?"

"No, I've just seen what it can do. Bad stuff happens when people drink. It's why I don't do it anymore."

"You drank?"

"A teenager living in Catalina? Yeah, I drank. But after getting pregnant, I realized you can only look into so many empty bottles before you learn it's not gonna help your problems. If anything, it's just gonna make your problems worse. I kinda realized a lot of things when I got pregnant."

"How old are you again?"

"Nineteen. Why do you always ask that?"

"You just say and do the most unexpected things. That's why."

I turned away to hide my smile and look at the burnt orange sky. A sense of peace washed over me as I took in the array of colors blurring together. My shoulders relaxed. Peter's attention was nowhere near the horizon. It was on me. His stare was just as warm as when the sun touched the tips of leaves so brightly, I thought they would catch fire. And he even had the same level of concentration as he had earlier this morning, sliding the blade across the layer of shaving cream on his cheek. Seeing the white foam and the twist of the blade leaving a bare and smooth surface seemed so foreign to me. It was with that same concentration that Peter traced the constellation of beauty marks on my face, his gaze briefly lowering to my mouth before returning to meet my eyes. I could see the need living inside him, only increasing in size, each time more difficult to control. That's when I first understood my own need matched his. A need that spoke to our most primal urges. Flustered by my own thoughts, I looked away. Out of the corner of my eye, I noticed he had turned as well.

"Well, uh, we should hit the road, yeah?" His arm reached out and patted my back.

"Uh-huh."

"Alrighty."

"Peter."

"Yeah?"

"You can stop patting my back."

"Oh, right, sorry."

He turned away again but not without flashing a boyish smile. Harley jumped down from the tailgate, and I followed. Peter held open the passenger door but before I climbed inside, I stopped and looked up at him.

"I got another question."

A smile spread across his face. "Of course you do. You wouldn't be Grace Callaway if you didn't."

I pushed myself onto the seat. "You said you were a spunky kid growing up. Just how much of a troublemaker were you?"

"It wasn't really anything serious. It was just me being a stupid kid wanting attention. Put your feet in."

I swung my legs inside, and he shut the door before I could ask anything else. Harley leaped into the backseat, and Peter sat down. Though I suspected he already felt somewhat drained from speaking so much these past two days, a part of me couldn't let it end so quickly.

"You know, I don't think that's stupid. I think every kid wants attention from their parents. It's only natural," I said and buckled my seatbelt.

"Well, I'll say this, Grace . . . I've never met a woman who talks like you do," Peter stated.

Afraid I would say or do something childish, something I'd regret, I remained quiet. Did he really just refer to me as a woman? I sat upright and rolled my shoulders back, conflicted as to what I should be feeling right now. Pleasantly surprised? Caught off guard? I bit my bottom lip, unsure as to what I should be experiencing. Just as he set down the cup of coffee, ready to drive, I finally mustered up enough courage to speak again.

"You think I'm a woman?" I asked, my heart quickening in anticipation of his response.

"I-I . . ." he stammered, quickly turning his face back toward the windshield, almost as if he realized the words he had just said aloud. "See, that's what . . .", he exhaled. "Grace, when you say stuff like that—I don't see you as a nineteen-year-old. And then I have to remind myself about the few times I've been to jail."

"You've been to jail?"

"That's what you got from what I just said?" His eyes danced with humor. I hesitated and turned away.

"I think the majority of people would focus on the word 'jail' if someone brought it up in conversation, don't you think?"

He thought for a moment as we turned out of the gas station.

"Yeah, okay, you got a point there. It's not something I usually say, but considering how we started, I thought it would be okay," he admitted and scratched his clean-shaven jaw as his other hand steered us onto the highway.

I couldn't help but smile as I leaned my head against the window. On the ride home, I dozed off, still exhausted from the day before. The hum of the tires on the highway and the melody of a song softly playing on the radio caused my heavy eyes to open. The sky was a clear blue with no cloud in sight. Shifting slightly, I felt Peter's shoulder against mine. Just even the slightest brush of his body against mine had become something I wanted more of. He was focused on the road, humming along to "Old Time Rock 'n Roll." He sang off-key and tapped his fingers to the beat, but paused as he realized I was awake.

"Oh, hey, have a good nap?"

"Mm-hmm." I wiped the layer of sweat from my forehead. "That Bob Seger you were singing to?"

"You know him?"

"I may be young, but I wasn't born yesterday," I said. "I like a few of his songs, but I like Elvis more."

He smiled as he kept his right hand on the wheel. "Elvis fan, huh? Gotta' love the King of Rock and Roll."

"Loved him since I was a kid," I said and sank deeper into the seat, stretching out my feet. Harley rested his chin on the windowsill, enjoying the breeze hitting his face at eighty miles per hour. "How far away are we?"

"Just twenty minutes. You slept for most of the ride," he replied and propped his left arm on the windowsill.

And like the last few times I'd been in his truck, a part of me prayed he'd keep driving or for the asphalt to never run out. Like a dust devil, there was nothing I wanted more to do than just run away. To drive some place far enough where my problems didn't follow. And to never look back. Though it frightened me to do just that, what had become more terrifying was I didn't want to go alone anymore. In a matter of weeks, all the things I had wanted to do on my own, I now wanted to do with him. I watched Peter out of the corner of my eye as he resumed humming to the song. Even if it never happened, all I'd want for him is to be happy.

We stared at the road for the remainder of the drive without looking at each other. And for some reason, that same anticipation from last night in the motel seemed to linger in the cabin of the truck. My palms were sweaty. My heart raced. It's then I caught Peter's eyes dipping down to my bare legs before he quickly caught himself. As we turned down the road and I saw the single-wide trailer coming into view, I sat upright but didn't find my hand reaching for the handle as fast as it usually did. He pulled into the driveway and shifted the gear to park, lowering his hands from the wheel. Neither one of us moved. I wasn't ready to go. I wasn't ready to see the inside of that trailer.

"Let me get the door for you." He hopped out of the truck.

I unbuckled my seatbelt as he opened the door and I slipped myself off the seat. "Thank you. And thank you again. I know I keep sayin' that, but really, thank you. I had a really good time."

A smile spread across his face and he nodded, saying, "Yeah, me, too. I had a real good time." He cleared his throat as he said, "I guess I should, uh, get your stuff," and rubbed the back of his left ear.

"Yeah," I said and looked to my feet to hide my smile. I noticed that his boots were now almost touching my toes.

And just like the first time, his hand reached up and tucked the fallen strand of hair behind my ear. There was a simplicity to his touch, both intimate and tender, that spoke to something deep inside me. I wanted to feel his hand against my skin. I wanted to know the exact angle of his face when and if he would lean in to kiss me. My eyes looked to his face. The crease in his brows had become prominent, just like it did whenever he was considering something. His gaze deepened the longer he lingered, letting his thumb glide across my cheek. Warm sensations tingled deep in my stomach and other places.

"You gonna kiss me now?" I asked, my own words causing my heart to quicken. He smiled. It was then his face drifted to the side, his nose grazing across my cheek. But he didn't close the last few inches between us yet. The palm of his hand reached up first, rested against my neck, and let his thumb trace my chin.

My eyelids fluttered closed when he tipped my face up. He exhaled a shaky breath and tilted his head further in. But the sudden sound of a screen door shutting made him pull away and take a few steps back.

And the fire in his eyes faded the instant Ray's voice called out, "Well, look who it is! You're back! Arlene, get out here! Grace is back!"

I leaned off the truck.

"Hi, Ray," Peter said, scratching the back of his neck. "How was your trip to Flagstaff?"

"Good. Good. I was just on my way out to pick up some things for dinner," Ray said and stepped off the porch, glancing between us, almost knowingly. "You two had fun wherever you went off to?"

I looked at my feet again to hide my smile just as Arlene walked out onto the porch. "Hey, you two." She leaned against the doorframe, her suspicious eyes glued to Peter, whose cheeks turned red. "Also, Ray, don't forget the ice cream. Not the chocolate. But the vanilla. And get those graham crackers and—"

"I got it, woman. I got it," Ray said. "Hey, Grace, we're gonna have s'mores after dinner. You should come on by."

"You gonna get those big marshmallows?" I asked.

"You know it. You can come on over, too, Peter, if you want any," Ray said and climbed into the car.

"Oh, thanks, Ray. Drive safe." Peter waved as Ray drove off down the road, waving back at us.

Arlene turned her attention to us and asked, "So, how was your trip? You gonna tell me where you took Grace?"

"Arlene," I said.

"Uh, it was good. Really good, ma'am." Peter cleared his throat and flashed a boyish smile. "And I-I was just taking her stuff up to the door. I have to get goin' and change one of the tires. I think we hit a nail on our way back."

"Well, glad you two are back. And Grace, you and I." She pointed to her feet before going inside the trailer, the same tell she used with each of her sons when she wanted details. Peter and I shared a look before he walked around to the back of the truck, grabbing my bag.

"What was that? What she just did?" he asked, following me up to the porch and setting my bag down at the door.

"It's what she does when she wants to know something. She's always done it with me."

"Got it. Well, uh, I should get going. Let you get settled in again," he said, his cheeks still red. He looked back at Arlene's trailer before facing me. That anticipation flourished again as I stood there, awaiting the one thing I longed for from him.

"Um, I do kinda wanna ask you somethin'. Again, you can say no, but after I come back from getting the tire fixed and take Harley for a walk, would you wanna get some lunch? We can go to Sunny's again and have a do-over of sorts."

I smiled. "I'd like that."

His expression lightened, and a big smile spread across his face. "Good, and maybe one day I could make those Sonoran-style eggs you liked so much this morning," he said and walked back to the truck.

"One day, huh?"

He smiled and climbed into the truck. Lowering myself down onto the porch, I stretched out my achy legs and watched Peter disappear down the dirt road. As the dirt and dust settled, my smile, bit by bit, became smaller and smaller. A pair of sandals came into view, and I looked up to see Arlene with her arms folded. She sat herself down beside me, propping her elbows on her knees and holding a red cup of ice and lemonade. Arlene took a sip and held out the cup. Taking the lemonade, I took a much-needed sip, relieved to feel the citrusy drink cool my body.

"Thanks." I handed her back the drink. "So, how was Flagstaff? You and Ray have fun?"

"It was good. They're expecting another baby. There's too many grandchildren to keep count of now." Arlene shook her head with a sigh and kept her focus ahead. "How was your little trip with Peter?"

"Good."

"I can tell somethin' is on your mind, though. You've been sitting out here for almost ten minutes," she said. "By now you would've gone back inside. So, tell me. What's goin' on? It must be somethin'."

I remained silent, fighting off the growing urge to cry.

"Grace, talk to me. I'm not gonna tell Ray anything."

"It's my mama."

"What about her? You better have not given her any money. I swear to God."

"No."

"Then what's wrong? You were smiling not too long ago. I haven't seen you smile like that in a long time."

"I don't wanna be like her, Arlene. My mama only stayed with Pa because no other boy wanted her. I know why we're doing this. Me and Peter. It's because we're lonely. But that's all it means. No man's ever gonna want me. It's different when a man is a single parent, but for women it's . . . like a shame," I explained and wiped my face to catch any tear that had fallen. "It's just different."

"You don't think you could find a man who would love you for being a mother, Grace?"

"You know what I mean."

"The right man will love you and will love your child. It won't matter to him, because he'll love you for who you are—a mother, a friend, a lover, and so many other things."

"That's if a man likes trailer park—"

"Don't you dare say that. You know I hate that. The right man won't care where you came from, Grace. Let me tell you what you deserve if it were up to me," she began. "You deserve a—"

A loud bass emanated up from the road. The neighborhood dogs began their howling.

"What on earth is that?"

Uncle Wayne's truck appeared. The tires skidded to a stop. Arlene and I waved the cloud of dirt from our faces. He jumped out and shut the door about to speak until he saw Arlene sitting by my side.

"Oh, hey, Arlene."

"Hey, Wayne," Arlene said, standing from the porch. "How have you been?"

"Fine. Just fine. Where were you and Ray? You guys are always here," Uncle Wayne said.

"We went up to Flagstaff. We just got back this morning. Well, I'll let you and Grace talk. I'll be right over there, sweetie. Okay?'

Uncle Wayne and I watched her leave and head back into her trailer. Our gazes fell on each other, and silence ensued. Just like the time he found out Pa had skimmed him in a poker game, Uncle Wayne took off his baseball cap and placed his hands on his sides, staring at me with expecting eyes. His foot started to tap. "Why didn't you call me and say that your father ditched you, Gracie? I had to hear from him that you were all alone up here. He's off God knows where. I dropped everything and came down here. But you were gone. So where the hell were you? It's like everyone just got up and left."

"I was at—"

"Don't say Sam's. You don't think I checked up there, too? I know more about you than you think, little girl."

"I'm here now, aren't I? So I'm obviously fine," I said, irritated, and stood from the porch.

"Uh-huh, and where'd you go off to that you needed your backpack, huh?" Uncle Wayne stepped onto the porch, causing me to halt in my tracks and look back at him. "Answer me right now, Gracie."

"You're not my pa, Uncle Wayne."

"You can't drive like that. So where did ya go, Gracie? Sam didn't even know. Was it that neighbor? I noticed his truck wasn't here either. You don't think your pa told me about him and how he's been lookin' at you?"

Panic pierced my lungs, and the only rational thought I had was to turn away and run inside. But before I could shut the door, Uncle Wayne's foot blocked the frame. "Hey! We're not done talking!" He pushed his shoulder against the door, and it swung open on the first try. I stumbled back. Uncle Wayne kicked the bag inside and slammed the door. He threw his baseball cap on the counter. "You went with him, didn't you? I knew something was off with him. That sick fuck. He tell you to do stuff with him?"

"No. He's not—"

"What, he's not like that? He's a good guy? He's a man, Grace! Did he ask you to try on stuff and shit?" He bent down and unzipped my backpack, rummaging through my clothes, carelessly throwing them in either direction. "Fucking bastard. Going after some teenager. I'm gonna kill him."

"Uncle Wayne, just—"

"Shut up! He's a sick fuck!"

"And what does that make you?! You've been looking at me since I was twelve years old!" I shouted.

Uncle Wayne went still and slowly stood upright, turning his head back at me. A slithering chill ran up my spine from the crazed look in his eyes, staring at me with a disgusted but lustful sneer. Uncle Wayne's eyes had always been more frightening than my pa's. Each time, just like now, his gaze would travel from my neck to my breasts, and down my legs, then to my face with a concentration that unnerved me. He pointed and said with gritted teeth, "You know, ever since that bastard came in here, you've been different. I knew something was different about you. You got more spunk now, Gracie."

"Don't call me that. I want you to leave. Now. I mean it, Uncle Wayne. I want you to go."

Anger brimmed his eyes, and he stepped closer. "I can call you whatever I like and leave whenever I fucking like. You don't get to boss me around just 'cause your daddy's gone. You're my niece. And here you are knocked up and spreadin' your legs for another man! You're just like my sister!"

"You're just pissed off that Mason was the first one!"

His eyes flared, standing there in blatant shock. When Uncle Wayne took a step closer this time, he grabbed my cheeks and squished my face together. "You're the one parading around in those little dresses of yours and smiling at me. Just because I hugged you and tried to feel you up that one time, you think I wanna fuck you?"

I pushed him off me. "I see it! I see it on your disgusting face every time you look at me!"

His mouth thinned into a scowl. In that second, the most frightening silence I'd ever heard enveloped us. I knew we had crossed a line that there was no coming back from. "I really want you to leave now. I mean it, Uncle Wayne," I pleaded with a shaky breath. "No. No! Don't touch me!"

Our hands and arms flailed as I struggled to break from his grip. The stronger his grasp wrapped around me, the louder my cries became. Freeing myself, I turned to run, but his arms seized my chest from behind. I kicked my feet. "No! Get off me!" I yelled. His hand muffled my mouth, and I struggled as he pushed me against the kitchen counter. And like the animal he was, he grabbed the back of my neck, pinning me down. He loomed over me from behind, breathing harshly as he lifted up my dress.

"You were right, you know. I did wanna be the first one who fucked you. Not Mason. Not that fucking neighbor. Me. How do you think I feel having their sloppy seconds?

My eyes frantically searched the counter as he removed his hand from my neck to unbuckle his belt. The sun's rays came through the window slats and settled on the handle of the cast iron skillet, like it was a sign from *Her*, giving me permission. I took the handle, turned, and swung. *Thunk*. Uncle Wayne fell against the chair and groaned, holding the side of his head. I stumbled into the corner, keeping a tight grip on the pan. My breaths came short and fast. I couldn't move or find the will to run. All I wanted to do was stay in this spot. I didn't know how to feel when I saw him tentatively touch his forehead and the blood on his fingers from the large gash. I only wanted to hit him more, because the longer I thought of those fingers touching any part of me or my child, the more the rage inside me became unearthed. A part of me was frightened, but it was also reassuring that my maternal instinct was more alive than ever. His furious eyes refocused, and he stood to lunge forward and grab me again. Instinct took over. I stepped to the side, raising my arm to swing the pan again.

Again. Again.

And again.

Bubbles of blood poured from his mouth as the pool of red spread across the linoleum floor. His eyes were stuck wide open. My shoulders shook as I stifled the long-repressed cries of the little girl inside who wanted nothing more than to feel safe in this world. The pan dropped from my hand, and I lowered myself to the floor, covering my ears to silence the gurgling sounds. By the time I opened my eyes, it was silent. The pool of red had formed a stream, traveling between the tiles, heading towards me. I scooted further into the corner, watching the thick liquid change direction, like a train switching tracks, as it filled another square.

I don't know what made me feel more guilty—the fact that I didn't *feel* guilty or the fact that I was relieved. Another worry was gone. I wouldn't have to worry about my baby girl being leered at by my uncle. No other worry existed now. Two of them were long gone, and this last one I made go away. That's all I've ever wanted for her.

# 14

I don't know how long I sat there on the floor, watching the red stain everything in its path. Though Uncle Wayne's fingers twitched randomly, every other part of his body remained still. Just like I was for years. Just like my mama.

I couldn't feel my body, but I knew my legs and arms were still there. Wayne was never an uncle to me. He was just a man. Now he was some man who had attacked me and was now lying on my kitchen floor. I looked at my round belly and then stared at the spattered dots of blood across my dress and arms.

A gentle knock at the door and Peter's voice calling my name was all it took for me to break down crying again. I heard the door open and shut, and my eyes closed tighter. The silence terrorized me until I felt a pair of sweaty hands touch my face. He pulled my hands away from my ears, and the more he pulled them away, the more I shook my head and sobbed, resisting. My chest began to heave, struggling to breathe.

"Grace."

"I had to do it. He was gonna . . . he was gonna hurt her. I couldn't let him hurt her. I couldn't let him hurt me. I'm sorry. I'm so sorry. I'm sorry." My eyes drifted toward the dead body.

"Don't. Just look at me. I need you to look at me, Grace. Only me, okay?" He cupped my face. His hands were steady, telling me he was as calm as he could be. No trace of fear or doubt was present in him as he held my face with such care, as if I was a baby, allowing me to cry it out. I could see the wheels turning in his mind. His eyes were serious but gentle as he inspected my face.

"Grace."

"I'm so sorry," I cried. "Please don't go. Don't—"

"Grace, I'm not gonna go anywhere," he said without any hesitation in his voice. "Can you stand up?"

I nodded and started to push myself up. Peter stood and grabbed each of my hands to lift me up to my feet. He brought me into his strong arms, and I buried my face in his chest, sobbing in relief that I was in his arms. Uncle Wayne's hand was near my foot, as if he was still reaching out to grab me. I slid my foot away.

"Okay, come over here."

He carefully inched back, avoiding the blood. I stepped over Uncle Wayne's arm, and Peter led me to the kitchen table. He grabbed one of the chairs and scooted it back.

"Okay. Sit down."

I sat down, and Peter kneeled, taking my hands in his.

"I'm sorry. I'm really sorry."

"Grace, don't be sorry. I'm gonna take care of everything. You just need to stay here. That's all you need to do."

"What are you—"

"I'm not gonna tell you what I'm gonna do. All anyone needs to know is that he left here. That's it. Okay?"

I nodded.

"I just need you to trust me."

I nodded. "Mm-hmm."

"Now, I'm going to turn you around, and you need to promise me that you won't look."

"Okay." My voice cracked, and I shut my eyes. The feet of the chair scraped against the floor as Peter turned me around. "T-there's a large plastic tarp outside that my pa used for his truck during rainstorms."

Though he didn't acknowledge he heard me, the slider door opened and snapped shut. For a fleeting moment there was a silence until I heard a *rustle*, like the crunching of plastic. A rush of hot air swept inside as the door opened and shut again. Peter's heavy footsteps returned. I heard the tarp billow on the floor, and the corner touched the side of my ankle. Sliding my foot away, I listened to Peter grunting, and I knew he was pushing Uncle Wayne onto the tarp. My toes curled at the sudden spew of water from the kitchen faucet falling into what sounded like a container. My eyes remained shut until the air was no longer laced with blood and the squelching sounds of water stopped. All that lingered was bleach and soap. I opened my eyes but kept them focused on my feet. I allowed myself to look out the window. It was twilight. And never had I been so grateful that in a couple of hours, it would be dark. My hands and my feet never moved. I never looked until Peter finally said my name.

"Grace."

I opened my eyes, feeling his arm brush against mine. "Yeah?" I asked, taking a much-needed breath.

"I'll be back soon. Okay?"

I nodded.

The sound of something heavy being dragged caused me to peek, and I saw the back of Peter in Uncle Wayne's baseball cap and flannel. He pulled the tarp out the trailer and shut the front door. Shortly after, I heard Uncle Wayne's truck revving to life. I quickly stood and pulled the curtain, watching Peter climb inside and drive off down the road. Turning away, I finally allowed myself to look at the floor. The freshly cleaned floor. Even the cast iron skillet was scrubbed and cleaned to perfection, sitting in the drain board. No one would ever guess something bad had just happened.

Death was always tragic.

But I was relieved. Relieved to feel my baby girl in my belly. I'd never been a vengeful person nor truly hated anyone. Yet deep down, I'd always prayed for one thing since I was a little girl and shamed myself for ever wanting it. I prayed for the monsters to go away. I never wanted a Prince Charming. All I wanted was someone strong and scary enough to keep all the bad things at bay, yet gentle to those they loved. But the realization that I had become that person for me and my daughter brought a peace to my soul that I never expected. I was that someone—strong and scary enough to take away the monsters.

For the first time, the invisible hands weighing on my shoulders finally disappeared. Nothing and no one was keeping me here anymore. Desperate to feel clean, I made my way down the hall and into the shower. Watching the last remains of the pink water spill into the drain, I dried off and pulled on my pajamas. I walked into the kitchen and stopped again to stare at the floor. Though it was clean, I knew I'd always remember the way Uncle Wayne's arms and legs splayed out on the floor. A knock at the door caused me to jump.

"Sweetie?" Arlene called out. "You up?"

I let out a deep breath before opening the door. "Hey, Arlene."

"I saw that your Uncle Wayne left a while ago. I would've come over sooner, but Ray and I were eating dinner. Everything okay?"

"Yeah. We just had a small fight, that's all. He was mad that I didn't tell him about Pa."

"He didn't know?"

"No."

"You think your Uncle Wayne will let you stay here?"

"I don't have a job. All I have is what's left in the Pampers box."

"That money you have is only gonna get you so far, Grace. Especially before that baby pops out."

"Arlene."

"Alright, alright. Well, you still want some s'mores? Ray's cookin' them up now. You and Peter can come on over."

"I'm tired. But thank you."

"Okay, well, have a goodnight." Arlene stepped down from the porch and looked at me one last time.

"You, too."

Throughout the night, I tossed and turned, worrying about Peter and where he might be. What was he doing? I felt guilty for bringing him into this. He wanted peace, and I'd given him no such thing. When the first light of day arrived, I did what I always did. I went outside and sat in my chair to watch the desert come alive. A chorus of howls erupted, and I closed my eyes to bask in the sound. Another howl broke, but it didn't sound far away. It sounded closer. I opened my eyes and saw a coyote in the middle of the road, stretching its neck to the sky. A feeling of wonder expanded within my chest, greater than all the times I'd ever opened a gift. Its pointy snout turned toward me and it canted its neck, staring at me with those big, golden brown eyes. Its gray and auburn fur was speckled with a layer of dirt.

The longer we stared at each other, the more I felt a sense of certainty and peace. That by some universal force, everything was going to work out in some strange way. Another set of howls broke free, and the coyote howled in response to its pack before running away. When I looked at the empty stretch of road this time, it didn't seem so empty. In fact, I saw limitless opportunities.

As the sky lightened, I saw Peter walking up the road, making way to his trailer. He wore a freshly cleaned white T-shirt and jeans. All I wanted to do was run to him, but something inside me wanted to stay put. He glanced over at me, and what I didn't know then was that that would be the last time we'd stop and look at one another for the next several days. But I didn't blame him. What he did for me would make any normal person not want to talk. My only glimpses of him would be from afar as I walked home from Sam's. Day by day, he tackled some new project on his uncle's trailer. The siding was stripped and replaced with new vinyl planks. A new gutter was installed. Even the wood porch was restored to its former glory. And when I did see him, I knew he wanted to tell me something. Something important. Just like I did. I wanted to tell him that I was leaving. That I'd be okay. That I'd be happy. But I didn't want to say goodbye just yet.

Not to him.

Though some part of me always believed we were only meant to know each other for a brief time, it didn't make it any less difficult to say it. But what I would never forget was how all at once, he'd become just as important as Arlene and Ray, if not more. And I now wondered how I had ever lived without him. That's what frightened me the most. Cause I knew he was the exception.

On my way back from Sam's, I saw the rear end of a squad car parked by Arlene and Ray's. A panic consumed me, and I stopped. Looking across the road, I saw Peter grabbing one of the many broken-down moving boxes from his truck. He turned his head, and just as quick as it was for him to look at me, he walked away. Though I knew he would leave soon, too, there was nothing that I could do to stop this sickly feeling in my stomach. One of the officers caught sight of me. He took his arm off the hood of the squad car and stood upright, giving me a once-over. His gut was about the same size as Ray's, telling me that he had somebody at home cooking for him.

"Oh, Grace!" Arlene rushed to my side. "Have you heard from your Uncle Wayne at all? It seems he's been missing for a week now."

"Really?" I asked.

The first officer walked over, shutting his notepad and taking off his hat to fan himself. "It's been a while, Grace. Don't know if you remember me. But I saw you quite a few times when you were just a youngin'. Your dad and your Uncle Wayne were always getting into some sort of trouble."

"I remember you. Liam, right?"

He smiled. "Yeah. How old are you now?"

"Nineteen."

"Time really flies, doesn't it? And here I thought I wouldn't ever need to come back down here. Thought your dad and your Uncle Wayne had straightened themselves out by now. But here I am. I'll try to keep this short 'cause it's gettin hotter than hell out here. Tina said he was comin' down to check on you."

"Yeah, he did. He only stayed a while. We had a fight. He'd been drinking. And then he passed out for a bit before leavin'. And that was the last I've seen of him," I said, catching Liam's partner's suspecting gaze.

"You the only one who saw him leave?" his partner asked.

"How many times you gotta ask that? My wife and I saw his big, loud truck leave. Mr. Taylor saw it leave. Even Mr. Emerson. You don't even need to see it to know it left. It's a sound you never forget, let me tell ya." Ray interrupted, standing by Arlene's side with arms crossed.

"Ray, he's just doin' his job," Liam said. "You all know more than anyone that Bill and Wayne have a habit of pissing off people wherever they go."

"You think someone hurt him?" Arlene asked.

"We're not rulin' it out. We know that Bill was seen at a hospital a few weeks back. All beat up. Haven't seen him like that in a long time. But now he's missin', too. It's why your Uncle Wayne came down here, Grace. You think you know where your dad might've run off to?" Liam asked.

"No," I answered truthfully. "I know him and Uncle Wayne sometimes take off for a while."

"And he left you here alone?" the second officer asked in disbelief. "Like that?" he gestured to my belly.

Liam looked at his partner, saying, as he gestured to us three, "Arlene and Ray here take care of her. They always have."

Arlene wrapped her arm around me and straightened her neck. "You bet we do. She's like a daughter to us."

"Well, if your dad or Uncle Wayne turn up here again, let us know," Liam said, handing me his card. "Joe, let's go. It was nice seein' you again, Grace. You, too, Arlene and Ray. Have a nice day."

Joe gave me one last look before turning away. "And thanks again for answering our questions, Mr. Lawson. Sorry again for your loss." he called out to Peter who was about to walk inside with another box and gave them a brief wave. "And thank you for your service." Liam and his partner tipped their hats and climbed into the squad car.

Arlene, Ray, and I watched them take off down the road.

"I swear I hate cops, Ray," Arlene said, shaking her head. "Didn't you see how Joe was lookin' at her? I git it that they need to think of every possible scenario. But a pregnant girl? Jesus Christ." She shook her head again and fastened her robe, walking back to their trailer. "And I ain't even had my cup of coffee yet!" she exclaimed as the door shut behind her. Ray exhaled and looked toward me.

There was something there. A knowing. An inkling of a knowing. Not big but big enough for him to be suspicious. Just as he was with Uncle Wayne.

"You worried, Grace?"

"No. Are you, Ray?"

"No. I never liked him anyway."

"Why have you never liked him? The times Uncle Wayne talked to you, you were nice to him."

"I didn't like how he looked at ya. That's why. I know I never say it much, but you're like the daughter I never had, Grace. And that means you're family. And families protect each other." Ray pulled me into his side, kissing the top of my head. "Now, walk over to that man and tell

227

him you're leaving here. Cause quite frankly, I think it would make him feel better. I think it's putting him out of whack how you two haven't been talking. I can see it on his face that he wants to."

"How do you know that?"

"Cause I'm a man, Grace. That's how." Ray turned away, heading back inside the trailer.

I looked across the road. At first I hesitated, but knowing I'd regret it if I didn't go, I walked over. Just as I came to the porch the door opened, and Peter came out. He lifted his head and stopped, his cheeks turning red.

"I know you're busy, but I'd really like to talk. If that's okay with you."

He stepped off the porch. "Sure. How've you, uh, been?" he asked, sticking his hands into the pockets of his jeans.

"Fine. I'm actually leavin' this weekend. That's what I wanted to come over and tell you."

He nodded and looked at his feet. "Oh, good . . . that's good," he said and raised his head.

"The trailer looks really good."

He turned back and regarded me. "Yeah, almost finished. Just another few days, and I'll be off, too."

To hear it with my own ears and see how serious he was gripped me with despair. My heart was suddenly heavy. Was this what Pa felt like when he saw Mama leave? Conflicted but utterly heartbroken? From the day my mama left, I had promised myself to never love again. To never trust again. And that was something not even the most hopeless of hearts could keep. To stop falling in love with people like Ray and Arlene. And like Peter.

I stood there, letting it all soak in.

Letting the loneliness nestle its way back into my chest. And it was just as suffocating as I remembered. For so long I had kept myself from loving for this very reason. Everyone I love had left at some point. First

Mama. Then Pa.

And now Peter.

"You heading back to Montana?"

"No. I don't know where I'm headed. I just know it can't be anywhere near here. You know where you're goin'?"

"No, not yet . . . Well, I'll let you get back to packin' up. If I don't see you before you leave, say bye to Harley for me. Okay? I'll miss him." I turned away but not without passing him a small smile.

"Grace."

My feet stopped and I looked at him. "What?"

I'd never seen him look so vulnerable. His eyes were soft but pained. Like he was about to say something important. A confession. And if he didn't, he'd break. And I knew with all my heart what he was about to say.

"No. Don't you dare say what I think you're gonna say," I pleaded. When he took those last few steps between us with such haste, I pointed at him and said, inching back, "No. No. Don't you say it, Peter. Don't—"

"Why? Why can't I say it? Why can't I say that I want you to come with me? Why can't I say that?"

"You said so yourself. You have a plan. I have a plan. That's why," I said, and in spite of my best efforts, my voice shook.

"You're the one who told me that you can't plan life. You think I expected any of this? You were never part of my plan, Grace. That's why I'm asking you this. Something I never thought I'd ever be asking. But here I am, Grace. Doing it. And I know what I'm asking for may be unfair, and I could say something arrogant like I'll make you happy. I know you don't need me to be happy. But I want you. I want you to come with me. And you can leave anytime you want. I won't keep you from experiencing the world," he said as he let out a shaky breath. "I'm just . . . I'm just scared of not ever seeing you again," he declared with such love and tenderness that all I wanted to do was cry.

"Why are you doing this now? Why are you making it so hard for me?" My voice cracked.

"Why am I doing this?" His hands held my shoulders, keeping me firmly planted in front of him. "Look at how you've made me, Grace. Look at me. You made me want to take that chance again. I know you still do, because you're probably the one person in the world who won't ever give up on love. And I want it. I want that thing. With you. I don't want it to be just Harley and me anymore. I want to see you every day. I want to be there when you hold your baby for the first time. I want to hold you in my arms and tell you everything's going to be okay. That's all I want. Cause if I don't get to hold you again, Grace, I don't know what I'm gonna do. I really don't know what I'm gonna do, and that scares me." His voice broke. "I don't want to leave here without you."

"You told me a person can't make you happy."

"I know, I was—"

"I'm no good for you. I mean, Jesus, Peter . . . look at what you did for me! Who does all this for someone out of the goodness of their heart? No one does. You told me a person needs to be—"

"I know what I said."

"Then who's to say you won't leave me if I go with you? What if I'm not the woman you think I am? I'm not even a—"

"Who's to say you won't leave me, Grace? I know that some day, if you change your mind, you'll leave. So what are you so afraid of? I'm finally telling you what you want to hear."

"You! I'm afraid of you!"

"Why? Cause I make you happy? You scare me, too, Grace. But the moment I sat at that diner with you, I knew I was in it with you. I knew it when you gave me a choice. I always had a choice." Peter took a deep breath, now holding my face in his hands. My lower lip quivered, my eyes continuing to water. "You . . . you and that baby have meant more to me than any person I've ever known. I'm falling for you, and I can't stop it. No matter how hard I try. I can't. And I see it in your eyes when you look at me. We haven't had any time. I want more time with you and that baby, Grace."

I knew he wanted me to say those words. I wanted to. Every fiber of my being wanted to. His eyes were soft and focused, as if he was memorizing the placement of the beauty marks on my face. A thick swallow passed through his throat and he leaned further in, pressing his lips against my forehead—a kiss that held such tenderness that my eyes squeezed shut. I was afraid that when I opened them, this would all be too real. That this wasn't a dream, and it would break me into a thousand pieces.

As if sensing my fear, his hands came up to cradle my face, and he allowed his kiss to linger a little longer, pleading again in a whisper, "Please." The pain swelled behind my eyes and in my throat, making it unbearable to breathe. Tears spilled over my cheeks. His thumbs swiped my tears away as I cried.

"I can't. I can't."

He didn't move at first. He just stood there for a moment and finally said, "Okay," and pulled back.

Peter walked away, his head down. I couldn't even feel my legs as I watched him return to his trailer. The sharp dig of my fingernails cutting into my palms didn't lessen the pain inside me. That light in my chest started to fade, and I felt that dark cloud moving out of the shadows of my mind once again. I never thought I'd feel fear like this again. To lose somebody I love. I stifled a cry and covered my mouth about to run back inside. I then saw Arlene standing outside. The look in her eyes told me that she knew that I'd regret this one day. Forcing my feet to move, I retreated to the trailer, finally allowing the sobs to break free. I felt heavy again, and I slid down. A part of me felt relieved to be inside, allowing myself to live in the darkness a bit longer. Yet there was this new part of me, aching to go back outside and to leave with him. The moment he asked me to come with him, I wanted to say yes.

I wanted to cry. Wanted to scream.

But mostly, I just wanted him to hold me.

Every bone in my body yearned to run free with him and to never look back. Every minute we had spent together was engraved in my memory. From the very first moment I beheld him, my heart was irrevocably his.

By nightfall, I was sitting outside, staring at the blanket of stars, hoping for one of them to point me in the right direction. To where I needed to go. I'd miss the smell of Arlene's scrambled eggs. I'd miss Ray's laugh. I'd miss Sam. I'd miss Peter. These were the moments in my life I wished I was in a book, and that I was just a girl heading towards a happy ending. It would be easier. But then it wouldn't be real. The swell of tears rose again, and I looked down in my lap. The sound of footsteps made my heart leap in hopes that he would be there. I looked over and saw Arlene in her pink robe and rollers, holding a card. Her eyes were tender, and she didn't say a word as she sat beside me.

"What are you doin' up? It's almost midnight."

"And what are you doin'? You've been out here for almost an hour."

"I'm just thinkin'."

"About?"

I stared at the sky, saying, "A lotta things. Usually I'd get an answer by now, but I haven't," and looked at her. "What do you have in your hand there? It's not another birthday card, right?"

"No. But it's for you."

"Arlene."

"Don't Arlene me. Just take it," she insisted and handed me the card. "But before you go on and open it, I wanna tell you somethin' real important. Cause when I saw that look on your face earlier today, I knew you needed to hear it. I told you that one day some man is gonna fall in love with you, and you will fall in love with him so much that it astounds you. And it will scare the ever lovin' shit outta ya. Cause you will experience so many things at once. And I think you're experiencing all those things right now, and it's scaring you. That's why you're sitting out here. And I bet it's scarin' him, too. Love scares everyone."

"Even you and Ray?"

"What? You think Ray and I were always perfect? Who is, for cryin' out loud? I know I'm not. Even Ray. But I believe there are very few times in life, if someone's lucky, that they might meet someone who's exactly right for them. Not because that person is perfect. But because their flaws and yours are shaped in a way that fit together. And as the imperfect people we are, we seek out the imperfect in others to fulfill our own imperfections. Do I believe Ray and I were meant to be together? Heavens, no. It's a choice we make every day, and we work hard at it. All relationships do."

"Don't you love Ray?"

"Of course, I do. You know what you told me one time? That you'd want a man like Ray. A good and loyal man to love you and your child. You didn't want a wedding. You just wanted the life that came with it. Do you know how crazy it was to hear that from an eleven-year-old?" She laughed and shook her head, exhaling. "You have so much love in you, Grace. I always hoped that you'd find a man who'd give you the same. Cause when someone loves you, the way they talk to you is different. You feel safe. You can be you. That's the best kind of love. It's the one that awakens something inside you and makes you feel free. And I see the way Peter looks at you, sweetie. I haven't seen that look on a man since Ray. I also see how you look at him. He makes you happy, and you make him happy. Now, don't get me started on the age thing, but let me tell you, it's hard to find someone who understands you. I mean really gets you and not just says it, Grace."

"I told him that I was gonna leave and . . . he asked me to leave with him. I didn't think I'd want to say yes, but I found myself wanting to. I still want to, Arlene. But I've never been on my own before."

"So are you sittin' out here because you're happy with your decision, or is it 'cause you wished you had said something else? Cause this is not how a happy person would be sitting."

"What does it say to him if I do? I don't need no man. All I need is me and my baby. I don't need him to be happy."

"That you love yourself."

I looked at her, surprised.

"Ray knows I choose to be with him every day. I can go on my own anytime I damn well please. He won't hold me back, but I'm happy. There's nothing wrong or weak in letting yourself be loved, sweetie. In fact, letting yourself be loved is a form of self love in itself. This decision you're making, this decision to leave, you're doing that because you want better for yourself and your baby."

"I don't wanna leave you, though," I said, my voice breaking. "You've been there for me since I was little."

"Grace, I want you to live your life. I want you to get outta here. Whether it's with Peter or not, I want you out. But you better call me every week. I wanna see that little girl grow up. You can come back for the holidays. Ray and I can even come up to wherever you decide to go and live."

"I still don't know what to do."

"You will."

"Arlene."

"Yeah, sweetie?"

"Will you and Ray take me to the bus station this weekend?"

"Of course. But you're gonna need to bring what's in that card with you," she gestured.

I sat upright and opened the card. A check was safely nestled in the middle. "Arlene, I told—"

"Nothin' wrong with having something to start with. You never know. Ever since your mama left you, Ray and I have been putting aside a little something whenever we could. It's not much. But it should be enough," she said and peeked at the check, then at my stunned face when I saw the three zeros. "Well, a bit more than enough."

"Arlene."

"You're takin' the money. You need it more than Ray and me. So suck it up."

I rested my head on her shoulder, looking at my round belly, knowing at least one thing for certain. Something I'd known for a long time since I was a child.

"Can I tell you something?"

"Sure."

"Thank you for being my mama."

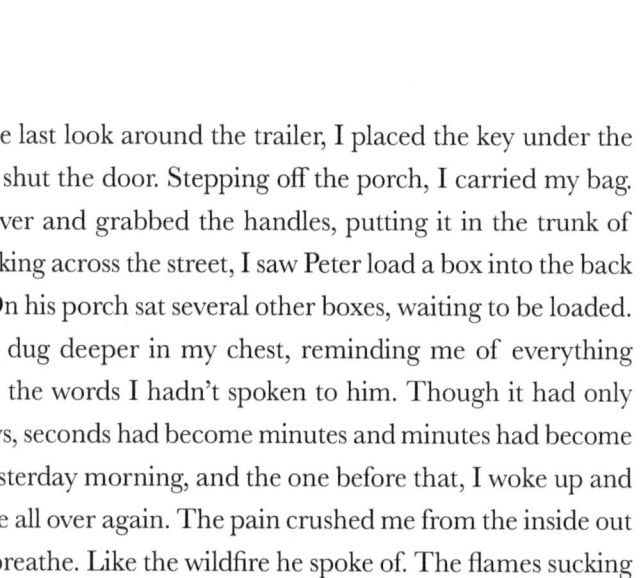

# 15

Taking one last look around the trailer, I placed the key under the mat and shut the door. Stepping off the porch, I carried my bag. Sam rushed over and grabbed the handles, putting it in the trunk of Ray's car. Looking across the street, I saw Peter load a box into the back of his truck. On his porch sat several other boxes, waiting to be loaded. And the ache dug deeper in my chest, reminding me of everything unsaid. Of all the words I hadn't spoken to him. Though it had only been a few days, seconds had become minutes and minutes had become hours. Like yesterday morning, and the one before that, I woke up and my heart broke all over again. The pain crushed me from the inside out till I couldn't breathe. Like the wildfire he spoke of. The flames sucking all the air and life out of me. I knew it would never leave me. No matter how far the years took me. But I felt happy, knowing that that pain would always carry the memory of him. Like the scorched earth. Even after the fire is gone, you can still see the burnt parts. Sam slammed the trunk, and I looked over to Peter's truck, knowing if I waited any longer, I might change my mind and go with him.

"Hey, careful, Sam. She's delicate," Ray exclaimed.

"Cause this is in such great shape to begin with? You'll be lucky to make it to the bus station with all three of ya."

"You have any other bags, Grace?" Ray asked.

"No, that's it," I said.

"Alright, I'm gonna grab Arlene. What's taking her so long? Probably doin' her hair." Ray stepped back into the trailer, yelling, "Arlene! Get your pretty butt out here, we're gonna be late!"

"I'm comin'!" Arlene yelled.

"Another for the road?" Sam spread his arms and I smiled, locking mine around him as best as I could, given the two bellies between us. He pulled back. "I can't believe you're leaving. I'm gonna miss you around the station. Who's gonna tell me all those *Reader's Digest* stories now? My wife's horrible at it. And you better tell me where you end up and what you name that baby. I want pictures. I need to see that little girl grow up. And you better tell her about Uncle Sam. The one who gave you all those Slim Jims."

"I promise, don't worry. I'll tell her all the stories about you. I love 'em, so I know she will."

"Good. I don't want you forgettin' about me. Oh, wait, wait, before I forget," Sam gasped in realization, rummaging in his pockets until he found the right one. "Ah, hah! Here it is!" He held out the saguaro keychain in his palm. "You said you were gonna buy it when you got outta here."

I grabbed the keychain from him. "Thank you, Sam." I hugged him just as Ray and Arlene came out of the trailer.

"Alrighty, we need to head out. Your bus won't wait forever, Grace," Ray said, jingling the keys.

"Where are you goin', anyway?" Sam asked.

"I don't know yet. But I was thinkin' some place with water. Maybe a lake or somethin'. I'll tell you when I get there," I promised him and gave him a kiss on the cheek before climbing into the back seat. Sam shut the door and waved. Arlene sat down in the front seat, waving at herself with a fan.

"Pete, you headin' out?" Ray called to him. Arlene and I shared a look through the rearview mirror.

"Yeah, I wanna get a head start. It was nice meetin' the two of you. I won't forget you," he said, shaking Ray's hand.

Arlene rolled down the window and hollered, "We won't either, hon!" she waved her hand.

Peter smiled, stepping back from the car. "Anyway, uh, I should let you guys get going. Drive safe."

"You, too."

My throat tightened, the swell of tears becoming harder and harder to resist as I heard his departing footsteps. I looked up from my belly and saw Arlene's knowing eyes watching me from the mirror. Turning away, I wiped both cheeks. Ray grunted as he climbed in and shut the door, shaking his head.

"I swear, Arlene, that poor man is leaving more depressed now than when he was comin'."

"Ray!" Arlene smacked his arm.

"What?"

"It's her choice. He's a big boy, Ray. He will get through it," Arlene said and shook her head.

"Are you sure about that, honey? Cause, from looking at him, I don't think he's gonna."

"It's none of our business, Ray. This is between the two of 'em. It's her choice. Her life."

As Ray and Arlene continued to bicker at each other, the sound of Peter's truck revved to life. Growing up, there was something that Arlene told me that stuck with me. That when I find my one exception, he'd be the first person I want to talk to in the morning and the last person I'd want to talk to at night before going to sleep. I hadn't known what that meant at the time, but I understood it now. Love was the fluttering in my tummy whenever Peter was near. The twinkle in his eyes when he laughed. The heat that the nearness of his body brought to mine. The way his words stirred my heart and mind in the best way possible. It was knowing without a shadow of a doubt that he was the person I would always want to talk to, no matter what time of day or night. I knew he was the man who would take the words "till death do us part" to his very core. Love was him. And I knew it and didn't want to ever let it go. The sound of tires hitting the dirt made me look over Arlene's seat, seeing Peter's truck move.

"Alrighty, I think we are ready to go everyone." Ray turned the key and the car stalled. "God dang it. Why does it always do this? Every time. Paul said he fixed it. I knew it. I knew he didn't know how——"

"Ray, just try again."

After the second attempt, the engine sprang to life and Ray began driving, following behind Peter's truck that was more than halfway down the road now. So dangerously close to the exit that would take him to Golder Ranch Road and out to the highway. Then he'd be gone. Just like that. Though I'd convinced my mind, my heart would never accept it. I didn't want to learn about life without him.

As the distance between us increased, my heart shrank as if he were taking what was left of it with him. That thin line of thread that connected us stretched further and further, and I was frightened that it would soon snap. It was then I noticed the brake lights of the truck had come on.

Ray stopped. "What's he doin', now?" he asked, looking over to Arlene.

Every part of me knew what he was doing. He was waiting. For me. Arlene turned around, looking at me. And I knew she knew I wanted nothing more than to get out of the car and run to him, but it was as if my mind and body hadn't quite caught up with each other. In the time it took me to realize this, the brake lights disappeared, and the truck inched forward some more—and I felt and heard one of those fibers snap from that thin thread. All I wanted to do was entwine them again

239

and never let it break.

"Oh, here we go. Guess he just dropped something."

Before Ray could hit the gas, I opened the passenger door.

"Oh, good heavens, be careful of the baby!" Arlene exclaimed as I ran towards the truck, cradling my belly.

I tried to control the gasping and the tears, but I could not run any further with the baby slowing me down. My feet came to a stop just as the truck came to an abrupt halt. Peter jumped out and Harley stuck his head out the window. I let go of all the fear. I was tired of holding back. I allowed my cries of joy and relief to be heard, unworried that anyone might hear. As Peter ran over to me, the burnt parts of my soul began to heal. I ran the last several steps until our bodies collided. Our arms wrapped around each other in a tight embrace. Peter buried his head in my neck and bunched the fabric of my dress around his fingers, showing me he had no intention of letting me go again. He pulled back and held my face in his hands, his eyes almost welling up with tears. Relief swept over his face, his loving gaze filling my heart. My lower lip quivered, and as desperation took over, I stepped up on my tip toes and kissed him.

And in this kiss, he knew that this was a love I wanted.

A love that I would never let go of.

# AUTHOR'S NOTE

Thank you for taking the time to read this book. The story you finished is deeply personal to me, coming from the first five years of my life that I spent growing up in a trailer park in Arizona. Those five years, and the stories told to me about that time and place, influenced my perspective on the world and now my storytelling. This story is not only for me, but for anyone who might see their own experiences reflected here and find solace from it.

This story's setting in no way suggests that such environments are more inherently prone to issues like abuse; instead this story was created to foster understanding and empathy. Abuse can happen anywhere, no matter the circumstances.

From the bottom of my heart, thank you.